Sisters of Willow House

BOOKS BY SUSANNE O'LEARY

The Road Trip
A Holiday to Remember

THE SANDY COVE SERIES
Secrets of Willow House

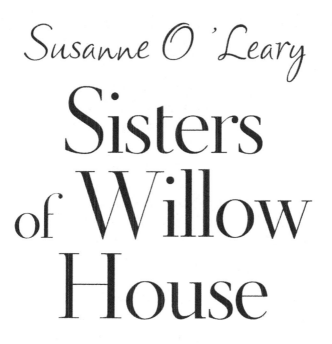

Susanne O'Leary

Sisters of Willow House

bookouture

Published by Bookouture in 2019

An imprint of StoryFire Ltd.

Carmelite House
50 Victoria Embankment
London EC4Y 0DZ

www.bookouture.com

ISBN: 978-1-78681-861-4
eBook ISBN: 978-1-78681-860-7

For my mother

Chapter One

It was the campervan that started it all. The big white van parked in the driveway of their house in Foxrock, one of Dublin's most prestigious suburbs, looked like a cross between an ambulance and a bus.

Roisin stood on the front step staring at it, thinking one of their neighbours was moving house and the removal company had come to the wrong address. It wasn't until she spotted the driver beaming at her from the open window that she realised what was going on.

'Hi, sweetheart,' he called. 'How do you like this, then?'

Roisin blinked and stared at her husband. 'How do I like it? What do you mean? What is this... this *thing?*'

'What do you think it is?' He opened the door and jumped out, running up the steps to her side. 'It's a campervan. Didn't I tell you to be prepared for a big surprise?'

'Yes but...' Roisin was stuck for words. She looked at Cian, feeling confused. 'I didn't think it'd be something like this. I thought, maybe, that you'd booked a holiday in the Caribbean or at least a week in the south of France. Some nice hotel with great food and...'

He looked slightly bewildered. 'Why? That's not my idea of a dream holiday. Not my style at all. But you know I've been dreaming of owning something like this all my life. I thought we'd go on an adventure, now that we're as free as birds, with the lads settled in boarding school and the business sold, plus we have all that extra cash from the inheritance. This super deluxe camper will be our rolling home while we tour Europe and maybe even further. We might end up in India. Wouldn't that be incredible?'

'India?' Roisin asked, staring at him. 'Have you lost your marbles? We'd have to go through several war zones on the way, not to mention deserts and mountain ranges.'

Cian laughed. 'Okay, I'm being a little bit ambitious. But we could go up the coast and do the whole Wild Atlantic Way from start to finish. I haven't been to Donegal in years.'

'It's the middle of January,' Roisin exclaimed. 'Donegal is being battered by storms at this time of year, it might even be snowing.'

'But we won't get there for a few weeks if we start in the south and travel slowly. The weather will have improved by the time we get there.'

'You hope.'

Cian looked only slightly deflated. 'Come on, Rozzie,' he urged, 'think about it. It will be like we're young again. We're free as birds. We could experience amazing things together. Let's have a little fun before we get too old to do anything. I want to go out there into the wild. Just imagine, bathing in rivers and lakes, fishing, listening to the birds, living like pioneers. It'll be amazing.'

'That's not my idea of fun,' Roisin replied.

'But you haven't really tried it. I think you'll love it once we're out there.' He put his arms around her. 'Sweetheart, I know it might be a little daunting, but won't it be romantic? Just like the old days when we lived in that tiny bedsit and showered together to save on hot water. Maybe we could find that romance again?'

Roisin smiled at the memory and kissed his cheek. 'That was lovely. But we're older now. It doesn't sound that romantic any more.' She stepped away from him and rubbed her arms. 'It's freezing. Let's go inside.'

'Good idea. I'll show you the amazing interior and the cute little shower and the double bunk and…'

'I meant inside the house,' Roisin corrected and went back into the hall. 'We need to talk about this.'

'Oh.' Cian ran his hand through his hair, looking only slightly deflated. 'Okay. Make a cup of coffee and we'll discuss this.'

'We certainly will,' Roisin replied, wondering how on earth she was going to handle the conversation.

Roisin went into the kitchen and started making coffee while she tried to understand what was happening. She knew Cian had been restless ever since they'd sold the business. They'd been planning to sell up for quite some time as they both felt they needed to start something new, something that'd give them a little more freedom. When their partner had offered to buy them out, they'd accepted at once, and nearly at the same time, Cian's uncle had died and left him a considerable sum, more money than they had ever had before. Suddenly, they had the financial security to do what they wanted and to pay the huge fees for the boarding school the boys were desperate to go to.

They'd decided to take a break before they started something new, something fun and different that they could invest in. Cian had spent long hours at his laptop and she had assumed he was looking around for a new business venture for them, hoping he'd come up with something exciting. She hadn't paid much attention to what he was doing and felt she needed a break from everything. Me-time, she thought. This was a buzzword she had read about in magazines and heard friends talk about, but had never tried for herself. It sounded lovely and she had often wished she had a moment to do something only for herself from time to time. She'd been working full time and raising children for seventeen years and had never, ever taken a break to do something even slightly frivolous. But now, finally she could.

Suddenly finding herself a lady of leisure, Roisin had looked around for new interests and hobbies. Yoga had always looked so relaxing and the women at the yoga centre nearby seemed so lithe and fit in their yoga pants and body-skimming tops. But after two sessions, she'd realised that it wasn't about stretching, breathing and lying on a mat smelling lavender and drifting off to some nirvana-land. To her it was a back-wrenching, exhausting way of doing static exercises. She never got the hang of the 'downward-facing dog' not to mention balancing on her hands, her body toppling forward banging her head on the floor, while everyone else was hovering elegantly in something called 'the crow'. 'It'll come,' the yoga teacher (a woman called Amanda with the body of a twelve-year-old gymnast) had assured her. 'Just keep practising.' Roisin knew she'd never be lithe and slim and that her generous curves would never look right in yoga pants and vests no matter how much she practised. The other women seemed to have been friends since birth and chatted to each other afterwards, making plans for coffee and lunch and never invited Roisin to join them. Oh, well, they weren't really the kind of women she'd want know better anyway, she'd thought, and she'd left the yoga centre for ever.

Then she'd joined a walking club but the other women there were too jolly for her liking, sprinting up the steep slopes of the Wicklow Mountains as if they were training for the Olympics. It seemed there was nothing left to do. Golf? Boring and the clothes were so naff. Bridge? She'd tried it once but found it a pointless pastime.

One of her friends from school invited her into town for shopping and lunch. She'd married a wealthy man and knew the ropes when it came to spending serious money. But as Roisin wandered through Brown Thomas, swiftly followed by a trip to Harvey Nichols in Dundrum, she'd glanced at the hair-raising prices of the clothes and felt a stab of guilt. Was she really going to pay five hundred euros for a silk shirt when half the people in the world were starving? She'd glanced at her friend, who happily bought anything that took her fancy, continuing to the cosmetic department where she stocked up on Crème de la Mer, easily spending the monthly salary of the average worker without blinking. After lunch at a plush restaurant they'd kissed each other and promised to do lunch again 'soon', which Roisin knew probably meant never, as she had made no secret of how bored and appalled she had been. Shopping for the sake of it was not as much fun as she'd thought and she realised she had grown apart from many of the women in her life.

Being a lady of leisure wasn't really all it was cracked up to be, she'd realised, missing those exhausting but challenging days of running a company, balancing childcare and housework and still finding time to have a bit of fun now and then. Those were the days. After a month of doing very little, she'd felt ready to scream with boredom and had started to look around for something new, as Cian hadn't managed to come up with anything.

The house was like a morgue without the boys, who had departed for boarding school in September, all excited about this new school which offered so many sporting activities they loved. Cian had been so happy they had started at his old school, and kept saying how it would make men out of them and how they'd do brilliantly academically as well as in sports. But Roisin had been devastated when they were all gone. She knew it would be good for them and that they'd get an excellent education which would give them a better chance to get into the best degree courses eventually. But oh how she missed them, even though she knew they loved it there and had taken to boarding-school life like ducks to water. Just as well, as they would stay there until they graduated and applied for college places.

They had been home for Christmas which had been lovely but it seemed like they had just arrived when they had to leave again and she had spent two days in tears, walking through their rooms and looking at their baby pictures. Why did kids have to grow up so fast? Why had they had them when they were so young, she wondered again and again. Roisin knew this was a watershed period, when she would have a chance to think of herself more and plan a new project.

She'd known since the New Year that Cian was cooking up something but he'd refused to tell her what it was. He'd spent long hours in the study surfing, looking coy and saying things like, 'You'll see,' or 'It's a surprise' whenever she'd asked. She had a feeling he was avoiding her. They had got on each other's nerves lately, having very little to do and all the time in the world to do it. There was no longer any focus to their lives, no struggle or striving for a goal, or simply to pay the bills each month. Money was more of a curse than a blessing, it seemed.

Roisin suddenly yearned for peace and quiet. For a sense of self she'd only had as a little girl. Something she'd only ever felt in one place. Willow House. Aunt Philomena's old house in Kerry. She found her mind drift like it often did these days, to the old house perched on a hill high above the beach with the sweeping views of the dramatic coastline. And far out at sea, the craggy outlines of the Skellig Islands, where the remains of a monastery had stood for over a thousand years. Sandy Cove, such a magic place that made her spirits soar every time she went there.

The house was having a huge make-over as her aunt had come into some money. She'd been writing romantic fiction and her novels had become hugely popular in America. Under the pen name Fanny l'Amour, her novels had been on the bestseller lists several times and she now had a huge following. It was amazing. She was now seventy-four but showed no sign of slowing down. This had earned her enough money to restore the huge Edwardian pile on the edge of a cliff overlooking the Atlantic.

All this had been revealed at her sister Maeve's wedding over a year ago. There were grand plans for the restoration of the house and Maeve had produced drawings and mock-ups of how it would eventually look, but it hadn't got started quite yet. But the house and gardens had been lovely in the spring sunshine and nobody minded the cracks and dents.

Roisin had been transported back in time as she and Cian had slept in her old bedroom the night before the wedding. The ceremony was held in the overgrown rose garden with Maeve in a long floral cotton dress and Paschal in jeans and a linen shirt. It had been a lovely ceremony which ended with the happy couple taking off in Phil's vintage Jaguar for a weekend on the island of Valentia where they'd first started their love story.

Rosin had made Cian promise that they'd go back for an extended visit later this year, and it was all Roisin could think about now. She'd even floated the idea that they'd move down there for a longer period, to help restore the house.

Cian. As she put two mugs and a basket of raisin bread on the table, Roisin tried to figure out what was going on with him. She'd thought he was looking into ideas for a new business while he spent hours in the study with his laptop but now she realised he had been searching for the perfect campervan. He had been into camping when they met in college and had taken Roisin on a camping trip to Wexford so she, despite her protestations, would get 'the feel' of sleeping in a tent and cooking over an open fire. She hadn't felt anything except back pain and mosquito bites. And washing in a freezing cold lake instead of a hot shower had soon lost its appeal. Cian had accepted that camping would never be her thing and instead gone on camping trips with his pals, and later their sons, who loved it.

The campervan idea had been raised many times during the years, but Roisin had always managed to shoot it down by changing the subject. In any case, running the business and looking after three growing boys had left little opportunity to consider the idea. He hadn't mentioned it for a long time and she thought it was a passing phase that had faded away. But now she realised she was wrong. He had surfed the campervan websites as if he was hooked on porn. And in a way it was. Campervan porn. A dream that had turned into an obsession. Roisin suddenly wished it had been real porn. Then she could have dealt with it. She laughed at herself. What was she thinking?

She looked up as Cian walked into the kitchen. 'Coffee,' she said. 'And raisin bread. I made it myself.'

He poured himself a cup of coffee from the pot and sat down opposite her. 'Let's talk about this.'

'Yes. Let's.' She looked at him and wondered what he was thinking. He looked the same as always, his brown hair cut short, his hazel eyes calm and determined, his tall frame relaxed. He didn't give the impression of someone whose dream was about to be shattered. Quite the opposite. Perhaps he was sure he'd be able to talk her into the idea and they'd go off into the wild blue yonder as if they were in their twenties and didn't have a care in the world. She wondered if he was going through some kind of mid-life crisis, like many men in their forties.

'Roisin?' His voice cut into her thoughts. 'Can I just tell you my side of this? From start to finish?'

'Just one question,' she interjected. 'How much did you pay for that thing out there?'

'Sixty-five thousand,' he muttered.

She stared at him, appalled. 'Oh, God. I had no idea they were that expensive.'

'We can afford it.' She took a deep breath but he put up a hand. 'Just listen,' he pleaded. 'Then you can have your rant.'

She sat back. 'Okay. Go on.'

He took her hand. 'You see,' he started, 'I have felt… I've been very lost since we sold the business. I know we both agreed it was time to give up the rat race and do something else, have more time for each other and the boys. But now that they're settled into school and really happy there, I felt we – you and I – needed to go on some kind of trip – or adventure. The campervan has always been my dream, a dream I never thought I'd be able to realise. But then we got all this money and all the free time, I felt it was meant to be. My dream could become real.'

'Your dream? What about me?'

'I thought you'd love the idea.'

'You know I hate camping.'

He sighed. 'But this isn't camping. It's more like living in a cute little house that travels. It has all the comforts of home and—'

'It's camping, Cian. Maybe on a more luxurious scale, but still – camping.'

He gripped her hand harder. 'I knew you'd say that. But… maybe you could come out for a spin in it? Just for the day? Tomorrow's Saturday and the weather forecast promised a sunny day. We could go to Brittas Bay and walk on the beach and cook lunch in the van, and roll out the double bed and try it out.' He winked. 'It's a big bed with a very comfortable mattress.'

She suddenly felt sorry for him. He was like a little boy with a new toy and she was the nasty stepmother who wouldn't let him play with it. 'Oh, okay, then. But it's not going to convince me. This is just an outing, okay? No promises and no twisting my arm or anything.'

'I swear. Thank you, sweetheart.' He beamed at her, his face transformed, looking suddenly years younger, very much like the Cian she had fallen in love with. It seemed churlish not to at least let him try to persuade her.

'I'll take care of lunch tomorrow,' she promised.

He got up. 'I'll go and get her ready.'

'Her?' Roisin laughed. 'It's a woman now? And does she have a name?'

He blushed. 'Yeah. I'm calling her Rita. But only in my head.'

'I should hope so.'

It wasn't until he had left that she realised where she had heard that name before. Rita was his first girlfriend.

Chapter Two

Roisin's phone rang as she was putting the mugs away. It was Maeve.

Roisin smiled as she thought of her sister. She'd ditched a brilliant career in interior design in London when she fell head over heels in love with Paschal and switched from city living to a windswept little village in Kerry. Roisin had understood her completely the moment she clapped eyes on Paschal and been bowled over by his good looks and charm. The house and the village were also a huge draw for the world-weary. The simple lifestyle, the friendly neighbours and the stunning ocean views were hard to resist. It suited Maeve perfectly and her move back to Ireland had brought the sisters closer after many years of not being in touch as often as they should. But now they were nearly as close as when they were teenagers, running wild on the beaches at Sandy Cove and sharing secrets while they lay on the back lawn at night wrapped in blankets looking at the stars. To Roisin, she felt as if she had been given her sister back at a time when she really needed her.

'Roisin, can you talk?'

Roisin sat down at the kitchen table. 'Of course. What's going on?'

'I have some news.' Maeve paused as if she was trying to find the right words.

'What news?' Roisin asked, sensing something big.

'I went to the doctor yesterday,' Maeve started, her voice shaking.

'The doctor? Are you sick?' Roisin asked, alarmed.

'Not sick exactly. But the results of the tests said that—'

'Is it a lump?' Roisin cut in, her heart beating. 'Please God, don't let it be a lump.'

Maeve laughed. 'It's a kind of a lump, yes. But a good one.'

'It's benign then? Can you have it out?'

'Definitively. It's due to come out in July.'

'Due?' Roisin squealed. 'You mean you're…'

'Pregnant!' Maeve laughed. 'Yes, you guessed it. I got myself pregnant at the age of forty-two. How's that for news?'

'It's the best news ever!' Roisin's face broke into a huge grin. 'But you must be at least three months by now. How come you didn't go to the doctor before?'

'I thought I was going through some kind of early menopause. I didn't have much morning sickness but my periods stopped and all the other signs pointed to that. I couldn't imagine in my wildest dreams that I could be having a baby. But then I felt a bit odd, so I went and then I found out.'

'Paschal must be over the moon.'

'He is still in shock, I think. I just told him. But…'

'But what?' Roisin asked, sensing a touch of concern in her sister's voice.

'Well, the thing is, I had a small bleed so the doctor told me I had to stay in bed for a couple of weeks and then take it very easy for the rest of the pregnancy. Nothing to worry about, he said. And the bleeding has stopped.'

'Oh, no!' A wave of dread washed over Roisin. 'I'm so sorry. You have to stay in bed until the baby is born. I had that same scare with Darragh, remember? It was so frightening.'

Maeve laughed. 'No, it's not as bad as that. I can get up in a week or so and live fairly normally, just not do anything strenuous. It's just that… Well, I promised Phil I'd oversee the last of the restoration of Willow House while she's on her book tour in the US. That seemed okay until this happened. But then I thought of you and Cian and how you're at a loose end, you said in your last email. So I was wondering if you could come down for a few weeks and take over?'

'Of course we can,' Roisin promised. 'We'll come down in a couple of days and stay for a month or two.' She mentally crossed her fingers that Cian would agree. He might like the idea of taking his precious campervan with them, keeping it on the west coast for day trips or something. And, as the school was only an hour's drive up the coast from there, they could go and see the boys and they could come down to Sandy Cove for the mid-term break at the end of February… A slow smile spread over her face. It was actually a perfect plan.

'That's okay with Cian?' Maeve asked. 'I mean, he might have other plans. And what about the house? Your house, I mean.'

'I'll deal with Cian tomorrow. And the house? We were thinking of letting it if we were going off somewhere. We don't want to leave it empty in case of burglaries and squatters. The rent will give us some extra cash, too, as we tied up a lot of the other money in investments and trust funds. We have no fixed plans yet. But now we'll be going down to stay with you… I'll have a chat with the letting agency and see if they can put it on their books a little sooner. I've already tidied away most of our stuff and put it in the attic.'

'Oh, that's good,' Maeve said, sounding happy. 'Thank you for coming down. Then I can stop worrying.'

'Stop worrying right now,' Roisin ordered, delighted at the prospect of this new project and being so close to her sister, who she had missed so much. Now they could be together all the time. She was suddenly looking forward to getting stuck in. 'I'll take care of everything.'

'Not a word to Phil that I've had a bit of a scare,' Maeve warned. 'She is so busy with her book tour and then she and Betsy, her editor, are spending a few weeks in Florida working on the next book.'

'I won't breathe a word. Except give her the news she's about to become a great-aunt again.'

'I'll do that myself. She'll be delighted. But I have to make sure she doesn't interrupt her book tour, so I'll pretend all is fine. She needs a holiday after all the stress of the tour.'

'Funny how she and Betsy have become so close. They seemed like chalk and cheese when I saw them together at the wedding.'

'The battle-axe and the party princess,' Maeve said, laughing. 'But they're the best of friends.'

'So it appears.' Roisin smiled as she thought of their aunt Philomena and how she had accidentally fallen into a writing career. The story was stranger than fiction. Phil's late husband had left behind an unusual legacy. He had secretly written several romance novels under a pen name, which had been discovered by Phil when she went through his affairs a year after his death. Phil had then picked up where Joe left off just for fun and sent a few chapters of her efforts to Betsy, Joe's editor in New York, who had loved it and offered Phil a very attractive four-book deal and the rest, as the saying goes, was history. Having no previous writing experience, Phil had nevertheless discovered a flair for writing fiction and it hadn't taken her long to find her voice as an author. Phil was now, two years later, a hugely popular author especially in the US, and her readers couldn't get enough of her books. Nobody, except Maeve and Roisin, knew their uncle had been the original author.

Maeve yawned. 'Sorry. I'm a little drowsy. I feel like taking a nap every half hour.'

'That's normal. I couldn't keep my eyes open the first three months of my pregnancies. You have a little sleep and I'll fill you in about our plans when we have it all sorted.'

'Sounds great,' Maeve said in a sleepy voice. 'Look, I should perhaps tell you that the house… the rebuild… it's quite a big project and not quite what you might expect…'

'I'll deal with it. Just rest and take care of yourself,' Roisin ordered.

Maeve let out a long sigh. 'Oh, that's fabulous. I'm so happy you're coming. We haven't had a chance to be together much like in the old days.'

'I know,' Roisin agreed. 'We were inseparable at school. But then life got in the way, and we only managed to get together during Christmas and Easter.'

'But we have been emailing each other regularly.'

'Not the same though, is it?'

'Not at all,' Maeve agreed with feeling.

'I've missed you and all our chats and laughs. Now we can pick all that up again.'

'It'll be fabulous,' Maeve agreed. 'Can't wait to see you, sweet-heart. Hugs and thanks.'

'Sleep tight, pet.' Roisin hung up and glanced out the window, shaking her head at the sight of Cian polishing the front of the campervan with her best tea towel. His new baby was getting a lot of attention. Her head full of what Maeve had told her and her own plans taking shape, she tidied the kitchen and went upstairs to wash her hair, her heart singing at the thought of seeing Maeve so soon. She decided to wait to break the news about the baby to Cian, and the plan she had decided on until the following day. She had always been the one to make the decisions and he had always agreed. But this time it was different. Rita reincarnated in the shape of a campervan might be more than she could handle.

'You look nice,' he said the next morning as they prepared to leave.

'Thank you.' Roisin touched her freshly washed blonde hair knowing she looked her very best. The new short style she had recently acquired suited her square jaw and the curls around her face accentuated her blue eyes and cute little nose. The rest of her wasn't bad either. Her jeans clung to her wide hips and showed off her tiny waist. She had put on the tightest wool sweater she could find and topped it with a smart little down jacket. Not exactly camping attire, but as they weren't really camping, she thought she'd dress up a little. She was dying to show him her sexy underwear too, which might result in some wild lovemaking… And then they'd talk and she'd convince him to come with her to Willow House. He was usually more receptive to new ideas after making love. This would work, she was sure of it.

'Have you got the lunch things?' he asked.

Roisin pointed at the picnic bag. 'Right here. I got those organic sausages you love, and some chicken legs and a few other bits and pieces.'

'And I put a mini bottle of champagne in the fridge,' he said with a wink. 'We have to christen this thing, don't we?'

'I thought you already had,' she said before she could stop herself. 'Sorry, didn't mean to be snarky.'

He laughed. 'I know what's going through that blonde head right now. But don't you worry. You're the only girl for me.'

After a little organising, they set off into the glorious morning with pristine blue skies and a soft breeze, unusually mild for January. The Japanese cherry trees lining the street were about to bloom, and the daffodils were already poking their green shoots through the grass. Spring was definitively around the corner.

They took the busy coast road and battled through the Saturday traffic on their way south and arrived at Brittas Bay only an hour later. Cian parked in the crowded parking lot.

Roisin peered out at the other cars. 'Not very private, is it?'

'It'll be better when we get further from the city on a real camping trip,' Cian remarked, looking disappointed. 'But I suppose everyone wanted to enjoy such a nice day.'

'By the truckload,' Roisin said.

'Let's walk on the beach. They might be gone when we get back,' Cian said hopefully.

'Okay.' Roisin opened the door, jumped down and ran up the dunes. 'Come on then,' she called to Cian as he locked the van. 'The walk will give us an appetite.'

'I already have one,' he replied, eyeing her trim behind.

'Not that kind,' she said with a laugh and held out her hand. 'Come on, slacker, let's get a little exercise. It's a fabulous day.'

He laughed, took her hand and they ran down the slope of the dune to the beach, where huge waves roared throwing salty foam in the air. The sea, the stiff breeze and the seagulls screeching above them made Roisin forget all her troubles, even if this beach didn't have half the magic or the wild beauty of the beach at Sandy Cove. Here, there was still a feel of a big city close by and the coastline was flat and uninteresting. In Sandy Cove, there was a sense of being on the edge of the world and the views of the endless ocean and the islands had a spiritual beauty. But it was still nice to be out in the fresh air and feel the wind in her hair and look up at the blue sky. She grinned at Cian, running away ahead, her arms outstretched as if she was playing aeroplanes. She laughed into the wind, her spirits soaring, feeling, knowing that this moment, this day would be the start of something new and exciting. It might not happen for a long time, but she could feel something shifting in her life that seemed to have been stuck in a rut for so long. *It's out there*, she thought. *Something new and fabulous.*

Cian laughed at the figure of his pretty wife running like a wild thing. She looked over her shoulder at him and knew what he was thinking. He often told her she looked like the proverbial dizzy blonde but he knew that inside that pretty head lurked a sharp brain that could do the most complicated calculations. 'You're such a quick thinker,' he would say in awe when they had struck a particular profitable deal. 'And so astute in business and PR.' She knew he was right and that her bubbly personality was a huge asset during business meetings and negotiations. She knew she could charm an army if she put her mind to it, and sometimes even had, if you could call bank managers and their assistants an army. That was the easy part. Managing work, childcare and running the household without a glitch had been the greatest challenge, but she had pulled it off most of the time even if it was exhausting and they'd often collapsed into bed not having had the energy to go out or enjoy much of a social life. And now, here they were with free time they didn't really know what to do with.

Roisin stopped and looked back at Cian studying her. Why weren't they happy? she wondered. Like retired work horses, they felt lost without the harness. Maybe the saying that 'it's better to travel hopefully than to arrive' was true? She waved him on and he stuck his hands in his pockets and shuffled after her.

'You looked lovely running there,' he called as she ran ahead.

'It's a beautiful day,' she called back, weaving her way through the crowds of people who had also come here on Saturday morning to enjoy the weather. This beach was nice, but not at all as wonderful as the beaches in Kerry that were never crowded and had that wild, Atlantic feel that she had never felt here, on the shores of the Irish Sea.

She looked at Cian again and could nearly see the tension in his shoulders. She knew that the past year had been hard for him, especially just before the business deal came through and the boys, now all teenagers, were acting up. And he had taken on most of the tasks of homework and housekeeping while she sealed the deals. But now, here they were, free as birds and with money to spend and he still wasn't happy. Why did he think that taking off in the spanking new campervan was the best thing for them to do? Couldn't he guess she wouldn't take to the idea? She sat down on a rock, waving at him to join her. It was time to talk. Feeling positive and hopeful, she smiled as he joined her on the rock and took her hand.

'Talk to me,' she said. 'Tell me what's been bothering you.'

He looked out across the beach. 'Not now. Maybe later.'

'After lunch, then?' she suggested, not liking the awkward feeling between them.

'Yes.'

He got up and started to walk again, back towards the van, glancing at her over his shoulder. He wouldn't be so easy to convince this time, she thought, watching him as he walked away.

With his hair ruffled by the wind and his eyes sparkling, he had for a moment been the Cian she had fallen for when she was nineteen and he had asked her out after looking at her all through a lecture about international trade. She had peered up from her notes and smiled, feeling something strange in the pit of her stomach. She agreed to a beer after lectures which had turned into pizza and a long snogging session outside her student quarters. She laughed at the memory. They had been inseparable ever since, sharing the same hopes and dreams and a curious love of spreadsheets and figures.

They were both hugely ambitious but also wanted a family. What a rollercoaster ride it had been trying to persuade their parents that getting married before they even had their degrees was a great idea. Meeting a stone wall of opposition from both sets of parents, they had run away and got married in Scotland, and then gone back to finish their degrees. Then they went to the bank where Roisin managed to charm the surly bank manager to give them a large loan to start their consultancy business. She did it so well that his brother turned out to be their very first client, as he was looking into importing tools and selling them online. Roisin, being an expert in international trade, and Cian, knowing everything that was worth knowing about tax and imports, had got that firm off to a very good start. Once they were up and running the business had taken off at once, to everyone's surprise, even their own. All they needed next was a house and a family.

Roisin had drawn up a plan on one of her beloved spreadsheets with a schedule for 'making babies' based on her menstrual cycle. Cian laughed and tore it up and said he wasn't going to be some kind of stud horse. They'd make love when they wanted, he said, and that was very often. But of course it resulted in their first baby they called Darragh, followed by Rory two years later and then after a gap of a year and a half, little Seamus, the cutest of them all. Now they were all teenagers.

Where did the time go? Roisin often wondered as she looked at her tall, handsome sons who had been toddlers only yesterday. The early years had been tough but so lovely and coming home to her noisy little crew every evening had been the best part of the day. Tucking them into bed, reading stories, Sunday mornings in PJs watching cartoons, trips to the beach in the summertime, all the birthday parties and holidays were magical times for them all.

She realised that between them, she and Cian had managed what most couples couldn't: running a hugely successful business, bringing up three children and, most importantly, staying happily married for nearly twenty years. That was some achievement. And now, when they were still young and energetic, they could finally break free of the rat race and enjoy life. But why did that seem frightening and lonely instead of exciting? Why did she dread the future instead of looking forward to years of freedom and happiness? Because she didn't have a plan. No spreadsheet to consult, no list with bullet points. It was like throwing herself into a dark void. Thank God she had Maeve and the baby and the building works on Willow House. She couldn't wait to get down there and sort everyone out. All she had to do was to tell Cian what they were going to do.

'Maeve is having a baby,' Roisin announced later as they were sitting at the table in the van, eating.

Cian gulped and stared at her. 'What? Maeve? But she's forty-two.'

'So? You can still conceive at that age, you know. It's a little harder but still possible.'

'Oh. Okay.' He looked at her blankly. 'And she's feeling okay? Very happy, I suppose.'

Roisin sighed and sipped some water. 'No. I mean yes, she's happy. You know she and Paschal have been trying for a baby since they got married. They didn't think it would happen. But now it has and they're over the moon. But she's having a few problems and has been told to stay in bed for a while and then take it easy for the rest of the pregnancy. So now she needs help.'

'I see. Of course she does.'

'So…' Roisin stopped, trying to find the right words.

'So?' Cian asked, raising an eyebrow.

Roisin swallowed. 'Well, you see, she needs me to come down there to help out with the building work at Willow House. She will also need someone to help out with her design firm, I can imagine. She didn't say anything about that, but I have a feeling she'll need someone to keep an eye on the website and the accounts. So I told her we'd go down and stay until it's finished and the baby is born and they're back on their feet again. And as it's so close to the boys' school...'

'You could go there and be the mother hen and make sure they have warm socks and dry their hair after swimming and take their vitamins, I suppose?' he said in a scathing tone that surprised her. 'And of course, the building project would be so much fun for you,' he filled in with just a touch of sarcasm. 'You're already drawing up plans and spreadsheets in your head.'

Roisin squirmed. 'Well... yeah, maybe I was.'

'And where would I fit in on that spreadsheet of yours?'

'You can keep the van there and we'll do day trips around Kerry or something.'

'When you're not rebuilding a house, managing Maeve's pregnancy, running her business and mollycoddling the boys?'

'Mollycoddling? Me?' Roisin snapped. 'What about you texting them good night every single night? And I heard you on the phone to the rugby coach telling him that Seamus bruises easily. And I thought you said that school would make men out of them.'

Cian coloured. 'Okay, yeah. I miss them as much as you do.'

'Well then,' Roisin cut in. 'Isn't my plan excellent in that case? We'll be there, much closer and go and visit often and they could come to Willow House for their breaks. We'll let the house here and get an income from that, plus the money from our investments, so we'll have plenty of time to figure out what to do next.'

'That wouldn't be good for them. And what you're suggesting leaves no space for me, except those day trips we're supposed to go on.' He shook his head, his eyes full of disappointment. 'Day trips are not what I wanted to do when I bought this thing. I was planning for us to cast off. Do something a bit crazy and go through our bucket list. See the world and discover new places.' He grabbed her hands. 'Maybe even get to know each other and who we really are.'

Roisin bristled. '*You* were planning? How come you never breathed a word about this until you drove up to the house in this… this fecking bus?'

'I wanted to surprise you.'

Roisin laughed. 'I've never been so surprised in my life.'

He sighed. 'I'm sorry. I should have told you. But I thought… I was sure you'd feel the same about this. We have always agreed on everything until now, done everything together, never been apart.' He stopped and drew breath, looking at her as if he was seeing her for the first time. 'Shit.'

'Shit – what?' she asked, feeling worried. 'This is the first time we haven't been on the same page.'

He looked down at his plate. 'I know.' He looked up. 'Is there any way I can make you want to come with me on a trip?'

'I don't think so, Cian. Maeve needs me and I want to help her. Can't you see that?'

'I'll go on my own, then.'

She stared at him, appalled. 'On your own? Without me?' She thought for a moment while it slowly dawned on her that this wasn't such a bad idea, after all. 'Why not?' she said, putting her elbows on the table, leaning forward. 'I just realised something. Do you know what we need?'

'No?'

'Space. We each need our own space for a little while.'

He looked thoughtfully back at her and nodded. 'Yes. You're right. I want you to be happy, to be able to do what you want, what you feel you need to do right now.'

'And I want you to go off in your lovely van called Rita and have your adventure.'

He looked taken aback. 'You mean… you really want me to go off on my own? Without you?'

'Yes. I think you need that wild holiday you've been yearning for. I think it would be good for you – and me. Just for a few weeks. Maybe ask one of your friends to come with you?'

'Like who?'

'Like your best friend Andrew. He's at a loose end after he broke up with his latest girlfriend and he's between jobs right now. I'd say he'd jump at the chance to do that trip with you. Make it an all-boys-together thing. Surfing, fishing, hiking all over the west coast. You've never done that kind of thing before. Maybe now's the right time?'

'Could be.' They looked at each other in silence. Roisin saw a glimmer of something in his eyes that looked like anticipation of something new and exciting. It was a great idea, she thought. A little bit of space would be good for them. Wouldn't it?

Chapter Three

Everything fell into place as if it was meant to happen. The rental agency called on Monday to tell Roisin that they had prospective tenant: an American banker moving to Dublin was very interested in renting their house on a long lease. Could they show him the house that day? Of course they could! Roisin raced around, tidying up, trying to make the house look attractive, wishing she had Maeve to consult for a bit of house-doctoring. But she had to do her best with the help of their cleaning lady, who arrived later that morning and whirled around the house like a tornado, dusting and polishing until everything shone. Cian sorted out the garage and put the boys' bits and pieces into the attic and swept the dead leaves from the drive.

At two o'clock, the house looked clean, tidy and very inviting in the pale winter sunshine. At least on the outside. With its Victorian brick façade and bay windows, it was one of the nicest houses on the street. On the inside, scuff marks on the floors and various dents in the furniture were the marks of the growing up years of three lively boys. But the rooms were large and bright and overlooked a garden that could have been tended a bit better, but the bare patches on the lawn spoke of many football matches and rugby tries which had also wrecked some of the flowerbeds. Hopefully charm would win over the lack of elegance.

Dressed in her best corporate pantsuit, Roisin stood at the door as the Mercedes swept up the drive and pulled up outside the front door. She smiled broadly as a man in jeans, a blue blazer and white shirt emerged. He was younger than she had imagined, as the word 'banker' always conjured up the image of an older man with grey hair and a three-piece suit.

He sprinted up the steps holding out his hand. 'Hi. I'm Jack Anderson. Great house you have here.'

Roisin nodded appreciatively. 'Thank you, Jack. I'm Roisin and this is my… I mean our house,' she added as Cian appeared at her side. 'This is my husband, Cian.'

'Hi there,' Anderson said. 'Really nice to meet you both. So could I have a quick look at the house? I have a meeting in about an hour, so not much time to lose what with the traffic in this town.'

'Of course.' Roisin stood aside to let him pass. 'Do you want me to show you around?'

'No,' he replied after a moment's hesitation. 'I'd like to see everything on my own. I'll be taking pictures to send to my wife, who's packing up in London. Hope that's okay with you?'

'That's fine,' Cian said.

'Of course,' Roisin replied, crossing her fingers behind her back, hoping he wouldn't mind the wear and tear of the house. 'We'll be in the kitchen if you need us.'

'Great.' He nodded, glanced around the hall and disappeared up the stairs to inspect the bedrooms.

Twenty minutes later, after a quick sprint around the garden, Jack Anderson joined them in the kitchen, beaming. 'Love the house and that big yard. I'd like to move in as soon as possible. My wife hates hotels and as the rental market here in Dublin is impossible, this is the best I've seen. The rent is…?' He paused. 'I don't think we've named a figure.'

'Three thousand a month,' Roisin said. 'Euros. And a security deposit of five thousand.'

'Oh.' He looked thoughtful. 'A bit more than I had hoped but okay. I knew apartments closer to the city centre go for around two K a month, so it seems fairly reasonable, given the size of the house and that fact that it's furnished. I've four kids, so they'll have plenty of space here and schools nearby.' He held out his hand. 'Got to go. The agency will be in touch. Good luck with that trip in the fabulous motorhome I saw behind the house. Bye for now.' He shook their hands and walked swiftly out of the kitchen, leaving Cian and Roisin staring at each other in shock.

'We've done it,' she whispered, her eyes stinging. 'We've given away the house… our house.'

Cian stared at her. 'But that was what you wanted, wasn't it?'

Roisin wiped her eyes with her fingers. 'I know. It's the best thing to do, but… Our home… We won't be able to come back if things go wrong. Or if…' She shivered as the front door slammed behind their new tenant.

'If what?' Cian put his arms around her. 'We'll have someone living in our house while we're away. It would be foolish to leave it empty. We're only renting it for a while anyway. And it'll give us a bit of extra cash while we think about our next business venture.'

'I know.' She sighed. 'But I suddenly feel homeless. And what will the lads say?'

'They'll love coming to Sandy Cove for their breaks. And we'll be back in our house—' He looked her. 'When? Long lease, they said. How long is that?'

'Two years, I think.' Roisin put her hands over her face. 'What have we done?'

'Three thousand euros a month,' Cian said. 'That's a great little income. We'll have a cash flow and can leave the rest of the money in the bank.' He shook her gently. 'Come on, Roz, you know we have to do this. We can't just sit here and rot. And you know what? Andrew has said he wants to come with me on my trip. We'll do the Wild Atlantic Way all the way to the north and then we were thinking we might go over to Scotland from Belfast for a bit of fishing.'

Roisin pulled away and stared at him. 'Scotland?'

He shrugged and grinned. 'Yeah, why not?'

'I don't know.' Roisin looked around the cosy kitchen and the old pine table where they had spent so many happy noisy evenings eating pizza or tacos or even her own Irish stew. The house seemed so empty without the boys, lonely and soulless. It was better to let it than live here, just the two of them. And this was supposed to be a new beginning. The beginning of what? she wondered with a dart of fear. Maybe they were taking too much of a risk…

The boys were neither shocked nor upset by the news that they'd be going to Willow House for their breaks instead of their house in Dublin. She called Darragh when she knew he was just out of study.

'Hi, Mum,' he said.

'Hi, sweetheart,' Roisin cooed. 'How are you?'

'Fine. Was that all you called about?'

'No. I have to tell you something important.'

'Oh? Okay. Could you make it quick? We have to hand over our phones at nine o'clock, so…'

'Right. What a good idea, by the way.'

'It sucks,' he grunted. 'But go on.'

'Well, you see, it's like this…' She paused, wondering where to start. 'Your dad has bought this campervan and is going off on a trip with his friend Andrew all the way up the west coast.'

'Really? Cool.'

'Yes, and I am going down to Sandy Cove to help your auntie Maeve with the building works at Willow House.'

'Good for you. Say hi to Auntie M.'

'I will. But this means you'll be going to Willow House for your break, because we've let our house, so…'

'Cool,' he said again. 'Is that all? Because I've got stuff to do.'

'So that's okay then?'

'Sure.' She could nearly hear him shrug. 'But only if there's broadband. And we can do some surfing.'

'Yes, of course.'

'Great. See ya, Mum,' Darragh said and hung up.

Roisin sighed and wondered how much he had actually taken in.

Rory called twenty minutes later. 'Mum, Darragh says Dad's gone off on a camping trip and we'll be moving to Willow House. But the broadband there is crap.'

'Not moving, exactly,' Roisin said. 'We'll just live there for a while. Auntie Maeve assured me there's fibre down there now.'

'Brill.'

'So that's okay with you?'

'Yeah, sure. Can we buy wetsuits and surfing boards? And invite some of the guys to come down?'

'I'll look into wetsuits. And maybe it would be better to invite your friends in the summer.'

'Maybe for Easter?' Rory interrupted. ''Cos I want to go to the Gaeltacht in June. Some of the guys are going and it's always great craic they said.'

'The Gaeltacht? You mean those camps where you go to learn Irish?'

'Yeah, them. I want to go. Can I?'

'Of course,' Roisin said, surprised by her son's sudden interest in improving his Irish.

'Great. Gotta go. Bye.'

'Hugs, darling,' she said, but he had hung up.

'What did they say?' Cian asked as he walked into the bedroom. 'Where they upset about going to Willow House and that I'm going to be away?'

Roisin laughed. 'Not at all. They were only worried that there would be no broadband in Kerry and asking for wetsuits and surfboards. The fact that you wouldn't be there didn't cause them much concern.'

'Typical.' Cian rolled his eyes. 'Only thinking of themselves as usual.'

'And we're not?' Roisin teased. 'They're teenagers so that comes with the territory, but what excuse do we have?'

Cian laughed. 'Yeah. I see your point. But we never had a moment to be young and carefree. This is our chance to try our wings and fly solo for a bit. We'll come back stronger and better after this.'

Roisin had agreed, even if she was getting seriously cold feet. Cian had been her rock for so long. How would she cope without him? How would she manage on her own? But as she travelled further away from Dublin, their house and Cian, she began to look forward to the time ahead. Maeve had said the building work on Willow House had got 'stuck', whatever that meant. And that she needed help to organise her online business so it would be easier to run after the baby was born. Paschal was often away as he was taking part in a huge marine life survey of the west coast. 'Whale spotting and swimming with dolphins is his new passion,' Maeve had said, laughing, when they'd spoken again on the phone. 'I'll soon look like a whale, so that should make him happy.'

The boys would come down to Willow House on their mid-term break at the end of next month, which would be fun. She had already looked up sports shops in Killarney that sold wetsuits and booked surfing classes for them at the mid-term holiday camp on the main beach in Sandy Cove. She had also made sure there was broadband at Willow House, which Maeve had confirmed. 'But not that fast, I'm afraid.' Which meant the fib she had told the boys would be exposed as soon as they tried to use it. Well, she'd deal with that when it happened. Right now, she just had to get there and settle in. And get used to being all alone.

Chapter Four

Roisin couldn't believe how quickly that last week went. As she drove down the slipway to the motorway, the rain beating against the windscreen, she wondered where Cian was. He had left two days ago, the campervan all polished, packed and organised for a long trip, looking excited at the prospect of his adventure. He had hugged her tightly and said he'd miss her but he hadn't looked exactly broken-hearted, more like someone dying to get away. Then he jumped into the van and started the engine, waving as he drove off, leaving her standing on the doorstep feeling abandoned. Would he ever come back or was this the beginning of the end of what had been a happy marriage?

After stopping twice for lunch and coffee, Roisin continued to Cork, where she took the road to Killarney and finally Sandy Cove, arriving in the late afternoon.

As she drove through the village, Roisin was struck by all the new shops and cafés lining the main street. She had only been back for Uncle Joe's funeral two years earlier and hadn't really paid attention to what was going on. But now, in the light of the setting sun, she saw how clean and tidy everything was, the old houses newly painted and the thatched roofs in good order. It was a huge contrast to the ragged look of the village in her teens. But tourism hadn't hit this part of Kerry then, and the people living in the village were mostly fishermen and shopkeepers who weren't well off. She felt a little pang of nostalgia as she thought of those days when life was simple. But it was probably better that the village thrived and its people prospered even if the bling of today seemed a lot less charming and cosy.

As she slowed down and looked around, she had to admit that the renovations to the cottages and the bigger Victorian houses had not been too brutal and that the old-world charm of the village was still present, the seaside theme even stronger with a lot of the houses now painted white with blue trims around the windows. As she glimpsed the ocean at the very end of the street, she felt her spirits lift, and she rolled down the window to breathe in the salt-laden air, closing it quickly as the cold wind made her shiver.

Her heart beat faster as she turned into the lane that led to Willow House, hoping the renovations so far hadn't been too extensive. It would be a pity to change the beautiful Edwardian façade and make it more modern. The pink stucco, the lovely sash windows and the ornate plasterwork needed restoring but with a very light touch. And what about the interior? It had been such a welcoming house, perfect for a family and for country living. Had that been turned into something more modern? She pondered this question while she drove through the ornate wrought-iron gates, coming to a screeching halt as she saw the house. She blinked and stared at the sight before her. What on earth…?

Roisin stared in horror at the façade covered in scaffolding, the windows swathed in black plastic and the state of the front garden.

It looked like a warzone, with the lawn dug up by trucks, the façade only half-finished and the brand-new roof sticking up above the scaffolding. Holy mother, what a mess. Why hadn't Maeve told her? And how was she going to sleep here with no windows? She dreaded going inside to see what she imagined would be an even worse disaster.

She suddenly laughed at herself. 'You wanted a project?' she said out loud. 'Well, your wish has been granted, with knobs on.' But where was Maeve? At her house probably, and it was only minutes away. But the path along the cliffs wouldn't be safe now that it was getting dark. She'd have to go along the road and then down to the front of the house.

Deciding to call first before she dropped in, Roisin picked up her phone and dialled Maeve. 'Hi. I'm here,' she said when her sister picked up. 'And what a sight that greeted me.'

'Oh.' Maeve laughed. 'Yeah, I should have told you that the builders are a little, ahem… unpredictable. They use the stop-start-stop method so common in Kerry.'

'You don't say. It looks completely unfinished from here, except for the new roof. I can't imagine the inside is any better.'

'Oh, but it is,' Maeve protested. 'There's even electricity.'

'Hooray. But there are no windows at the front of the house. I'm looking at black plastic here.'

'But that's only at the front. The windows at the back and sides are finished. These windows had to be ordered from a firm in Limerick because they are exact replicas of the period ones that were there before, so they take longer to make.'

'Mm,' Roisin said, still looking at the house. She knew it had needed to be saved from falling down, but the restorations seemed a little too heavy-handed somehow. 'Did we really need to replace the windows? Couldn't they be repaired?'

'No,' Maeve replied. 'They were all rotten. The house needs intensive care before it can live again. A patching-up job isn't enough, I'm afraid.'

'Oh, God. And what about the rest?'

'Go inside and take a look. The kitchen is in working order. It hasn't been done yet. I asked Paschal to light the Aga, so it should be nice and warm. Your bedroom is at the back so it has a new window and you can light the fire in the fireplace. There are some logs and stuff in the shed outside the kitchen. Get Cian to do that for you.'

'Cian isn't here.'

'Oh? Why?'

'Long story. I'll tell you later.'

'Okay. But go and get settled in and then come over and have dinner with me. Paschal's gone to Cork, so it'll be just the two of us.'

'How are you feeling?' Roisin asked, suddenly concerned about Maeve's condition.

'I'm fine. The nausea is gone and the doctor gave me the all clear to get out of bed yesterday. But I'm taking it easy.'

'Keep doing that,' Roisin ordered. 'I'll be over in a little while. Don't cook anything. I'll do dinner.'

'You don't have to. Nuala was over a while ago with a lamb casserole. Enough there for twenty. But you know Nuala. Always there for you.'

'Nuala?'

'Yeah. Remember her? The girl with the loud voice and even louder laugh. She was at the wedding.'

'Oh, yes.' Roisin laughed. 'I liked her. She was great craic.'

'Still is. Slimmed down to about half and married the owner of the Harbour Pub. Three kids and a lovely husband. Still the life and soul of the village with a heart of pure gold, even if she can be quite raucous at times.'

'Looking forward to meeting her again.' Roisin glanced up at the house. 'I'm going in. Call the troops if I'm not out in half an hour.'

'You'll be fine. See you later, Roz.'

Roisin got out of the car and walked to the front door, suddenly remembering she didn't have a key. There used to be one under the flowerpot beside the front steps, but the space where it had been was empty. She pushed at the door and found it swung open easily. *How secure is that?* she wondered, stepping into the hall, dimly lit by a bare bulb in the ceiling. Paschal must have switched on the lights.

She looked around the hall that used to be crammed with coats and boots, the shelf over the old hall stand stacked with hats of all kinds and the tall urn bristling with umbrellas. But the hall was empty and the smell of beeswax and wet wool replaced by the odour of new paint and drying plaster. The floorboards were still the same wide oak planks but needed sanding and polishing, a job she put at the top of her mental list. She looked up the stairs and noticed the bannisters had been replaced with something that looked too new and modern, but was probably safer than the one made of carved oak that threatened to give way at any moment.

Where to next? The bedrooms, she decided and started up the stairs, carrying her suitcase. Cian would normally do it for her but now she had to do everything herself. Character-forming, she told herself as she lugged the heavy case. It felt scary, but good at the same time to be alone, to meet each challenge on her own and not shout for help every time she had to do some heavy lifting. She had been strong and assertive at school, she remembered, and always coped in the toughest situations. But then, when she got married, Cian had been there always at the ready, and she had lost that can-do attitude. She had been bossy at times which had been easy as she had Cian – her rock – to fall back on. But where had that strong, independent young girl gone? she asked herself, suddenly wanting to be her again.

The top-floor landing was dark, as the window was covered in black plastic. But she could feel the smooth oak planks under her feet and imagine the way it had been, with framed photos from the nineteen twenties and a seascape on the far wall. Were they still there? She flicked the light switch but nothing happened and she felt her way down the corridor to the large back bedroom with the four-poster bed and the window with a view of the ocean that used to be hers and then, years later, shared by two of her boys one summer holiday when they were small. There was a small box room beside it, she remembered, handy for toys and clothes.

She felt the door handle and opened the door, feeling for the switch on the wall. The room sprang into view, transformed by the builders who had obviously managed to finish it. What an amazing space. The old wallpaper with birds and flowers had miraculously been left but that was the only thing reminiscent of its former look. The floorboards were covered in a light green carpet which matched the new curtains. The window frames and shutters had been painted white and the door to the box room was open to reveal a brand-new bathroom with a shower and hand basin and a heated towel rack. Roisin stuck her head in and turned on the spotlights in the ceiling. Oh my God, this was so elegant. Her old room had an en suite and looked like something in a boutique hotel. The only furniture, a large double bed, was made up with clean sheets and there was a note on the pillow:

Hi Roisin, welcome to the all-new Willow House. The new bathroom isn't finished yet, so don't use the shower or toilet. The old bathroom down the corridor is perfectly okay (or should be). The kitchen is still fine, and the Aga there works, but be careful walking through the rooms downstairs. So much still to do. Maeve will fill you in.
    Cheers, Paschal.

Roisin smiled. Typical. Maeve's new husband was the kindest man on earth but not one for overdoing the explanations. She had to look for herself to find out what he meant by 'so much still to do', and why she needed to be careful walking through the rooms downstairs But it was getting dark and she was hungry. She decided to leave the rest of the inspection for the next day when she could see it all in daylight. The builders would be there so she could talk to the foreman and see what kind of schedule they had, if that was what Maeve wanted her to do. There didn't seem to be much of a plan, but this was Kerry and things worked to some kind of ancient law which was hard to understand. 'The dark side of the moon,' her friends in Dublin called this part of Ireland. Kerry people were tricky, a little secretive, proud and very stubborn, that was all she knew. But under all that beat a heart of solid gold. She was half-Kerry herself as her father and aunt had grown up here. She just had to awaken her Kerry spirit and then all would be fine, she told herself, trying to conjure up that strong-willed young girl she had once been.

Without Cian's support and reassuring presence, she felt suddenly very small and very alone. But then something told her not to be a wimp and to show the world – or mostly herself – that she could do it: cope alone and deal with stubborn Kerry men who made their own laws, unlike Dublin where everything happened according to well-drawn plans and a modern work ethic. Here in Kerry it was completely different. But she would crack it, she told herself sternly, trying her best to believe it.

Having washed her hands in the old bathroom down the corridor, Roisin put her jacket back on and went to join Maeve. She left the hall light on and got into her car, deciding to drive the short distance up the lane and down another driveway rather than stumble on foot along the path that went beside the cliffs.

It was a dark, cold evening with the crescent of a new moon rising above the weeping willow at the gable end that gave the house its name. She could see the ocean glinting in the distance, but it was too dark to enjoy the sweeping views. At least they hadn't removed the willow in the rebuilding frenzy that seemed to be taking place. Roisin decided to make absolutely sure it wouldn't be touched when she spoke to the builder the next day.

Maeve and Paschal's cottage glowed like a jewel through the darkness. The little white house with its thatched roof and smoke rising from the chimney looked as inviting as a house in a fairy tale. You wanted to go inside, take off your shoes and snuggle on the sofa in front of the fire. Maeve had even put a candle in the window beside the red front door to welcome Roisin and light her way down the flagstoned path. She pushed the door open.

'Maeve? I'm here!'

'I'm in the kitchen,' came the muffled reply. 'Feeding her highness.'

Roisin walked into the small hall, hung her jacket on a peg beside the jumble of outerwear and kicked off her shoes. Then she went into the cosy living room, which bore the marks of a Maeve-makeover. With its two plump red sofas flanking the fireplace where logs blazed, the armchair by the window and the green wool curtains pulled against the cold night, it could be featured in a magazine as the cosy cottage home of the year. Lamps on small tables cast pools of light on the colourful rug and the smell of turf smoke blended with Irish stew from the kitchen, making Roisin's stomach rumble. She padded across the rug and went into the kitchen, where she found Maeve putting cat food into a bowl while Esmeralda, the Siamese, wound herself around her legs meowing loudly.

'I see Esmeralda is top cat here too,' Roisin remarked.

Maeve whipped around and smiled. 'Hi. Yeah, she's doing the I-haven't-been-fed-for-years act.' Maeve put the bowl on the floor beside the Aga. 'There you go, your highness. Food.'

Esmeralda threw a haughty look at Roisin before she turned her attention to the food.

'She's not too happy to see me,' Roisin said and went to give her sister a hug. 'Hi, pet. How are you at all?'

Maeve hugged her back. 'I'm fine. Much better now that you're here. The doctor says the danger is over and that it was just a little glitch due to hormones. I can live normally except no stress and no heavy lifting.'

Roisin pulled back and looked at Maeve. They hadn't seen each other since the summer but the pregnancy hadn't changed her much. She had put on a little weight and her normally slender waist had thickened. But apart from that, she was the same Maeve with curly auburn hair, large green eyes framed by black lashes and smatter of freckles on her nose. 'You look wonderful. Pregnancy suits you.'

'It seems like a miracle. Can't really believe it's happening.' Maeve put her hand on her stomach. 'I felt the baby move yesterday, so there must be someone in there, or Paschal's curry last night was too hot.'

Roisin laughed and let go of Maeve. 'No, it's the little rascal you're expecting. They usually start moving around this time. It'll get worse, I promise. Darragh was like a whole football team before he finally emerged.' She sat down at the large pine table by the window admiring the new look of the kitchen with its white cupboards and red-and-white checked curtains. 'Lovely kitchen. You've done wonders with this house.'

'It took a while to get it ready. But we love it now that it's finished. I'm doing the nursery in the small bedroom at the moment. I'll show you when we've eaten and I've told you about Willow House and what we're planning to do.' Maeve spooned Irish stew from the pot onto a plate and handed it to Roisin. 'There. That should warm the cockles of your heart.'

Roisin drew in the delicious aroma of lamb, carrots, onions and potatoes in a rich gravy. 'Mmmm. Nothing like a good Irish stew.'

Maeve helped herself to stew and sat down opposite Roisin. 'So, where's Cian? I thought he'd come down with you.'

Roisin stopped eating. 'No, er… Well, we… We're taking a break from each other for a while.'

Maeve stared at her. 'What? A break? Is there something wrong? Are you breaking up? Is there another woman or something?'

Roisin started to laugh. 'Yes. Another woman. Her name is Rita and she is a brand-new shiny campervan.'

'What?' Maeve dropped her fork. 'Campervan? He finally did it?'

'Yup. After all that talk for years and years that I just went along with. I thought the idea would go away, but he finally bought her.'

'Oh my God.' Maeve picked up her fork. 'I never thought he'd do it. He must have known you hate camping and that you'd never want to travel around in one of those things. I mean, that has been a family joke for years.'

Roisin laughed. 'Yeah. Remember when I said that I had only one thing to say about camping and that was: why?'

'Exactly. Why did this never sink in?'

'He refused to believe it. Wishful thinking in a way, I suppose. He must have thought he'd be able to persuade me one of these days. Then he bought that stupid campervan and tried to make me come with him on a tour across Europe. He was even thinking of going on to India before I pointed out that there are several warzones on the way. Now he's just taken off up the Wild Atlantic Way with his best friend. I think they might end up in Scotland.'

'Really?' Maeve stuffed a forkful of stew into her mouth, peering at Roisin. 'You just let him go?'

Roisin pushed away her plate. 'Yes. But it was all very amicable. I wanted to come down here to help you and he wanted to…' Roisin burst into tears as it suddenly hit her. The impact of the loss of her home combined with the separation from her children suddenly felt too much to bear. 'We let the house to an American family,' she sobbed. 'The boys are in boarding school and now Cian is gone off on this mad camping trip and I'm here all alone. What's happening to us?'

Maeve put her hand on Roisin's arm. 'I'm sorry. I had no idea you were going through all this. Now I feel guilty to have asked for help.'

Roisin wiped her eyes with her napkin. 'No, don't. This is a good thing, I swear. It feels hard now, but I think we need to be apart and find our own feet before we can carry on with our life together. It sounds mad, I know, but that's the way we want it. I don't want to go on a camping trip and Cian doesn't understand that. But I'm so happy to have something to do. Otherwise I'd be in that big house in Dublin on my own going mad. You know how I love a project.'

Maeve made a face. 'You might change your mind when you see the reality of what we've taken on. It's one hell of a project.'

'Surely it's a simple job.' Roisin frowned. 'Is there a problem with the house?'

Maeve finished her stew and wiped her mouth. 'A problem? No, more like a thousand problems. Let's go into the living room and I'll show you the plans of the rebuild.'

'Rebuild?' Roisin asked. 'I thought it was just some repairs and redecorations.'

Maeve looked a little embarrassed. 'Er, no. A bit more than that. And then there's the marketing of the house for guests and…'

'Guests? What…? You mean you're turning Willow House into some kind of…' Roisin suddenly realised her now so elegant room with the en-suite bathroom was for something other than just family. 'Why didn't you tell me?'

Maeve squirmed. 'I forgot.'

When Roisin studied the plans at the small desk in the living room, she saw the enormity of the task ahead. The whole of the upstairs was being remodelled to house guests, with en-suite bathrooms put into box rooms and what had been walk-in closets. The house was big enough to take it but it would change the whole feel and character of the once-so-welcoming family home.

'The period feel won't be touched,' Maeve tried to reassure Roisin. 'It'll be a little gem of a boutique guesthouse.' She pointed at the plans. 'And look, downstairs is relatively unchanged, except we're turning the study into Phil's bedroom with her own bathroom in the utility room and then the kitchen is so big that there's plenty of room to section some of it off to make a sitting room for her.'

'Yes… okay.' Roisin looked at Maeve. 'But why? I thought she was just going to do the place up to make it more comfortable. Why a guesthouse?'

'Five star, but still a guesthouse.' Maeve sighed and went to sit down in one of the sofas. 'Come and sit here and I'll tell you.'

Roisin left the plans on the desk and joined Maeve by the fire. 'Okay. I'm listening.'

'Maybe we should have a cup of tea first?' Maeve suggested.

'No. I want to hear the full story now,' Roisin said sternly. 'No ifs or buts or cups of tea. You could have told me weeks ago, so now I need to know. Come on, let me have it, warts and all.'

Maeve nodded and sat up. 'Okay. I'll tell you.' She took a deep breath. 'There's a lot more we haven't told you.'

'I'm sure that's an understatement,' Roisin cut in.

'Possibly. But just listen,' Maeve ordered in a big-sister voice. 'As you know, Willow House originally needed extensive repairs and renovations. We didn't know it would be so extensive but once we got started, new problems popped up. The roof, which was the first thing we did, cost a fortune, but we knew it would. But then there was rising damp in the living room and dining room coming from the basement, so a new damp-proof course had to be installed, which took a lot of time. Then some of the walls had to be partially torn down and built up again with new bricks and mortar. I don't know the details but I can tell you it's extensive. Then the bills started to come in.'

'But I thought Phil was earning mega bucks from her books and all the foreign deals and everything,' Roisin remarked. 'She was very positive about the sales. At least that's what she said when I was here last.'

Maeve nodded. 'Yes at first, she managed to pay off the larger bills. But then it kind of grew and grew. Once you start taking an old house apart, more problems pop up. Phil earns a good living from her writing, that's true. But she needs money for herself too. And remember she is now seventy-four years old. Who knows how long she can keep up the pace? She might want to retire one of these days. Not that I think that is on the immediate horizon, but you never know. In any case, we have decided to try to earn some money from Willow House. It's not big enough to be a hotel or even a B&B. So we have decided to run it as a as a small boutique hotel. We'll be applying for tourist board approval too, so we can set up a website. Phil likes the idea because she can live in the quarters we're organising for her when she comes back after the summer. She can run the hotel with a little help from some extra staff. And we can close it down at any time, should her – or our – circumstances change.' Maeve paused and looked at Roisin. 'So that's some of what's going on.'

'I see.' Roisin tried to digest what Maeve had said. Even though it made sense, it didn't fit into her plans at all. She had thought the house would be restored to a large family home, perfect for holidays and breaks. She had looked forward to seeing the boys enjoy it the way she had as a teenager. 'I thought it was just going to be restored as the family home it once was.'

'What family?' Maeve asked. 'It's too big for us.'

'Yes, but maybe *we* could… I mean, we have nowhere to stay when the boys are on holiday.'

'But…' Maeve stared at her. 'You mean you wanted to take over the house? You never said anything about this before.'

Roisin shrugged, feeling foolish. 'It just came to me. Okay, that was silly,' she said, deciding not to tell Maeve that she had been sitting there imagining a big Christmas tree in the newly restored living room and everyone, including Phil, Maeve, Paschal and their parents around the large dining-room table for Christmas dinner. Their parents had retired to Spain and didn't come home very often. It would have been nice to invite them to Willow House for Christmas, a way to gather the whole family together. But now she knew this would never happen. 'Some of what's going on?' she asked, suddenly remembering what Maeve had just said. 'You mean there's more?'

'Not really. It's just that... well, the builders are a bit of a problem. We hired a local firm based in Killarney. The builder's name is Johnny O'Shea. He was supposed to be free to see this job through to the finish.'

'But he's not?'

'You know what those people are like in rural Ireland. They tell you what you want to hear. The reality is quite different.'

'You mean he quit?' Roisin asked, alarmed.

'No, he's still on the job, he says. But he's also on another job at the same time. So he only appears occasionally, whenever it suits him.'

'But... but haven't you set a deadline?' Roisin stared at Maeve. 'You haven't paid him in full, have you?'

Maeve put a cushion on her stomach. 'No, of course not. He's paid in stages. But now that the economy is taking off again there is a new building boom, and everyone is building around here. You should see some of the holiday homes that are going up along the coast. You'd think you were on the Riviera. Anyone with a bit of cash wants a house in Kerry. No idea how they manage to get planning permission. I suspect there is some money being paid under the table.'

'Oh, God. So this means the house won't be ready as soon as you hoped?'

'Yes.' Maeve sighed and leaned back in the sofa. 'And we already have a booking for June, which is four months away. A family of five. They live in the UK but want to spend Whit weekend here as the dad grew up in the area. And I'm sure there'll be more as that weekend is the start of the summer season. We were right on target when Johnny decided to start his new project. He said he would be back when that was underway. But that was two weeks ago and I haven't seen him since.'

'That's terrible.' Roisin got up and put another sod of turf on the dying embers of the fire. 'So how do we get him back on the job?'

'I have no idea. I'm afraid that might be your first job while you're here. I haven't been able to get in contact with him, since I've been stuck in the house. Paschal thinks it will take a lot of negotiating to get Johnny to come back to finish – the other project is that huge house he's building for some celebrity.'

'Yeah, but he promised to finish Willow House,' Roisin protested, suddenly angry with this builder who made up his own rules as he went along. That was both unfair and unprofessional, and poor Maeve had had to deal with all of this as well as being pregnant and having that awful scare. 'I suddenly feel the need for that cup of tea,' she announced. 'I might as well make it while I'm up.'

'There's a bottle of Bushmills beside the cooker if you want something stronger. But I'd love a cup of tea.'

'I'll make it,' Roisin promised.

Maeve closed her eyes. 'I'm so glad you're here,' she said gratefully, looking like she was relaxing for the first time in months. 'I feel all the tension going as I sit here, talking to you. You can't imagine how good that makes me feel.'

'Me too. And I'll get that house finished on time even if it kills me,' Roisin vowed, feeling a surge of energy at the thought. 'I'll take those plans and draw up a spreadsheet on my laptop. And a list with bullet points for the builders. If we can get them focused on what's left, be specific with what needs to be done, maybe we can get them to finish. Where's the contract he signed?'

Maeve opened her eyes. 'Er… there's no contract as such. They don't do that here. We shook hands and then we drew up a plan. It's in the drawer. Brown paper bag.'

Roisin walked to the desk and pulled out a drawer. 'In a brown paper bag?'

'No. *On* a brown paper bag. He must have run out of paper. He stuck it through our letterbox early one morning and then he came around later and we shook hands.'

Roisin froze and stared at Maeve. 'You're joking, of course.'

Maeve giggled. 'No. It's true.'

Roisin looked into the drawer and found a torn piece of brown paper that had once been a shopping bag from the garden centre. On it was scribbled a list in pencil with an undecipherable signature at the bottom. 'I don't believe it.' She stared at Maeve. 'How can they work like this?'

Maeve was still laughing. 'Welcome back to Kerry, darlin'.'

Chapter Five

In the early morning light the next day, Roisin walked around the upper floor, discovering just what an enormous project she had got herself into. Upstairs, her bedroom was the only one that had been finished. The other ones still had the old furniture and the new en-suite bathrooms were either empty or had the pipes and drains but no showers or toilets. The only functioning bathroom was the old one beside what had been Phil's bedroom. In a way that was a relief as the boys would have beds to sleep in. A month from now the boys would arrive and it would be a few months before early June, when the first guests arrived, but even so, there was so much to do which had to be finished in time. The central heating didn't work because the old boiler had broken down and a new one hadn't been installed yet, Maeve had told her. Roisin sighed and went downstairs to see what had – or hadn't – been done there.

The living room had been stripped back to the bare floorboards and the wallpaper had been pulled off revealing plaster on the walls that showed cracks and patches of damp. The windows had been replaced, but that was the only sign of any real work being done. In the dining room, the wallpaper hung in strips and some of the floorboards had been taken up revealing rotting timbers that had yet to be replaced. All the furniture had been removed and put into storage, Maeve had told her, which was a relief. At least the beautiful antique pieces and the lovely paintings were safe from this destruction.

The kitchen was much the same as before with the Aga working perfectly, a blessed relief now that the boiler was no more. Paschal had bought tea, bread, eggs and butter for her breakfast, so she could eat before she headed to the supermarket in Waterville to buy supplies. Johnny O'Shea's other building project was on the way there and Roisin planned to call in and try to talk him into coming back to Willow House and finish it. Fat chance, Maeve had said, but Roisin would have a go. She usually succeeded in making people deliver, even if it looked impossible at the start. If anyone ever doubted her ability to do something, she worked extra hard to prove them wrong. And this was a prime example. She'd show that Kerryman how to rejig his schedule and get him to come around. How hard could it be?

Roisin had plenty of time to plan her attack during the drive on the winding coast road to Waterville. It was a blustery day, with clouds scudding across the blue sky and waves crashing onto the shore below, sending sprays of water over the road. The car shook as the gusts hit it sideways, and Roisin had to keep a tight grip on the steering wheel to stop it veering off the road.

She laughed out loud, feeling a surge of pure joy as she glanced out across the ocean. She had forgotten how exhilarating Kerry could be and how the light changed from one minute to the next.

She wished she could paint the wild seascape and got out and took a shot with her phone, just to catch the amazing sight. Then she got back into her car and continued her journey, keeping an eye out for the new house Johnny O'Shea was building, preparing her first attack.

Ten minutes later, she saw the huge two-storey construction high on a hill just outside Waterville. It was an imposing house, with a tower at each end and a long terrace below. The views from the picture windows on the top floor would be spectacular. The roof was finished, but the scaffolding was still up and she could see men putting in windows and finishing the façade. Roisin pulled up below the terrace and climbed the steps to what would be the front door. She peered into the hall, where the smell of paint was overwhelming.

'Hello?' she shouted. 'Is Johnny O'Shea there?'

'Who wants to know?' came the reply from deep inside the house.

'Roisin Moriarty,' she replied. 'From Willow House in Sandy Cove. I'm Maeve's sister.'

'Right. I'll be there in a minute,' came the reply.

Roisin realised that 'a minute' in Kerry was more like half an hour, and she paced around, her frustration rising, before anyone appeared. Just as she was about to give up and go into the house, a short, wiry man with receding fair hair appeared. 'Yeah?' he said, peering at her with suspicion in his small dark eyes. 'I'm Johnny. What do you want?'

Roisin straightened her back, ready for battle. 'I want to talk to you about coming back to finish what you started over there.'

'I will when I can.'

'And when would that be?' she enquired, trying to keep the sarcasm out of her voice.

He glared at her. 'When this bastard is finished.'

'But you started our house first,' Roisin argued. 'Why not come over and finish it? You agreed on a date. It's all in the plan you drew up for Phil and Maeve and then you shook hands on it.'

'I know what I did,' Johnny replied. 'And I will finish it. Soon.'

Roisin stamped her foot, knowing it was childish but she couldn't help herself. 'You have to come back *now*. There is so much to be done. The central heating for a start, then the floors in the living and dining room, the bedrooms upstairs still have no bathrooms, not to mention the windows and the plasterwork on the front of the house. We need to get the house organised and there's a booking for the guesthouse for June. If you don't start now, you'll never have it done in time.'

'Says who?' He kept staring at her. 'You think you can come here from Dublin and order me around? On whose authority?'

'Well…' Roisin stuck out her chin. 'Phil made me the project leader of the building work. So I'm the one to call the shots from now on.'

He let out a laugh. 'The shots?' He smirked and turned, disappearing into the house. 'I'm busy right now,' he said over his shoulder. 'I'll be around when I have the time.'

'But… but couldn't you come and install the new boiler? Or ask the plumber who works for your firm, at least,' Roisin called after him. 'It's freezing in the house.'

'Put on a sweater,' he shouted back from somewhere inside.

Seething with anger, Roisin marched inside, across the plastic sheeting, nearly tripping on a pot of paint and walked into a huge room where kitchen units were being installed. 'I think this is outrageous,' she shouted. 'You agreed to the job on our house and then you leave it half-finished and start another project, while Willow House is like a… a warzone,' she ended. 'And I have to live there while I wait for you to get your arse in gear. Without heating in the middle of fecking January. I'll be complaining loudly all over the village, which might not be so good for your image.'

Johnny sighed and stuffed a wrench into a pocket of his cargo pants. 'Okay. I'll be there in the morning with some of the lads.'

Roisin blinked. That seemed nearly too easy. But maybe he had been scared by her threats? She sighed and smiled. 'Great. Thanks. See you tomorrow, then.'

'Yeah. See ya.' He turned back to the kitchen units.

Roisin drove off, feeling she had won the first battle. That'd show Cian she could hack this without him. They had always worked together, but this time she was on her own. Part of her wished he was there with her, but then she wouldn't know if she would manage this by herself. This was the real test. She wondered where he was and if he had forgotten all about her. He was probably having a ball with Andrew, fishing and surfing and drinking beer. Maybe even chatting up women? The thought made her shiver. Was this so-called break a good idea?

Roisin emerged from the supermarket with a trolley full of supplies in order to load the freezer so she wouldn't have to go back soon again. She remembered that living miles away from a supermarket required stocking up regularly with things that couldn't be found in the small village grocery shop. Country life was so different from the city, where you could run to a well-provisioned shop for anything at any time of the day. As she was stuffing bags of shopping into the car in the parking lot outside the supermarket, someone called her name.

'Yoohoo! Roisin McKenna, isn't it?'

Roisin turned around to come face to face with a large woman with brown hair and a wide grin. 'Oh, hi. You're… Nuala?'

'Sure am.' Nuala squeezed Roisin's hand in an iron grip. 'Howerya at all? Haven't seen you in ages, but I recognised you straight away. That blonde hair and the pretty face and of course the fancy clothes make you stick out around here.'

'Fancy?' Roisin laughed, easing her hand out of the vice-like handshake. She glanced at her cream down jacket and blue jeans. Not brand new but still fashionable and maybe a tad too glam for this part of the world. 'Hi, Nuala. I remember you from the old days. You haven't changed a bit, except you've slimmed down and grown up. You look great, I have to say.' That wasn't a lie. With her rosy cheeks and warm smile Nuala did look fit, healthy and happy. They had been friends as teenagers during those summers long ago, but then lost touch.

Nuala smiled. 'Thanks. Sure, life here isn't bad at all. But it's busy with the pub and three teenagers, all pains in the butt in different ways.'

Roisin nodded. 'I know. I have three of those monsters myself. All boys.'

'Then you got off easy. I have two girls and a boy. The girls are the worst. Always having some kind of drama, falling in and out with boys and friends and fighting with each other.'

'Not to mention their phones and their social media stuff.'

Nuala rolled her eyes. 'Drives me nuts. Thank God Seán Óg gets them to behave when they start killing each other. The best dad ever. What about yours?'

'Cian?' Roisin squirmed. 'Well, yeah, he's great.' Roisin drew breath, wondering how she was going the get away without telling Nuala the story of her life. 'But he's not here at the moment. He's taken off in a campervan around Ireland. And the boys are in a boarding school up the coast in County Clare.'

Nuala looked at her with envy. 'Oh, that's fabulous. So you get to have some time for yourself? And now you're here to help Maeve, she told me.'

'And to get the house finished,' Roisin filled in and closed the boot.

'Yeah, I heard. That's a job and a half. Getting Johnny to stay, I mean. He's got about half a dozen different jobs going at the same time and everyone is screaming to get him to finish what he started.'

'I had a word with him just now at that big house on the way here.'

'You did?' Nuala raised an eyebrow.

'Yes. And he's coming back tomorrow with the lads to get started again.'

'Is he now?'

'Yes. That's what he said.'

'Doesn't he always?' Nuala sighed and shook her head. 'If he arrives tomorrow morning and starts working on your place, it'll be a bloody miracle. Everyone will think you've said a thousand novenas and sprinkled holy water on Johnny or something.'

Roisin stared at Nuala. 'You mean he lied to me?'

'Not exactly. He says what people want to hear so they'll leave him alone. Johnny is a law unto himself. Shame he's the only builder around here and he's also very good. He can do what he wants when he wants it. You just have to be patient. He will finish the house. Eventually.'

Roisin winced, panic clenching her stomach. 'Oh, God. What am I going to do? My boys are arriving for their mid-term break at the end of next month. I must at least have heating by then.'

'I'm sure they'll cope. As long as there's broadband they'll be happy. But maybe I can get you someone to install the boiler for you. I'll have a word with the plumber who helps us out.' She patted Roisin's shoulder. 'Don't worry. It'll be fine. I'll give you a call at the house later to let you know what the plumber says. Bye for now, and good luck.' Nuala got into the big four-by-four parked beside Roisin's car and took off, the engine rumbling loudly.

Roisin stared at the lights disappearing up the road, feeling she had learned more about Kerry men in the last few minutes than she had ever known before. They were a force to be reckoned with and it would take more than spreadsheets and lists with bullet points to crack this particular project. But she was half-Kerry, she reminded herself. She could do this. She only had to figure out how.

Chapter Six

As Nuala had predicted, there was no sign of Johnny and his lads the following morning. Roisin wandered around the house taking note of what needed to be done. Upstairs, five of the six bedrooms had no bathrooms as the designated en-suites were bare and had not even been tiled. The toilets, hand basins and bathtubs were being delivered during the week, but there was nowhere to put them. Downstairs, the floorboards in the living and dining room needed to be replaced and some of the walls had to be plastered. Phil's new sitting room was nearly ready, but needed a final touch of plaster around the window and the partition wall finished.

The list seemed endless but she kept going until every job was recorded. Then she went along the path to Maeve's house to see if she needed help with anything. She stopped several times to look at the old house, thinking how well it fitted into the landscape standing on a grassy hill overlooking the beach where the waves crashed onto the shore sending sprays of foam over the cliffs just below the house. It looked so proud standing there, like an impregnable fortress, protecting its territory. She said a little prayer that it would always stand there, cared for by the generations to come. Roisin cast a last affectionate look at the house and resumed her walk along the path to the cottage.

She found her sister at the desk in the living room working on her laptop.

'Hi,' Roisin said as she walked inside. 'How are things?'

Maeve looked up. 'Great. I was doing a bit of work but then I switched to Facebook to catch up with some of my friends.'

'How are you feeling?'

Maeve stretched and smiled. 'Fine, apart from needing to go to the loo every five minutes and a touch of nausea. Is that normal?'

'Perfectly normal. The nausea will be gone completely soon and the need to run to the toilet should ease. It comes back during the last few weeks, so enjoy the easy part.'

'I am.' Maeve put her hands on her stomach. 'I'm amazed this is happening. It's so wonderful to share this with you, Roisin. Not just because you can reassure me, but because it's so lovely that we're together during this special time.'

Roisin kissed Maeve on the cheek. 'Me too. I'm glad to help in any little way I can.'

'I feel less nervous now you're here. It's nice to have an old pro to ask silly questions.'

'Ask away,' Roisin replied. 'No question is silly, you know. The first time can be scary.'

'Thanks, darling.' Maeve turned to her laptop. 'Have you seen the photos Cian posted yesterday?'

'No. I was too tired. I had dinner and then I had to look around the Internet to see if there might be someone else who could finish the work on the house. But there's nobody in this area.'

'I could have told you that. Did you find Johnny yesterday?'

'Yes. In that mansion he's building for his noveau riche cousin. I'm afraid I shouted at him.'

Maeve sighed. 'Thought you might lose it. That temper of yours isn't a great help in these kinds of situations. Should have warned you to grovel a bit.'

'Grovel?' Roisin exclaimed. 'Why should we have to do that? He's promised to do the job and he's not doing it. He even lied to me and said he'd be here this morning but of course there is no sign of him.' She sighed and sat down on the chair opposite Maeve. 'Show me Cian's photos. At least one of us is having fun.'

Maeve turned the laptop around. 'Here. They were surfing in Sligo yesterday. Andrew must have taken the shots.'

Roisin peered at the photo of Cian in a wetsuit riding on a surfboard, then at the picture of him grinning into the camera raising a pint of Guinness in some pub. He looked carefree and happy and very handsome. 'Oh, God I miss him.' She sighed and turned away from the screen. 'But he doesn't seem to be missing me much.'

'I'm sure he does,' Maeve soothed. 'But maybe it's good for him to have a bit of a boys' holiday with his best friend.'

'Yeah, of course. And I'm glad to be here with you.'

Maeve reached across the desk and took Roisin's hand. 'Me too. It feels so good to have you next door and know you're taking care of everything.'

'I'm not doing a great job so far,' Roisin remarked. 'But I'll get the hang of how to deal with Kerry builders. I'll even grovel if that's what it takes.'

'I'm sure you will. But you need to work on Johnny and get him to like you first. He can be a little full of himself. You need to tell him what a wonderful builder he is and so on. I've been dealing with him for a while now, and I've discovered that weak spot, at least. You need to channel your inner Kerry woman and see things the way he does.'

'Inspirational,' Roisin said, impressed.

Maeve winked. 'Inspired by our ancestor, you know. Do you want to walk on the beach before lunch?'

Roisin jumped up from her chair. 'I'd love to. It's such a nice day, nearly like spring.'

'A pet of a day as they say here.' Maeve took her jacket from the back of a chair. 'It's going to be wild tonight, as well, with high winds, so let's make the best of it.'

They walked out of the house and the short distance to the steep path that led to the beach. The wind had dropped and the sea lay like a mirror across the bay. Seagulls screeched above them and a flock of oystercatchers fed on the seaweed at the water's edge, fluttering away as they approached. Further out they could see gannets diving into the water catching fish, hardly making a splash, elegant as ballet dancers, emerging seconds later with their catch in their yellow beaks. Roisin stopped and watched, breathing in the salty air, basking in the warmth of the sun on her face. She tucked her hand under Maeve's arm, happy to be there and being free to enjoy the beautiful day with nothing much to do other than walk along the beach watching the wildlife and breathing the fresh, salt-laden air. Was this what Cian felt too? Free and happy? She hoped he did, even if he had agreed to her scheme so easily, which meant he wanted a break from her.

'Look, there's someone coming towards us,' Maeve exclaimed.

Roisin glanced in the direction Maeve was pointing and spotted the figure of a man walking swiftly along the water's edge. As he came closer, she saw he was tall and wore a navy anorak, jeans and walking boots. Soon he waved and shouted, 'Hello!'

'Hi,' Maeve shouted back. 'Nice day.'

He increased his speed and was soon at their side. 'Lovely,' he panted. He had close cropped fair hair, piercing grey eyes with black lashes and dark stubble on his chin. 'Hi,' he said when he had caught his breath. 'I'm looking for Johnny O'Shea.'

'Isn't everyone?' Roisin remarked dryly.

The man looked at her. 'You too?'

'Yeah,' Roisin said and gestured towards Willow House on the hill above the beach. 'That's one of his unfinished symphonies.'

The man glanced at the house, where the scaffolding could be seen clearly in the bright sunshine. 'Oh hell, that looks like some big job. Mine looks puny in comparison.' He laughed and stuck out his hand. 'I'm Declan O'Mahony. I have a house with half a roof near Ballinskelligs.'

'I'm Roisin Moriarty and this is my sis—' Roisin stopped and stared at the man. 'Oh my God, it's you!'

Chapter Seven

The man frowned. 'Who do you think I am, exactly?'

'Declan O'Mahony. The journalist,' Roisin replied, feeling a buzz of excitement.

He laughed and bowed. 'That's right, ma'am. The vilified, spat-upon whistleblower and former crime and political reporter. Now in hiding in a remote part of Ireland where nobody would recognise me. Or so I thought.'

'We recognised you immediately,' Roisin said, laughing. 'Didn't we, Maeve?'

'Er… No?' Maeve looked from Roisin to the stranger. 'Should I know you?'

Roisin rolled her eyes. 'He was only the most famous reporter in all of Ireland a year or two ago.'

'Three,' O'Mahony corrected. 'That's when the shit hit the fan about that corruption scandal in the Irish parliament.'

'Oh, that,' Maeve said, looking relieved. 'That's when I was still living in London. I heard something about it but it seemed to die down after what was going on in the UK at the time. And then I moved here, where nobody gets excited about anything except hurling and whatever the county council gets up to.'

O'Mahony laughed. 'Why do you think I moved here?'

'So you're building a house here?' Roisin asked.

O'Mahony nodded. 'Yes. Well, not exactly. I'm doing up an old house and they just stripped the roof ready for the new slates. It's up the road near Ballinskelligs. I'm writing a book and working freelance for a number of different newspapers. RTE let me go, as they so diplomatically put it when those politicians threatened to sue after that special I was involved in. They didn't have a leg to stand on, as everything I revealed was true, but the top people in the media felt I was too hot to handle. So no more TV for me.'

'Pity,' Roisin said, looking at his ruggedly handsome face.

He grinned at her. 'I'll take that as a compliment, if I may.'

'Of course,' Roisin purred, smiling. God, he was attractive in the flesh. She had seen him on TV many times and thought he was an excellent reporter with a fantastic delivery. His political review programmes had been among her favourites and his crime reporting had been like watching a good detective movie. But he had been too hard-hitting, revealing some uncomfortable truths about the goings-on in both politics and the police force, which had rattled the top people and then he suddenly disappeared from the TV screens. She had thought he was good-looking, but up close like this, his charisma was more obvious.

'I'm Maeve O'Sullivan,' Maeve interrupted, holding out her hand. 'Roisin's sister. 'Nice to meet you, Mr O'Mahony.'

'Sorry,' O'Mahony said and shook hands with them both. 'I should have said hello properly. Please call me Declan,' he continued. 'I take it you don't know where the elusive Johnny is? I was told he was around here today.'

'I wish,' Roisin sighed. 'He said he'd be here in the morning. But he forgot to say if it was this morning or Christmas morning next year.'

'He told me he'd be around soon, whenever that is,' Declan said with a sigh. 'At least you have a roof. I have to stay in a B&B in Ballinskelligs which isn't that great. They're usually closed until after Easter but they took pity on me and let me stay in the annexe which has no heating.'

'Ah, no heating. Join the club,' Roisin said. 'But at least I have a functioning Aga.'

'You don't know how lucky you are. But hey, this is a beautiful day.' He made a sweeping gesture at the glimmering ocean. 'Can't think of a better place to be on a day like this.'

'Neither can we,' Roisin agreed.

'I love it even in the rain,' Maeve stated.

He smiled at her. 'It kind of grows on you, doesn't it? Is your house one of Johnny's projects too?'

'No,' Maeve replied. 'I live in the cottage next door.' She pointed at the roof sticking up above the dunes. 'The one with the thatch.'

'She has central heating,' Roisin remarked.

Declan looked impressed. 'I'm rapidly turning green. But why aren't you staying with your sister, Roisin?'

'No room,' Roisin replied. 'The cottage is small enough as it is and they're expecting a baby in the summer.'

'Congratulations,' Declan said.

'Thank you.' Maeve looked at him with interest. 'How about you? Are you married, or…?'

'No.' There was a guarded look in his eyes as he moved away. 'Well, I'd better get going. If Johnny shows up will you let me know?'

Roisin laughed. 'Of course I won't. If I see him first, he's mine and I'm not going to let him go until he's finished.'

Declan laughed. 'Good luck with that. And vice versa. If I manage to grab him, there's no way he'll come within a hundred yards of this place until every slate is up on my roof. See you around, girls. Nice to meet you.' He turned and walked swiftly back the way he had come, scrambling over the rocks to the main beach like a mountain goat.

'Gee, he's fit,' Roisin said, watching him disappear.

'And cute.'

Roisin nodded and sighed. 'Oh, yes.' She turned to Maeve. 'But did you have to ask if he was married? I could tell it made him uncomfortable.'

'And you telling him about my pregnancy was perfectly fine, then?' Maeve looked annoyed.

'It just came out.' Roisin took Maeve's arm. 'I'm sorry. Did it embarrass you?'

Maeve shook her head and laughed. 'Nah, of course not. It's all over the village already. But why would being asked about his marital status make whatshisname uncomfortable?'

'Because he has been married three times. It's been all over the tabloids. I'm sure he's sick of talking about it. It's also probably one of the reasons he wants to keep a low profile.'

'I can imagine.' Maeve shot Roisin a probing look. 'You seem a little starstruck.'

'God, yes.' Roisin sighed. 'I loved him on the telly. Nobody could expose a crooked politician like he could. He was also on that *Watchdog* programme that reported on all kinds of scams and frauds. There was one where he revealed a huge insurance fraud. He had to stay in hiding for weeks after that.'

Maeve pulled up the zip of her jacket. 'I had no idea. I haven't been very good at keeping in touch with the news. We hardly ever watch TV and we read the papers online. I'm afraid I'm going from the newly married bubble right into the baby one.'

Roisin tucked a strand of hair behind Maeve's ear. 'You've been nesting. That's lovely. Stay in that bubble as long as you can. You'll never get that time back. I remember those days,' she said wistfully. 'Cian and I were only just out of our teens and trying to live on a shoestring while we finished our degrees. And then we had Darragh and started our business and then it was like getting on a train we couldn't get off.'

'But now you've stepped off that train.'

Roisin started to walk. 'Yes. And it feels strange. And Cian so far away, both geographically and emotionally. But we need this time and space to ourselves, I think. Just so we can get together as two independent people.'

'As long as you don't become too independent.'

Roisin looked at Maeve, squinting in the bright sunlight. 'Oh, I'm sure that won't happen. We needed a little space right now. We need to be apart for a while, just so we don't end up leaning on each other too much. You can get too dependent on the other person if you live and work together for as long as we have. So I feel it's good to fly solo for a bit, and then we'll be stronger than ever before.' She bent and picked up a large shell and admired the scalloped edges. 'I love looking at these shells. I had no idea you could fish for scallops here until Paschal told me last year, or that there was such a variety of marine life on this beach.'

'Yes, you did. Uncle Joe taught us. Or tried to.' Maeve picked up a small shell with a pearly inner surface. 'Look, this one is called mermaid's toenails. Isn't it pretty with the mother of pearl inside?'

Roisin took the shell from Maeve. 'It's gorgeous. I have a vague memory of what Uncle Joe tried to teach us, but I don't think such things stick in a teenage brain.'

'I know.' Maeve put the shell in the pocket of her anorak. 'But when I came back here, I began to see all the beautiful, miraculous things in nature. Paschal was a huge help. He is so at one with this landscape and the sea. And he knows everything there is to know about marine wildlife. It's fascinating to learn about the tiniest creatures in the ocean that make up the whole ecosystem. But that is in great danger now. We have to protect what's left and make sure it stays alive.'

'It's really scary to see what humans have done to the planet.' Roisin looked out across the bay. 'I've only been here a short time, but I have already noticed how there is very little regard for the impact all these new buildings will have. That huge house Johnny is building near Waterville is an example of how people just go ahead and do what they want without thinking about the environment.'

'I know,' Maeve said with feeling. 'Not only is that house a blot on the landscape, it could also be damaging the land around it with a septic tank so close to the seashore. I heard they're putting in a swimming pool, as well. And I'm wondering how they got planning permission for a huge two-storey house when the other new houses in the area are only one-storey, with dormer windows being the tallest.'

'I thought there were laws about that.'

Maeve shrugged. 'Easy to get planning permission if you know the right people. The person whose house Johnny is building is the cousin of a local politician. And they're all related to each other. But…' She looked thoughtful. 'It's possible to check with the planning office and see if they really got the permission. Sometimes they build anyway and hope for the best.'

'And if they don't have permission and someone objects? What happens then?'

'They have to stop building and wait until they get it.'

Roisin forgot about the blue sky, the beach, the seabirds and the lovely view. 'Stop building!?'

Maeve laughed. 'I know what you're thinking, but I wouldn't go there if I were you. Forget what I said. Don't mess with the locals. You have no idea how fast gossip and all kinds of talk spread around here. And once they find out someone has come down from Dublin and started poking around in their business, you will never get Johnny to finish Willow House.'

'I'm half-Kerry,' Roisin argued.

'Yeah but the Dublin half is all they see.'

'Hmm, okay…' Roisin thought for a moment. She was desperately looking for a way to get Johnny away from the other job so he could come back and finish Willow House. Maybe there was a way around it… 'I need to be really sneaky in this case. And find someone even sneakier to do the dirty work for me.'

'What? Who? I don't know anyone like that around here.'

'Yes we do. We just spoke to him.'

'The reporter guy?'

Roisin nodded, feeling a spark of excitement. 'Of course, dear sister. We're going to get him to do the research. And then the rest will be easy.'

'You nutcase. He'll never agree.' Maeve stuck her hands in her pockets and started to walk back.

Roisin fell into step with her. 'Why not? It'll be in his own interest. He'll get his roof done a lot sooner if my plan works. It's a quick job really. All they need to do is to stick up the rest of the slates. If he helps out he can move into his house very soon and then Johnny will be free to tackle our job. I'm sure Declan will jump at the chance.'

They had reached the steep path from the beach to the cottage. Maeve looked further away at the big house on the hill overlooking the ocean and sighed. 'Poor old Willow House. Will it ever be finished?'

'Yes,' Roisin said with feeling. 'It will.'

Maeve shook her head and laughed. 'You haven't changed since you were seven. Nothing was impossible for you then. Not even diving from the pier even though the other kids didn't dare.'

'I practised for weeks. But I was scared stiff when I finally did it.'

'Really? I had no idea. I thought you were the bravest girl in the world. I always have ever since. All the things you tackled and came out smiling. You were like Pippi Longstocking. I was in awe of you.'

'I was good a faking it.' Roisin started up the path. 'And now I'm going to get in touch with Declan O'Mahony and see if he'll join forces with me so we can get our houses finished.'

'How are you going to do that? You don't have his number.'

'I'm going to find his house. On the road to Ballinskelligs, he said. A roofless house can't be that hard to find.'

There was a rumble in the distance as a blue van drove down the lane to Willow House and drew up at the front steps. 'I wonder who that is?' Roisin said.

'Maybe Johnny has arrived like he said?'

'That would be a miracle.' Roisin ran up the path. 'I'll go and see. I'll be with you in a minute when I've found out what's going on.'

She arrived at the house as two men in boiler suits were dismantling the scaffolding and loading some of it into the van.

'What are you doing?' Roisin screeched. 'Why are you taking down the scaffolding?'

One of the men, ruddy-faced with the shoulders of a wrestler, turned around. 'Johnny needs it all at the big house in Waterville.'

'But…' Roisin said, near tears. 'What about this house? And the new windows? And all the rest?'

'Haven't a clue,' said the other man, who looked friendlier than his partner. 'We were just told to get this stuff and bring it over. Just following orders, like.'

'Oh, God.' Roisin let out a sound halfway between a sigh and a groan. 'This is terrible. This house will never be finished.'

'Ah sure of course it will. One day,' the ruddy-faced man said. 'You just have to be patient. It'll be done eventually.'

'Eventually?' Roisin whispered. 'That sounds like never to me. Tell me, is there *any* way I can get him to come and finish this place? At all?'

'You could try and talk to him.'

'I did and he said he'd be here this morning, but of course he wasn't.'

'I'd catch him later in the day at his own house,' the friendly-faced man suggested. 'No use talking to him when he's in the middle of something. Try going over there around eight or so. He'll be after his dinner then and more inclined to listen.'

'Where does he live?'

The man jerked his thumb over his shoulder towards the west. 'Down there on the other side of the village. Down a lane just after The Two Marys' café.'

'The two Marys?'

'Yeah. You know, the two Keating girls who opened the beach-side café last year. Mary and her cousin… Mary. It's more of a fish and chip joint but they call it a café. There's a sign with a cup on it over the door. Can't miss it.'

'Okay, thanks.' Roisin gave a start as a four by four drove in and pulled up in a shower of gravel behind the van.

Nuala stuck her head out the window and glared at the man. 'What the hell are you doing? Put that scaffolding back or I'll tell Johnny.'

'He won't mind. He was the one who told us to do it. He needs it for—'

'For that pile of shite he's building near Waterville?' Nuala filled in. 'Just a wild guess but it seems it's going to be bigger than the Taj Mahal.'

'The what?' the man asked.

'Big place in India,' Nuala informed him and got out of the van. 'Hey, Roisin, I brought you someone who can help you with the boiler. Best plumber in the area. You'll have the central heating up and running in no time.'

'Johnny won't like that,' the smaller workman said. 'He doesn't like other people than his own men working on one of his projects.'

'Well, tough,' Nuala snapped. 'If he wants to do it himself, why isn't he here? Why is he leaving that poor woman with no heating in the middle of winter?'

'That's none of your business,' the ruddy-faced man said. 'Move your car out of the way so we can get past when we have finished.'

Nuala put her hands on her ample hips. 'What if I won't?'

'I'll call the Guards.'

'You're on private property,' Nuala shot back. 'In any case, I doubt the Guards will come all the way from Waterville to move me out of the way. I'm sure they have better things to do.'

The man shrugged. 'Okay, whatever. We can stay here until you have to move. We brought lunch and all.'

Nuala's eyes narrowed. 'You're not from around here, are you?'

'No,' he replied. 'I'm from Cork.'

'Thought so. A Kerryman would never be so rude.'

'A Cork woman would never be this stroppy,' he shot back.

Roisin watched them, trying not to giggle. Nuala was such a character, standing up to these men in a way Roisin would never dare. She should have joined in but felt it would be impossible to get a word in. And in any case Nuala was on a roll. She looked from one to the other, wondering how it would all end.

'Stroppy?' Nuala snorted. 'You caught me on a good day. You should see me when I'm in a bad mood.'

'I don't think I'd like that,' the man retorted. 'Move your bloody car so we can get on with our job and get out of here.'

'Oh, for feck's sake.' Nuala got back in her four by four. 'I'll move out of the way just to get rid of you. We don't want rude Cork men loitering around here.' She backed the car down the driveway and parked it, leaving space for the van to get through when they had finished taking down the rest of the scaffolding. Then she got out and gestured to someone sitting beside her. 'Okay, Olga, come out and meet Roisin.'

'Olga?' Roisin asked and walked to the jeep.

A tall woman with short dark hair dressed in dungarees with what looked like a thousand pockets over a grubby fisherman's sweater stepped onto the gravel. She took Roisin's hand in an iron grip, smiling broadly. 'Hello, Roisin. I'm Olga Lindblom,' she said in a thick east European accent. 'I fix your boiler, yes?'

'Eh, yes.' Roisin glanced at Nuala. 'That'd be lovely.'

'Olga is from Russia,' Nuala announced. 'She came here last year and has saved many a house from flooding and disasters. One of the most popular women here, isn't that right, Olga?'

'Oh yes,' Olga said, laughing. 'Even in the middle of the night I get calls. But I switch off my phone now and only work in the daytime. Except if there is a big flood and much water, then I come at once.'

'Sounds great.' On closer inspection, Roisin saw that Olga's hair had purple and pink highlights, she had studs in her ears and a ring in the side of her nose. Her eyes were so dark it was difficult to discern a colour and there was a gap in her teeth that made her look young and cheeky. The warm expression in her eyes and that wide, lopsided smile were all so charming that Roisin instantly warmed to her. 'If you can get the heating sorted, I'll cook you dinner,' she offered.

'Wonderful,' Olga said. 'But I can't fix today. I need to look first.'

'Yeah, I only brought her here to introduce you anyway,' Nuala interrupted. 'Olga has her own little van with all her tools and stuff outside her house in the village.'

'Not my house,' Olga protested. 'Just half of a house that I rent. But it's very nice.'

Nuala nodded. 'That's right. Hey, why don't you show Olga around and I'll come back later? I have to get going. The kids will be home from school soon and they'll be starving.'

Olga nodded. 'Yes, that's good. You pi—'

'No!' Nuala interrupted. 'I know what you were going to say but…' She sighed and shook her head. 'Olga, what have I said about using that expression?'

Olga laughed. 'Oops, so sorry. I forget. This is what I learned from television. P… pee off meaning going away, no?'

'No,' Nuala said sternly. 'I told you. That's not polite. Nor is that other word I told you about, the one starting with "f".'

Olga nodded. 'I know that one. I have to say feck instead of fuck. So you feck off now, right?'

'Jesus,' Nuala muttered. 'I give up.'

'No, no, no!' Olga exclaimed. 'Jesus is not good. We must not say his name except in church.'

'Exactly,' Roisin said primly, trying not to laugh out loud. 'Shame on you, Nuala.'

Nuala sighed and laughed. 'I can see the two of you will get on like a house on fire. See ye later, lads.' With that, Nula jumped into the jeep and took off behind the van that was just rounding the corner.

'So,' Olga said. 'The boiler. I take a look. You show me, okay?'

'This way.' Roisin walked to the house and led the way through the hall and down the corridor to the cellar door next to the kitchen.

Olga glanced into the rooms as they walked, letting out a long whistle. 'Holy shite. Much to do here.'

'You can say that again.'

'It will take a long time, I think. A very long time.'

'I know. But it'll be okay in the end, I'm sure.'

'How do you know?' Olga asked, looking glum. 'That builder is not very nice to you. He come and start, then stop. Why is this? He signed contract?'

'A kind of contract.' Roisin opened the door of the cellar and turned the light switch. 'But let's not go into that now. The new boiler is down there. Please let me know what you think.'

Olga nodded and went down the stairs. 'I look and then I must see radiators and pipes in the house.'

'Great. How about some lunch when you've finished?'

'Yes, please,' Olga said and disappeared into the depths of the cellar.

Roisin left the door open and went into the kitchen to see what she could put together for lunch. Olga looked as if she had a good appetite. She also looked as if she knew what she was doing and if what Nuala said was true, she'd have the central heating going very soon. One step forward, Roisin thought. But that was only one of what seemed like several thousand. How would she get the rest done?

*

'No problem,' Olga declared over a lunch of tomato soup and cheese toast. 'I can do this for you quickly. And if you need me to fix the new bathrooms, I can do that too. If the builder says yes. I've never worked with him. He has a lot of people from Cork working for him. And Polish people. They're good.'

'So I've heard.' Roisin finished the last of her soup. 'How did you come here?'

'With Nuala in her car.'

'No. I mean to Ireland. What's your story?'

Olga took another slice of cheese toast from the plate and crammed it into her mouth. 'Was married to Swede,' she mumbled through her mouthful. 'Then we broke up when I found him with another woman in our bed.'

'Oh, God that's awful. I'm so sorry. That must have been tough.'

Olga gave her a glimmer of a smile. 'For him, yes. I broke his front teeth and threw the woman out of the apartment. Naked.'

'Really?' Roisin stared at Olga with respect. 'You clobbered him?'

'What would you do?'

Roisin tried to imagine what she would do if she found Cian with a naked woman in their bed. 'He'd have more injuries than a few broken teeth,' she said with feeling.

Olga nodded. 'But of course. Then I packed up and came here.'

'Why did you choose Ireland?'

Olga shrugged. 'Don't know. Nice country. Friendly people, someone told me. So I booked a flight to Dublin and then the train to Killarney. I found work straight away with a plumbing firm. No problem with papers because I have a Swedish passport. And Swedish last name. That was the only good thing about my marriage, becoming Swedish. If I was still Russian, I couldn't work without a permit. But Sweden is in the EU, so…'

'That was lucky.'

Olga winked. 'More than lucky. I married him for the passport. But then I fell in love with him after the wedding and I thought he felt the same thing.' She gulped down the last of her soup. 'But he didn't. Any more soup?'

'Of course.' Roisin took Olga's soup plate and filled it up from the saucepan on the stove.

'What's your story?' Olga asked.

'My story?' Roisin handed her the plate and sat down. 'Oh, nothing much to tell. I've been married nearly twenty years. Three kids. All in boarding school right now.'

'And your husband? Where is he?'

'I don't know.' Roisin laughed. 'That sounds a bit strange, but it's true. He's on a kind of camping trip with his friend. We decided to take a break and be on our own for a bit. We've been together since we were in college so it was getting a bit…' Roisin stopped. A bit what? she asked herself. Boring? Stale? Unsatisfactory?

Olga looked thoughtful as she noisily slurped her soup. 'Not good idea this taking a break,' she remarked. 'You could get too used to it. Or he could meet someone new. Younger perhaps? Men are like that.'

'Not Cian.' Roisin laughed to hide her discomfort. This was getting far too personal. And scary. 'But hey, what about the boiler and the central heating?' she said to lead Olga back to a safer subject. 'It looks like quite a big job. Do you think you can do it on your own?'

'Not on my own,' Olga protested. 'I have two lads working for me. Young and strong. We can do this.'

'That's terrific. When can you start?'

'Tomorrow if you like. I have another job this afternoon but that will be finished tonight.' Olga looked thoughtful. 'As I said, if you want we do the bathrooms in this house, yes?'

'Well…' Roisin hesitated. 'I will speak to the builder first and see if we can work out some kind of deal about the plumbing. And then I'll draw up an agreement with you. Deadlines and payments and things like that.' She looked sternly at Olga. 'I don't do handshakes and scribbles on bits of paper. This has to be a proper contract with a schedule that you'll have to stick to.'

Olga smiled, showing a dimple in her left cheek. 'I like this. Much more professional. Kerry people are…' She shrugged. 'They make their own rules. Very difficult for people not from Kerry but we have to go with the flow and smile.' She tapped her forehead. 'But in here we are angry and saying bad words.'

Roisin giggled. 'That's for sure. And now I have to go to his house and tell him you're doing the plumbing.'

Olga nodded and got up from the table. 'Yes. Good idea. Get him when he has eaten. He will listen better then and not be in a bad mood.'

'I certainly hope so,' Roisin said with a feeling of dread at the thought of facing Johnny O'Shea again. If he had taken a dislike to her, the whole building project was doomed.

Chapter Eight

There was a chilly wind and a smattering of rain against the windscreen as Roisin drove through the village later that evening. The weather forecast promised strong winds and a sharp drop in the temperature later that night.

Roisin mentally blessed Nuala for introducing her to Olga. If the heating didn't work, the boys' mid-term break would be miserable. She imagined their long faces as they huddled around the Aga in the kitchen after a day's surfing. They were used to their creature comforts and the lack of heating in the middle of winter wouldn't go down well. She had to sort this out with Johnny and maybe even make him at least put in the windows at the front of the house, otherwise they'd only have two bedrooms that were fit to sleep in. Hopefully Olga was right and Johnny was in a sunnier mood after his evening meal and maybe also a glass of beer or two. If this didn't work, Roisin would have to put her plan B into action: trying to get Declan to find out if there was planning permission for the big house in Waterville. But that would be quite an undertaking and difficult to achieve. She hoped the need for that wouldn't arise.

She passed the last house of the main street and took the first left down the lane to the main beach, where she spotted the beachside café run by the 'two Marys', then she turned right into a driveway she hadn't spotted before and pulled up outside a white bungalow with a slate roof and a porch with a green door. Johnny's van parked outside confirmed this was the right house. But the red Audi parked behind it puzzled her until she saw the Dublin registration and the familiar figure in the driver's seat. Shit. Declan O'Mahony had obviously had the same idea. He got out, looking less than delighted to see her.

'What are you doing here?' he asked, looking at her with ill-disguised irritation.

'The same as you, I suspect,' Roisin replied and marched to the front door and pressed the doorbell.

Declan leaned against his car and folded his arms. 'He won't talk to you. I just tried and got the door slammed in my face. So I was just about to leave.'

'We'll see.' Roisin rang the bell again.

They waited while the wind whipped around them, tearing at their clothes and hair. Roisin shivered, knowing she should have put on her warm jacket instead of the flimsy cardigan. But she stiffened as she heard footsteps inside. The door was flung open and Johnny's angry face appeared.

'I thought I told you to clear off,' he snapped.

'That wasn't me,' Roisin started. 'It was him over there with the snazzy car.'

'Yeah, okay. I don't want to talk to you either. Call my office tomorrow.' Johnny started to close the door but Roisin put out her foot in the gap to stop it.

'Hang on just a minute. I need to tell you that I have a plumber who'll fix the heating and she'll do the bathrooms as well, if you agree.'

'Agree to what?' Johnny demanded.

'To letting her do the plumbing job in the whole house. It'll save us a lot of time and maybe even money.'

'Save us money?' Johnny glared at her with his dark eyes. 'In what way?'

'You won't have to pay that plumber you use and the job will be done much faster. Then all you have to do is put in the windows next week and start the rest of the work to be finished in the spring.' Roisin produced the plan she had drawn up and printed on Maeve's printer. 'It's all on this list with all the dates. If you do it this way, we can have the guesthouse operational by late May. And I'll be out of your hair and pay the rest of your fee. All done and dusted. What do you say?' She drew breath and shoved the plan at Johnny. 'Here. Take a look.'

He shot her a glimmer of a smile. 'You got yourself a deal, Miss McKenna.'

'Mrs Moriarty, actually,' she corrected.

'Nah, you're a McKenna through and through,' Johnny grunted. 'Never knew women more persistent than the McKenna girls. Your aunt is just the same.' He took the piece of paper. 'I don't do plans and stuff but I'll take a look and let you know. But you can go ahead with the Russian woman. She's good. Except keep her away from my lads. She's inclined to get up their noses and I don't want any trouble.'

'Absolutely,' Roisin promised. 'Thanks, Johnny.' But he had closed the door leaving Roisin in the dark, looking triumphantly at Declan. 'See? I got him to agree. How about that, eh?'

'How about what?' Declan replied with a touch of scorn in his voice. 'He agreed to take a look at your plan. I'd say he'll throw it in the fire as soon as you're gone. He only agreed to let you use that plumber. I'd say the rest is still up in the air.'

'Ha, we'll see about that.' Roisin walked back to her car and opened the door. 'You didn't even get to talk to him, except for being told to clear off. I think you can whistle for that roof.'

'Pretty stroppy, aren't we?' Declan drawled.

Roisin stiffened. 'Why don't you go back to Dublin?'

'Why don't you?'

'I'm from here, so I don't have to.'

Declan laughed. 'No you're not. You're just pretending. So you're a McKenna? Is that a big deal?'

'It is around here.'

'But you're from Dublin, if I'm not mistaken. What part?'

'What's it to you?' Roisin snapped and got into her car.

Declan walked across the gravel and stopped her closing the door. 'Hey, what is this? Some kind of warfare?'

Roisin looked up at his face and the probing grey eyes. 'Warfare? Not at all. You're just annoyed because I won.'

'Congratulations. Not annoyed at all. I just don't like arguing like this.'

Roisin raised an eyebrow. 'Really? I thought you would be used to this kind of conflict by now after all your tussles with the big guys.'

'You're a tougher nut to crack.'

Roisin smirked, beginning to enjoy herself. 'That's Kerry women for you. We never give an inch.'

'You're scaring me now.'

'Ya big chicken,' Roisin said and pulled the door shut.

'Hey, wait a minute,' he said as she started the car.

She glanced at him through the half-open window. 'Yes?'

'Let's not fight about this. I admit my defeat and bow to your superiority as a Kerry woman. Could we call a truce? No need to be enemies, is there?'

Roisin relaxed and turned off the engine. 'No, of course not. I'm sorry. I didn't mean to be bitchy. But your tone made me bristle a bit.'

'I'm sorry, too. I'm a bit touchy at the moment. Nothing personal at all. How about a drink in the pub up the road to make peace?' he suggested.

Roisin laughed and shook her head. 'The gossip will be all over the place in an hour. Roisin Moriarty drinking with a man behind her husband's back, they'll say.'

'But it's just a friendly drink in a public place,' he protested.

'That's what you think. In their minds it'll be a lot more. This is a small, quiet village where people know each other very well. Gossiping is the spice of life here. Especially in the winter when nothing much happens. And in some ways, it's still the nineteen fifties around here, like a little time warp.'

She paused, wrestling with the problem. A drink with him would be a welcome relief from all her problems that seemed to pile up with every day. He was probably feeling a little lost here, all alone in Kerry in the winter with no kindred spirit to talk to. The locals were nice and friendly but she was sure he didn't get to socialise much or even talk about things that went on in the world. She had Maeve and Paschal and the boys arriving later, but he didn't seem to have anyone to call on.

She smiled, feeling foolish for being over-sensitive. It would be nice to have a chance to know him better. It would take her mind off the problems with the house, and missing Cian. Besides, she had always wanted to meet Declan O'Mahony and here he was, asking her to have drink with her. Why was she hesitating?

'Okay. You're right,' she said. 'No big deal. So let them gossip about us. I don't really care.'

'Are you sure? I don't want to compromise a lady's reputation.'

'Nothing much to compromise. See you there in a few minutes.' Roisin slammed the door shut and started the engine with just a small dart of guilt. Should she be doing this? But it was just a chat and a drink with a nice man, she told herself. Nothing that Cian should worry about. Or anyone else.

Chapter Nine

The village pub was dark and nearly empty. It was lovely to step in from the cold to the warm cosy interior with its turf fire blazing in the fireplace and the little lamps casting a warm glow on the wooden floor and the wood panelling. Roisin glanced around to see if anyone had noticed them, but nobody looked up as they came in. An old man sat at the bar talking to the bartender and two women were gossiping over a glass of beer and a bowl of crisps at the far end of the pub. Declan led the way to a table near the fireplace and pulled out a chair. 'Here, let's sit by the fire and get warm.'

'Good idea.' Roisin sat down and held out her cold hands against the flames. 'It's a little chilly out there tonight.'

'What would you like?'

She looked up at him and saw something in his eyes that made her suddenly wary. 'I'm not in the mood for anything strong. A cup of tea would be nice, though.'

He nodded. 'Fine. I'll just have a glass of beer as I'm driving.'

'Of course,' Roisin agreed. 'Driving under the influence is not a good idea, but the Guards are never around at this time of year. Too busy setting up speed traps around Cahersiveen and other small towns. Much more lucrative for them.'

'It's not the Guards I'm worried about.' Without another word, he walked to the counter to place their order. 'They have sausage rolls that look fresh,' he called to her.

'Lovely. Get me some, please.'

He returned and sat down opposite her. 'Nice pub,' he said glancing around at the small space. 'One of my favourites around here. It still has that feel of the old days with all the old beer bottles on the shelves and those stone flagons they used for whiskey. And look at the pictures of what it was like in the beginning of the last century. Talk about a one-horse town.'

'More like a one donkey-town,' Roisin remarked. 'They were all dirt poor back then.'

'That's for sure. But are we better off, apart from our central heating, running water and Internet?'

Roisin laughed. 'Hey, I don't have any of that now, remember. But I know what you mean. And I think we are better off, to be honest. We have time to enjoy the fantastic scenery and nature. Back then all they were worried about was to be able to feed and clothe their families. You can't eat the scenery, you know.'

'Of course. But still, maybe we have gone too far with all this technology and our cushy lifestyles.'

Roisin knew it was only small talk to cover up some kind of reserve or maybe even shyness. They had only just met and he looked a little uncomfortable to be sitting here with her in such close proximity. 'But we can't wind the clock back,' she said. 'We have to deal with what we have created and try not to go overboard.'

He nodded. 'True but very difficult.'

Their order arrived and Roisin busied herself with pouring tea from the teapot while he paid. She bit into a sausage roll and waited while he took a sip from his beer, glancing at her over the rim of the glass.

'Do I qualify?' she asked.

He looked startled. 'What?'

'You're studying at me as if I'm some sort of subject for an article on Kerry women in the wild.'

'Or wild Kerry women?' He waggled his eyebrows and grinned, finally looking relaxed. 'I'm sorry. I didn't mean to stare at you like that. I suppose I'm a bit jumpy after all I've been through. Never trust anyone. Everyone is up to something behind a perfectly normal façade, that kind of thing.'

'And how about if this person is hiding something juicy worth revealing?' Roisin parried, beginning to enjoy herself.

He grinned. 'Everyone hides something they don't want anyone to know. But is it worth reporting? Most of the time it's not.'

'I suppose.' Roisin added milk to her tea and took a sip. 'So,' she started. 'What made you come here to the bog of beyond? Old local joke,' she added, in case he thought she was sneering at the village and its people.

'I think I told you that. I wanted to go somewhere remote and beautiful. Where I could look out across the ocean and just sit and think, away from people and...' he paused, 'women.'

'Women?' Roisin laughed. 'But here you are sitting in a pub with one of those.'

He shook his head. 'You're not one of them. I mean, you're not the kind of woman I usually mix with.' He sighed and took another sip of beer. 'Look, I don't want you to misunderstand me. I asked you to come for a drink because I needed a bit of company.' He sighed and shot her a sad little smile. 'I think I meant that I need a friend. Someone who trusts me and I can trust back, someone who is from around here but still not.' He drew breath. 'A Kerry Dubliner like you fits that description perfectly.'

Roisin nodded. 'I think I know what you mean.' She met his eyes and felt relieved that there was not the slightest hint of flirtatiousness there any more, only a deep sadness and a plea to be his friend with no strings or demands or judgement. 'Tell me about them,' she suddenly asked despite her resolve not to be inquisitive. 'The women who made you so sad and disillusioned.'

He looked at her thoughtfully. 'I will,' he said. 'But not now. It's such a long story and not fit for a cosy evening by the fire. But I can tell what I've learned the hard way.'

'What was that?' Roisin asked, surprised by the fire in his eyes.

'Don't expect to find the key to your happiness in someone else's pocket.'

'Oh.' Roisin looked at him and nodded. 'That's true. It kind of fits in with what we… I mean, I felt before I left Dublin. My husband and I…' She stopped. 'But maybe that's not a good subject for a night like this either.'

'Later perhaps?' he asked.

'Or maybe never.'

'Absolutely. Up to you.' He pushed his empty glass away and glanced at her. 'I'm very impressed with you, you know.'

'Me?' Roisin sat up straighter. 'Why?'

'Roisin Moriarty, head of Moriarty Consultancy. One of the best-known consultancies in Dublin. The go-to firm for new business consultancy. And that PR firm as a kind of annex. You started all of that.'

'Oh.' Roisin laughed. 'You googled me.'

'Of course. I always google interesting people I meet. Your sister is pretty impressive too. Very high profile in interior design. Didn't she do that new hotel in Cork? And the government offices in Dublin that were just refurbished?'

'Yes she did. She's an incredibly talented designer.'

'Not as talented as you.'

'Well, it wasn't just me,' Roisin protested. 'My husband did half of it.'

'A lot less than half, if I'm to believe what I saw on the Internet.'

'I don't know what you saw or who did what and how much, but the truth is that we did it together as a team. The business, the kids, the house. Everything.'

'And now?' He sat back and looked at her through half-closed eyes.

'Now we're taking a break,' Roisin said, trying to keep a positive tone. 'We need it after all the hard slog. We sold the business to our partner and let the house to an American. The boys are in boarding school so we're free to do what we want. Cian took off on some kind of sabbatical up the west coast in a campervan which has been his dream all his life.'

Declan raised an eyebrow. 'Sabbatical? From you?'

Roisin squirmed at the probing gaze from his luminous grey eyes. 'Yes, from me and everything: pressure, duty, responsibility. God knows he's earned it.'

'You're a very understanding woman. And what about you? Don't you need a break too?'

Roisin shrugged and laughed. 'Me? I'm the original Duracell Bunny. Can't stop and when Maeve cried for help to finish the building work and get the guesthouse up and running, I jumped at the chance. And my boys are only a little over an hour away and can come here for their breaks and I can go and visit them.' She drew breath and looked at him archly. 'There. You did it.'

'Did what?'

'Got everything out of me without really trying. You're one hell of a reporter, I have to say.'

He laughed and sat up. 'It's hardwired into me. I didn't mean to get all that out of you at all. I was just interested in what makes you tick. I'm great admirer of women.' He held up a hand. 'Not in a sexist way, but as a feminist.'

Roisin stared at him forgetting her tea and sausage roll. 'You're feminist?'

'Yes. One hundred per cent. I'm the only child of a single woman. My mother is also a journalist who had to struggle with men's ideas of what women should and shouldn't do. She's coped with a lot of harassment, sexual and otherwise, in her different workplaces and dealt with it beautifully. Never took shit from a man.'

'Your mother—' Roisin stopped and gasped. 'Derval O'Mahony is your mother? The editor-in-chief of *The Irish Times*? I read her leader all the time. She's amazing.'

'She certainly is,' Declan said proudly. 'But she's retiring this year.'

'Oh, that's a pity.'

'Don't worry. She won't stop. She's going to travel for a bit and write articles about what goes on in other countries. I think it'll be interesting to see what she gets up to next. She'll be eighty next year so she thought it was time to let the younger generation have a go.'

'I didn't know she was that old.'

'You have to google her.' Declan sat up and looked around the pub. Roisin followed his gaze and noticed that everyone had left and they were alone.

'I think it's time to leave,' Declan declared. 'The bartender is giving us funny looks.'

Roisin glanced at the man behind the counter and smiled at him. 'We'll be off in a minute,' she called.

The man nodded and wiped the counter. 'No problem. I wasn't trying to get you to leave. I was just looking to see if I recognised you. Roisin McKenna, they say. Maeve's sister, right?'

Roisin got up and walked to the counter. 'That's right.' She peered at him. 'I recognise you from somewhere. Have we met before?'

'Sure have,' he said. 'I was at the party in the Harbour Pub the night before the wedding last year. I'm Jack MacGillicuddy. Like the reeks.' He held out his hand. 'Welcome back to Sandy Cove.'

Roisin shook his hand. 'Thanks, Jack. It's been a while, except for Maeve's wedding but then we only stayed a couple of days. I'm here for a lot longer this time.'

He nodded and winked. 'Yeah, I'd say you will be. Johnny is a tough nut to crack. Especially now that he's doing that big house for… well, you know who.'

Roisin frowned. 'I don't know, actually. I mean yeah, I've heard it was for a local politician. But who is he really building that house for? I have a feeling it's someone else altogether.'

Jack squirmed. 'Well, it's just a rumour so I won't say it in case it isn't true, but…' He leaned over the counter and whispered something in her ear that made her gasp.

'What? Are you sure?'

'Nearly.' Jack jerked his head at Declan. 'But don't tell yer man over there or it'll be all over the country in an hour. And we'll be sued for spreading false rumours. Keep it to yourself, okay?'

'Okay,' Roisin whispered and winked at him. She jumped as Declan came up behind her.

'Ready to go?' he asked.

'Yes,' she said and walked to the door. 'See you, Jack,' she called over her shoulder. But he had disappeared through the back door.

'A new friend?' Declan asked as he held the door open for her.

'Not new, but someone I used to know.'

'And he had some startling news?'

Roisin glanced at Declan as she went through the door. 'No, not at all. He was just telling me that…' Roisin paused while she frantically tried to come up with something plausible. 'The county council have decided to have fibre broadband installed in this area. They'll start laying out the cables next week. Should be up and running by the summer.'

'I know. I read it in the local rag yesterday. Exciting, huh?'

'Well, it is to me.' Roisin walked ahead down the street to her car. 'My three sons are coming to stay for their mid-term break. They'll have to cope with the Internet the way it is now, but it'll be great to have fibre by the summer.'

'I can imagine. But I have a feeling you were told something a lot more startling than that.'

They had reached Roisin's car. She opened the door and got in, looking up at him standing there leaning against the bodywork. 'You know, Declan, you might be a hot shot reporter but around here you're just a blow-in.'

'I know,' he said calmly. 'But I have eyes and ears and a very twitchy nose. I can smell a story from miles away. Not that I'm looking for one, but there's something going on to do with that big house, isn't there?'

'Not as far as I know.' Roisin pulled at the door. 'I really have to go now. Thanks for the tea and chat.'

'I enjoyed it.' He stepped away. 'Good luck with the house. And if you find out for whom Johnny is building that house, will you let me know?'

'I will yeah,' Roisin said and banged the door shut, laughing as she drove off. Of course he knew that she meant she wouldn't as 'I will yeah' was Dublin speak for 'In your dreams.' Her mind buzzed with the news Jack had just told her and she couldn't wait to share it with Maeve. What a day it had been. Arguing with Johnny. Meeting Declan and Olga and now this. She had only been there twenty-four hours and all that had happened. So much for the peace and quiet of the countryside.

'You have no idea who's going to live in that big house,' Roisin exclaimed, standing in the door of the nursery with Maeve.

Maeve looked up from her task of stencilling dolphins on the wall. 'How about "hello, how are you this fine evening?"'

'Yeah, yeah, hi, how are you?' Roisin took off her cardigan. Her eyes focused on the wall Maeve was decorating. 'Oh, this is so sweet.

What a lovely little room.' She touched the old cradle making it rock gently. 'I love this. Where did you find it?'

'In the attic at Willow House. I think both Phil and Dad slept in it when they were babies. I painted it white and got a new mattress.'

'Gorgeous. And that rocking chair is perfect too.'

'I found that in an antique shop in Killarney. I thought I could sit there when I feed him or her.'

'Yes, that'll be great. Babies love rocking.' Roisin sat down in the rocking chair and looked at Maeve with tears in her eyes. 'I'm nearly jealous. There's nothing like having the first baby. Such a special, precious time.'

Maeve put her hand on her stomach. 'I can't wait. But it'll be months before anything happens. So I just have to be patient.'

'You need that time to adjust. Have you bought a lot of baby stuff yet?'

'No. I thought I'd wait a while. I'll do a big shop just before the birth.'

'Ooh,' Roisin said dreamily. 'Baby shopping. I love that. I'll come with you.'

Maeve nodded. 'I was going to ask if you'd come. I need the expert's advice on what to get.'

'It's a date. We'll go to Killarney and spend the day there. I'll take you to lunch in that great fish restaurant in the main street.'

'Fantastic. Thank you, Auntie Roisin.'

Roisin laughed, feeling a surge of pure joy. 'Oh my God, it never occurred to me that I'll be an auntie. How fabulous. I want to be the cool auntie who spoils her niece or nephew rotten. Especially if it's a niece. She'll make up for the girl I never had.'

Maeve smiled and bent to kiss Roisin on the cheek. 'I'm so glad you're here to share this with me.'

'Me too.' Roisin suddenly remembered why she had come. She got up from the rocking chair. 'But you have to hear this.'

'What's going on now? You got Johnny to come back?'

'Yes, but there's more. Could you just listen for a sec, okay? It's about who he's building that big house for, and it's not who you might think.'

Maeve laughed. 'I can see you're bursting to tell me and I can't wait to hear. Who?'

'Come into the living room and I'll tell you.'

'Okay. I need a break anyway.' Maeve put her paintbrush and stencil on a newspaper on the floor and followed Roisin out of the room and joined her on the sofa. 'Right. So tell me.'

'You know Elaine O'Halloran?'

'Not personally. You mean the supermodel?'

'Of course not personally.' Roisin leaned back against the cushions. 'But yeah, her. The Irish supermodel and now actress and singer with the rock star boyfriend. She is the one who's going to live in the house when it is finally ready.'

Maeve turned off her laptop. 'How did she get planning permission so fast? I mean the rule, if it's not the law, is that only someone from here can…'

'Her uncle is Richard Healy. Our local member of the Irish parliament. He must have fixed it for her.'

'How do you know all this?'

'Jack whatshisname in the village pub. Whispered it in my ear when I was having a drink with Declan.'

Maeve sat up. 'You were having a drink with Declan O'Mahony? In the village pub? Was that a good idea? I mean it might start people talking. And isn't it tempting fate a little? Going out with another man during this break or whatever you and Cian are doing. Especially with that man?'

'Calm down,' Roisin soothed. 'It was just a drink – a cup of tea, actually. And he had a glass of beer. We chatted for a bit and then I left about twenty minutes ago. I didn't think it was that big a deal. It was fun to chat to him and get to know him a little better. It was good to take a break from everything. And I am also trying to lull him into trusting me, while I find out what his plan is. He might have something up his sleeve to tempt Johnny to do his roof before he has a chance to get back to our project. Anyway,' Roisin breezed on. 'That's when Jack told me, making me promise not to tell Declan. Of course I wouldn't. Me tell a journalist an official secret like this?'

'It must be something new though,' Maeve remarked sitting down beside Roisin. 'Otherwise I would have heard it somewhere. Probably at Locks to Dye.'

'What's that?'

'The hairdressers' in the main street. It's run by Nuala's sister Kate. She thought the old name was boring so she came up with this one.'

Roisin laughed. 'I love it. Are they any good?'

'Yes. Kate trained at Peter Mark's in Dublin. She's a whizz with the scissors. But she loves dyeing hair so you have to make sure you don't come out with purple streaks.'

'Ah, that explains Olga's hair then.'

'You met her?'

'Nuala brought her to the house and she's doing the central heating for us. And she'll hook up the bathrooms and everything. I just squared it with Johnny.' Roisin leaned her head back on the cushions. 'God, I'm tired. What a day it's been.'

'But you love it,' Maeve teased.

Roisin stretched her arms above her head. 'God, yes. You know me, I'm a workaholic. And this project is so much fun. I get to meet people and I have to figure out how to get everything done in time. Can't understand how Cian can enjoy lazing around in that campervan. We're too young to retire.'

'You achieved a hell of a lot more than I could. I had a call this morning from the window people. The windows will arrive on Friday so then Johnny's men can put them in.'

'Hold on a minute,' Roisin interrupted. 'I'm a little confused here. Doesn't the window firm handle the installation of those windows?'

'No, they just deliver them. Johnny is supposed to put them in. That's why the scaffolding was there.'

Roisin nodded. 'Oh. Okay. I see now. But he took the scaffolding away so now we have to get him to put it back and finish the job when the windows have arrived.'

'Yes. And I'll get the furniture delivered and we're nearly ready for the agent.'

'The agent?' Roisin asked, mystified. 'Stop for a minute. I don't think you've filled me in on everything. What agent?'

'From Hidden Ireland. If we can get the house listed there, we're away in a hack and the bookings will start coming in.'

'Hidden Ireland?'

'Yeah, you know, the collection of historic houses that aren't on any tourist websites, only on their own and in their booklet. Off the beaten track kind of thing. But we have to qualify first. I know I should have told you, but I seem to be very forgetful these days.'

'Oh. Okay. But we're far from ready for that. Especially since Johnny's lads just nicked the scaffolding.'

'We'll have to beg him to get it back before we even get to the windows.'

'I will. Somehow,' Roisin promised. 'But I think we should put Hidden Ireland on hold for now. I know I might have sounded confident that it would all be ready, but I can't guarantee anything. I'm not Superwoman, you know.'

'Okay. I'll wait until you're ready. But back to Elaine O'Halloran.' Maeve fluffed up the cushions and sat back. 'Is she going to live there permanently or is it just a summer house?'

'A house of that size? I wouldn't be surprised if they put in a jacuzzi and an indoor pool and a cinema. I'd say it'll be her permanent hideaway.' Roisin shrugged. 'Not really earth-shattering news but it'll be fun to tease Declan with it before he finds out.' Roisin got up. 'Shall I make some tea?'

'Sure, go ahead. I'll have some camomile.'

'Coming up. You don't have some wine by any chance? I think I need something stronger than tea after this weird day.'

'In the wine rack. There's a bottle of red Paschal says is nice. I can't even remember what wine tastes like.'

'You'll remember when the baby comes out.' Roisin went into the kitchen and turned on the kettle. 'But tell me,' she shouted, rummaging around in the cupboards for a corkscrew. 'If everyone in the village knows about Elaine and the house, how will they keep it from leaking to the press?'

'You don't know how it works around here,' Maeve called back. 'None of us tells anything like that to outsiders. If any journalists come here asking questions, they won't say a word.'

Roisin came back with the tea and a glass of wine on a tray. 'I feel sorry for him. He's a nice guy and very lonely behind that tough exterior. We had a fun chat.'

'In full view of everyone.' Maeve took the tray and put it on the small table in front of the sofa. 'They'll have you divorced and involved with O'Mahony in a week.'

Roisin sat down and took a sip of her wine. 'So what? They can gossip all they want. I know the truth and so does Declan.' She winked. 'I'm going to have a bit of fun teasing him. I'll get Johnny to do our house before Declan can blink.'

Maeve's green eyes took on a stern look. 'Be careful, Roisin. You might get pulled into something you can't stop. You're in a vulnerable situation. With Cian off on that mad trip and the two of you not communicating… An attractive man in the neighbourhood… And someone you used to have a bit of a crush on. This could escalate into something very complicated.'

Roisin squirmed. Maeve had hit a raw nerve and touched on something she had felt but was afraid to face. But no, it wasn't possible. She and Cian had parted on a very positive note and there was complete trust between them. Nothing could break that, she told herself. Was it so wrong for her to enjoy being on her own for a while?

Chapter Ten

Time flew with astonishing speed as Roisin's plan was slowly implemented. Not quite as perfectly as she had hoped, but at least the house was coming together and it looked like it would all be finished by late spring. A month after her arrival, the central heating was up and running and Olga was finishing the bathrooms. The new windows for the front of the house had been delivered but not yet installed. But Johnny had, after several late-night visits to his house by Roisin, promised to provide the scaffolding so that they could get the windows up in time for the mid-term break. At least the outside of the house would be completed.

The past month had been hectic, but Roisin had also managed to take breaks when the weather was fine and had walked on the beach, often bumping into Declan and they had managed short hikes up the hills together, Declan being a seasoned hillwalker.

They had talked a lot during those walks, as if being up there in the mountains with the bracing wind and challenging climbs freed them from inhibitions. At least that's how Roisin felt when they were up there, looking down at the world below.

'Up here, I feel I could fly,' Roisin said as they rested at the top after a particularly tough climb.

He laughed and ruffled her hair. 'You're like a kid when we're up here.'

'I know.' She bit into her cheese sandwich. 'It's like being on a different planet. I feel ageless, weightless and free.'

'Yes.' He looked at her thoughtfully. 'This is where I do my best thinking. And when I get down, I have a whole new take on some of my problems and life in general.'

Roisin drank some water from her bottle. 'Exactly. For me, sitting here, I sort everything out in my mind.' She looked out over the rolling hills below. 'The world is far away now but every time we get back from a hike I feel better about everything. I thought the idea of "finding yourself" had become such a tired cliché, but I know what it means now. I feel I have caught up with myself since I came here, and I'm beginning to see what I want for the future. With Cian, of course. He might be surprised when he comes back and discovers the new me.'

'And who is the new you?' Declan asked, sounding amused.

Roisin ignored his teasing tone. 'I'm more mature. More content, I think. Less frantic. And much more in tune with my surroundings.' She made a wide gesture at the mountains above them. 'All this, the lovely countryside and being in touch with nature, makes me feel humble and quite small. But it has also made me see how frantic and wound-up I was before. I was looking for a project to get my teeth into and draw up fancy plans. But now that it's all nearly finished, I can take a step back and enjoy myself. I think I understand Cian and what he was looking for better now. It's like a kind of serenity.'

'That sounds terrific.' Declan finished his sandwich and glanced up at the sky. 'Those dark clouds might mean some heavy showers. We'd better head back before we get soaked through.'

Roisin scrambled to her feet. 'You're right. Let's get going.'

They walked back in companionable silence, each in their own thoughts, but Roisin felt she had talked more to herself than to Declan, even if he had been a good listener. They were becoming close friends, she felt, without any sexual tension on either side, which was a huge relief. And each time they met, they found out more things they had in common.

As if by a silent understanding, they never discussed the building works or whatever Johnny was doing, as it would ruin the feeling of camaraderie they had built up. They only talked about their likes and dislikes in other areas. Roisin had discovered they shared the same love of books, liked the same movies and laughed at the same jokes. They had bonded as friends in an astonishingly short time and he felt like the brother she never had. Nuala had been great company too and Roisin often sat in Nuala's large kitchen while they were having a good moan about teenagers and life in general. Sometimes Olga joined them and made them laugh with her take on life in Ireland and her stories about the weird people she met during her work.

She didn't hear from Cian much, but he texted her from time to time, telling her where he was and what a wonderful time he was having as he and Andrew slowly made their way up the west coast, discovering many parts he had never visited before. He suggested they go back in the summer with the boys so he could show it all to them. She said she'd think about that and that they could talk about it when he came to Sandy Cove in a few weeks' time. She was beginning to look forward to seeing him again, and showing him how much she had changed.

The boys would arrive for the mid-term break the following Saturday and Roisin had already organised the bedrooms. Rory and Seamus would have to share one of the bigger rooms, and Roisin would move into Phil's new bedroom downstairs to make room for Darragh to sleep in the new bedroom. The router for the Internet connection was in the living room, but as that room was still a complete shambles, she had asked the phone company to install a second one in the kitchen. She hoped that would placate three teenagers who needed to be online most of their waking hours.

As she was paying the bill and saying goodbye to the technician, she could hear Olga talking to someone upstairs. Roisin listened. Was she on the phone? But the man's voice told her someone was up there. Maybe it was Johnny? Roisin hurried upstairs to catch him before he left. She needed to discuss the replacement of the floorboards in the living and dining room and the repairs to the walls that had been damaged by rising damp. Not much left to do, but it had to be finished before he started on Declan's roof. But the man talking to Olga wasn't Johnny but Declan. They were chatting and laughing, Declan doing most of both. He turned and smiled at her as she entered the bathroom where Olga was kneeling in front of the toilet.

'Hi, Roisin,' he said. 'I was just asking Olga here about Johnny.'

'Yeah,' Olga grunted. 'And you ask a lot of other questions too.' She threw a wrench on the floor and got up. 'There. I finished this one. I just have to turn on water and check it's all working.'

Declan shook his head. 'My God this woman knows her stuff. Never saw a neater job in my life.'

'And she's fast,' Roisin added.

'Oh, thank you.' Olga made a little bow. 'It's nice when the customer is happy. That makes me happy too.' She hitched up her dungarees. 'I'll go and turn on the water. You flush and turn on the taps when I shout "go", okay?'

'Will do,' Roisin replied, her hand ready on the button. 'God, I hope it'll work,' she said to Declan when Olga had left. 'If not, we have to start again and I couldn't face that.'

'I'm sure it'll be okay.'

'Fingers crossed. What are you doing here anyway?'

He shrugged. 'No real reason. Just thought I'd come and check on the progress.'

'The windows will be put in on Friday, if they put up the scaffolding like they promised. And then I hope they'll get started on the rooms downstairs.'

'Where is Johnny now? Still at the house he's building for that big wheel in government?'

'How did you know about that?'

'It's common knowledge. Everyone knows who it is by now.'

'You might be wrong, though.'

Declan frowned. 'What do you mean?'

'Oh, nothing,' she said airily. 'Just that the locals know the real deal and they might not want to share it with a blow-in.'

'You're having me on.'

'Maybe.'

They were interrupted by Olga yelling 'Go!' downstairs.

'Wish me luck.' Roisin closed her eyes and pushed the button on the toilet. There was a whooshing sound when the water cascaded into the toilet bowl and then disappeared down the U-bend. 'Phew.

Perfect. And no leaks.' She turned one of the taps of the hand basin which worked perfectly too. 'We're in business.'

'Congratulations,' Declan said with a wink. 'But now to Johnny. I know we kind of agreed not to talk about him and what he's up to. But is there any way at all you might inveigle him to do my roof? I can't get him to talk to me even on the phone and he never returns my calls. The weather is dry right now but the long-term forecast promises rain and storm-force winds next week. I would hate to think what would happen to the house if there was only half a roof when it hits. The tarpaulin they put there protects from the rain but a storm would rip that off very quickly. It's only a couple of days' work, as it's just a question of doing part of the roof, if he gets his lads to do it. The slates are there and everything is ready to go.'

'I'll see what I can do,' Roisin said, suddenly feeling sorry for him. Here he was with a half-built house and nowhere to live. Staying in a cold B&B for months couldn't be much fun. 'I might get him to do it if I beg.'

'I'd be eternally grateful. And as a thank you, I was wondering if you'd like to come with me to a do in Kenmare at the weekend? Friday, to be precise. I'm going to a party for someone who is getting an award. Kerry man of the year. Kerry person, actually,' he corrected himself. 'All in the name of equality. It's in Sheen Falls Hotel. It's quite fancy, but not black tie or anything. Should be fun.'

'Who's the celebrity?' Roisin asked. 'And why in Kenmare of all places?'

'It's Alan Sheehy, the golfer. He's from Kenmare, so that's why.'

'Alan Sheehy? I've heard of him,' Roisin said. 'He's been very successful lately, I think.'

'Yes, he has. Should be a fun party. I was invited because I did a feature on him years ago when he was just starting to win big tournaments. So how about it?'

Roisin laughed. 'You've got yourself a deal,' she said, asking herself how on earth she would convince Johnny to tear himself away from the big house. 'The lads are arriving for their break the next day, so I won't stay the night,' she said to Declan, wondering if this was a good idea. But it sounded like it would be a fabulous party with loads of local celebrities. Not something she'd normally be going to, but it was a nice break from everything. It'd be fun to meet all these people who were connected to Kerry in some way or another. It wasn't an invitation she felt she could turn down. But what on earth was she going to wear?

'You can't go,' Maeve said sternly, lying on her bed. 'You're married.'

Roisin opened the wardrobe and peered inside. 'What's that got to do with anything? Now what do you have that would fit me and is suitable for a glamorous event in a five-star hotel?'

'Nothing,' Maeve said and gathered up Esmeralda in her arms. 'I haven't been to anything remotely glamorous for a long time. Why don't you go to Cork and see if you can find something there? Or online?'

'Too late. The party is tomorrow.' Roisin pulled out a black skirt and a light blue silk top. 'How about these?' She held them up. 'The skirt can be shortened and taken out and the top…' She held it across her bust. 'Looks like it'd fit.'

Maeve glanced at the items. 'Oh, that. It could fit you, actually. I bought it in Cork for a wedding about two months ago. My boobs were already getting big so I got the next size up. The colour was awful on me though but it'll suit you with your blue eyes. It would look great on you as a matter of fact.'

Roisin held it up to her face in front of the mirror. 'It's lovely. I'll do a job on the skirt if you tell me where you keep your sewing stuff.'

'I don't have any,' Maeve mumbled into Esmeralda's fur. 'But there's a sewing box in Phil's cupboard in her new bedroom.'

'Oh, great!' Roisin blew Maeve a kiss. 'Thank you!'

'Don't know why I'm helping you to get glammed up for a date with some other man.'

'It's not a date, silly. I managed to get Johnny to finish his roof and this was the deal. We're just friends, you know. What's wrong with that?'

'Everything.' Maeve sat up, making Esmeralda meow in protest. 'Declan O'Mahony is a very attractive man. And a bit of a lad as far as women are concerned.'

'How come you suddenly know all about him? A month ago you didn't even know who he was.'

'I googled him.' Maeve glared at Roisin. 'I saw a lot of old items from the gossip magazines about the women he's been dating and all about his divorces and stuff like that. You know what I mean. And what will Cian say?'

'He won't say anything because he won't know.' Roisin sank down on the bed with the clothes in her lap. 'Come on, Maeve. I need a bit of fun. I've been knee-deep in building work since I came here. The windows are going in and the bathrooms are done. The boys arrive for their break at the weekend and then I'll be busy trying to amuse them. Declan is just a friend and this was his way of saying thanks for getting Johnny to do his roof. They've just started working on it.'

'I still wonder how you managed that.'

'Me too.' Roisin laughed. 'But I pleaded and Johnny suddenly said yes. I couldn't believe it myself.' Roisin put her hand on Maeve's leg. 'Don't worry about me and Declan. It's truly just a friendship. A very nice one, but that's all it is.'

'I'm probably overreacting. It's just that I'm worried about you and Cian. I don't want you to do anything that might damage your marriage.'

'My friendship with Declan won't affect my marriage in any way,' Roisin protested. 'I'm not even his type, he's told me.'

'That's what they all say.' Maeve sighed and got up. 'I can't stop you, but just be careful with that man.'

'We'll be with hundreds of other people. What could possibly happen?'

'I still don't like it. But you have to make up your own mind.'

'I already have.' Roisin jumped up and kissed Maeve on the cheek. 'Thank you for this. Got to go and fix this skirt. The boys are arriving the day after so this will be my last free night.'

'Take your own car.'

Roisin froze on the way to the door. 'What?'

'Go in your own car, not with him.'

'Why?'

'Because that way you have no control. If you take your own car, you'll be able to get away if you have to.'

'Why would I have to? Declan isn't like that. He's my friend, nothing else.'

'I know, but… That kind of situation can create all kinds of temptations. And then something could happen that you'll regret.'

'Oh, well…' Roisin felt hot all over as she considered the possibilities. Maeve had been around men a lot more than she had, having married Cian when she was just out of her teens. In fact, he was the only man she had ever slept with. Not that she wanted to sleep with Declan, the thought couldn't be further from her mind. Declan was truly just a friend, and their friendship was deep and meaningful. But he appealed to her frivolous, fun side, which she hadn't allowed to come out in a long time. 'I see what you mean,' she said. 'Not that he's that kind of guy, but I'll take my car. I'll have to drive home after the party anyway. The lads are arriving the day after on the bus to Cahersiveen and I have to pick them up.'

Maeve nodded. 'There you go. You have your excuse and won't have to tell any lies.'

'That's true.' Roisin gathered up the clothes. 'I'll be off then. Say hi to Paschal if you talk to him.'

'He'll be home tomorrow for a bit. You'll be able to see him yourself.'

'Oh, great. I'm looking forward to seeing him again. I'd better go and get things organised. Thanks for the clothes. Bye, darlin'.'

Roisin left, running down the path, the clothes in her arms, for once not stopping to take in the view of the ocean or enjoy the sight of the many sea birds gathered on the beach picking at the seaweed. All she could think of was her night out. Her excitement was more about the party and meeting interesting people from the area than the fact that she was going with Declan. He might think this was some kind of date, but to her it was just a bit of fun. It was a good idea to take her own car, she realised. And she had the best excuse. This way she wouldn't have to tell any lies. Except maybe to herself.

Chapter Eleven

Paschal arrived for one of his occasional weekend breaks later that evening. 'I'm worried about Roisin,' Maeve said to him the next day as they sat in the kitchen having lunch.

He put down his fork. 'Why? Is she having trouble with the builders?'

'No, she's managing that perfectly like any project she ever took on. It's her marriage and how she and Cian are now on some kind of break.'

'Maybe that's normal, considering they've been together since they were students. It's been a hard slog for nearly twenty years. I can imagine they'd want to do something mad now that they're free.'

'Yes, but shouldn't they do it together?'

Paschal helped himself to more salad. 'Well, you know, all couples are different. Some can't bear to be out of each other's sight, others like being apart now and then. And in any case, it could be good for her to try to figure out who she is when she's on her own and maybe also see if she can handle being alone.'

'She handles it a bit too well,' Maeve mumbled as she finished her omelette. 'And now she's going with Declan O'Mahony to some do in Kenmare.'

'Why does that worry you? It's not as if she's going to have an affair with him. Didn't you say they're just friends?'

'Yes. That's what she says in any case. I know what you're saying, and I don't distrust her in any way. I know she was a little lost in Dublin and needed to break out a bit and be on her own. It's been good for her and she is really blossoming, which is lovely. And her friendship with Declan seems very sweet and genuine. But I don't know how he feels. You know what she's like, so bubbly and friendly. That could be misunderstood by a man on the prowl.'

'Oh, come on,' Paschal protested. 'He's a grown man. Who says he's on the prowl? I'm sure he has no ulterior motive other than wanting some company. So she's off on her own for a bit. I'm sure that's good for their relationship in the end.'

'I wouldn't like that at all.' She looked at him and yet again felt a sense of wonder at them being together and their child growing in her womb. 'I hate it when you're not here with me. I know the marine wildlife study is important, but…'

He reached out and held her hand. 'I was going to tell you later, but now is a good time, I think. I'm here to stay this time. The research project is nearly over and I can write the reports from here. Plenty of marine wildlife to study in the area, anyway. I'm not going away again, except a short visit to Cork for the day now and then.'

Maeve brightened. 'That's wonderful. But you don't have to give up the project for me. I didn't mean—'

His eyes were suddenly serious. 'I'm not doing it for you, but for me. I can't stand being away from you, worrying that something might happen.' He ran his hand over his face. 'Well, you know…'

'Of course.' Maeve touched his cheek, knowing he was thinking of Lorna, his first wife, who had died so tragically in a hit and run accident, pregnant with their child. It had happened four years before they met but it still haunted him from time to time. The fear that it would happen again was natural and she hoped the birth of their child would help heal the wounds and make the trauma disappear. 'I'm glad you're here to stay, of course.'

He nodded and picked up his fork. 'I don't want you to worry about Roisin. She's a sensible woman with a very practical mind. I'm sure she can resist temptation if it should come her way. O'Mahony is a decent man, you know. I've read his articles. He seems to be someone who knows right from wrong.'

'Maybe,' Maeve said, still not convinced. 'But what about his relationship with women? He's been married three times.'

Paschal shrugged. 'It takes two to tango, as you know. You don't know what goes on between a couple when they're on their own. Sometimes people just grow apart. And some people are bad at picking the right partner. It might have been all their fault in the end.'

'The women's?' Maeve asked, bristling.

Paschal sighed. 'Who knows? Let's not turn this into an argument about men and women and whose fault it is and blah, blah.'

Maeve giggled. 'No. Because you'd lose.'

'I'm sure I would.' Paschal got up and started to clear the table. 'Can we get back to us? And leave Roisin and her marriage alone?' He bent over and put his arms around her. 'Please relax and stop worrying. You have another little person to think about now.'

Maeve smiled and kissed him. 'You're right. I'll try not to worry. Roisin is a big girl now. It's her problem, not mine.'

He returned her kiss. 'Exactly. Let her sort it out. If she gets herself into trouble it won't be your fault.'

'No, it'll be hers. And that O'Mahony guy,' Maeve said with a sigh. 'But okay. I'll do my best to forget about it. I can't stop her anyway when she wants to do something. Nobody could.'

The drive to Kenmare proved very enjoyable. Roisin hadn't been on that leg of the Ring of Kerry for a long time and now she was reminded of how lovely it was. She had left early in order to give herself plenty of time to enjoy the drive and to relax away from the problems of the building works. She was relieved Paschal was home and would not leave again, so Maeve was being looked after in the best possible way. She had stayed up late to take out the skirt and shorten it slightly and with the help of Phil's old sewing machine, she had done a very good job. The silk top was lovely, the blue a perfect match with her eyes and she had found a pair of sixties Chanel shoes in Phil's wardrobe, which was an Aladdin's cave of classic fashion pieces, and discovered they were, if a tight fit, nearly her size. She'd only wear them for an hour or two anyway, so she wouldn't suffer too much. She mentally blessed Phil for keeping such stuff for emergencies and for maintaining them in such good condition so they looked nearly new. Good old Phil. Always so chic and perfectly dressed for all occasions. Roisin hoped she had a good time in America on her book tour and that her subsequent holiday in Florida would be wonderful.

Roisin had spent days perfecting a management system for the guesthouse that she and Phil could use when she returned. The detailed list with bullet points was all there on a big noticeboard in the kitchen now and it would be a huge help for Phil.

She was beginning to think about what she'd do once Phil returned. Perhaps when Cian came they would look for a house to rent in the area so they could be together and make plans. She already had her sights on a big house she had seen in the local paper with sea views and a path to the main beach, which the boys would love. Everything would fall into place. If everyone behaved the way she thought was best. Including Cian, who seemed to have disappeared into the wild blue yonder. She hadn't been able to contact him during the past week and then got a text saying he would be out of range for a few days and not to worry. She had heard that he and Andrew were now camping on an island off the coast of Donegal which, she assumed, was the reason. Well, good luck to him. That camping lark would soon pale when the next storm hit.

Her thoughts drifted to Declan. She thought he was a nice man, but somehow a bit wary of women, Roisin being the exception. But of course he saw her as a friend, not a woman to flirt with. It was probably because she wasn't his type, and only sent out friendly, sisterly kind of vibes. Maeve was worried this would turn into something else, but Roisin was sure it never would. To her he was like some kind of big brother figure, someone she could laugh and joke with and who'd offer a hand to hold and a shoulder to cry on should she need it. Their friendship combined with the effect her weeks at Sandy Cove had had on her set her free from all that ambition and stress of a career in business and showed her a whole new way of thinking. She would always associate him with the relaxed, friendly atmosphere of Sandy Cove. It had also proved that a man and a woman could be close friends. Sex never raised its ugly head whenever they met. Not for her, anyway. But who knew what went on in his mind? Nothing of that kind, she fervently hoped. But you never knew with men. Especially men like Declan.

Chapter Twelve

Having driven through the loveliest countryside with many stops to take in the view or to just sit on a rock and breathe in the mild air and stare out across the ocean in a kind of meditative state, Roisin arrived in Kenmare as darkness fell. She had always loved this little town, preferring it to the more touristy Killarney. With its pretty square and beautiful church, it was an idyllic place where time seemed to have stood still. Except for the square no longer having a weekly cattle market, nothing much had changed since the old days. Some of the shops in the main street had been there since the early days of the last century. New shops had sprung up too, mainly craft shops and small, cosy restaurants. At the top of the street, she spotted Lansdowne Arms Hotel, where she had planned to have tea and change into her party clothes before she drove the short distance to Sheen Falls, the five-star hotel where the party was being held. Then she would drive back to Sandy Cove the way she had come, even if the party ran a little late. She parked around the corner of the hotel and took out her bag, turning around as someone called her name. Declan was here already.

She smiled at him as he walked up to her car. 'Hi. What are you doing here so early?'

'I was in Killarney and took the scenic route through Moll's Gap. It's a beautiful drive if a bit hairy. The road is so narrow that you have to hang over the edge of a cliff if you meet anyone. I thought I'd plunge to my death at times. But the views are spectacular. Which way did you come?'

Roisin took her bag out of the car and banged the door shut. 'I took the coast road through Sneem. Lovely drive too.'

'It seems silly to have been in separate cars. We should have driven here together.'

Roisin shrugged. 'Yeah but I wanted to be on my own for a bit before the stampede tomorrow. My three sons will be arriving and then it'll be hectic.'

'But this way you won't be able to have more than one drink.'

'Neither will you,' she shot back.

He smiled and took her bag. 'I'm staying the night. Splurging on a room at Sheen Falls as a fat royalty cheque came in yesterday and I can now move into my house. The roof is nearly finished, all thanks to you twisting Johnny's arm.'

'I didn't force him. It was my diplomacy that did it in the end.' She started to walk to the hotel entrance. 'Must have been a very fat cheque. I've heard a room there is at least three hundred a night.'

'Three fifty.' He fell into step with her, taking her elbow and pulling her back as a white sports car came racing down the street nearly running her down. 'Careful. Don't get yourself run over. Fecking eejit anyway. I hope the Guards catch him.'

She looked at the car disappearing around the bend at breakneck speed. 'They never get caught. That was a woman by the way. Maybe on her way to the party.'

'Could be.' They crossed the street together. 'Are you planning to have tea here?'

'Yes. And change into my party gear in the ladies'. How about you?' she asked, eyeing his jeans and anorak.

'Don't worry,' he said with a laugh. 'I'll be all dolled up in white tie and tails in time for the party.'

Roisin stared at him. 'Is it that dressy?'

'Nah, only pulling your leg. There's no dress code really. May I join you for that tea? I haven't checked in at Sheen Falls yet but it's early and a cup of tea would be great.'

Roisin pushed the door open. 'Of course. I think they do a nice afternoon tea here.'

'How splendid,' Declan said and followed her inside. 'Do they serve cucumber sandwiches and scones with jam?'

Roisin laughed. 'Absolutely.' She smiled at the girl behind the desk in the reception area. 'We just want to have tea and a bun or something.'

'High tea?' the girl asked.

Declan held up his thumb. 'That's it.'

The girl pointed across the reception. 'The lounge is through that door. High tea for two?'

'Perfect,' Roisin said and walked to the door and into the deserted lounge where she settled on a pink-and-yellow striped sofa near the window. 'The décor is a bit naff but I'm sure the tea will be great.'

She was right. High tea at Lansdowne Arms was everything one would wish for after a long drive. Tiny smoked salmon sandwiches, muffins, cupcakes and scones with jam and whipped cream were placed before them along with a huge pot of tea and two cups.

Declan rubbed his hands together. 'This looks amazing. May I pour you a cup of tea, ma'am?'

Roisin held out her cup. 'Yes, please. And then I'm going to have' – she eyed the display of cakes – 'a bit of everything. How about you?'

Declan poured tea into her cup and smiled. 'Oh, yes. Absolutely everything.'

They dug into the delectable array and munched in companionable silence, laughing through mouthfuls of cupcakes and scones laden with cream and jam.

Declan wiped his mouth with the napkin. 'Now I know a little bit more about you.'

Roisin's hand with the rest of a pink cupcake froze. 'What?'

'I know you have a sweet tooth. And that you're left-handed. And that you look cute with cream on your upper lip.'

'Oh, shit.' She wiped her mouth with her napkin.

'And that you let out the odd swearword from time to time which ruins the goody-two-shoes image.'

Roisin bristled at his patronising tone. 'Goody-two-shoes? What the hell do you mean?'

He adopted an innocent air while topping up their cups from the teapot. 'That's not quite the right description of you, but it's the running around fixing everything and being nice while you do it. I sense the proverbial iron fist in a velvet glove. Very scary.'

She smiled sweetly. 'But that's the best way to get things done. Nobody can say I was being nasty. I just ask and sometimes tell them what to do with a big smile.'

'That pretty face helps a lot too.'

Roisin glared at him. 'It's pretty sexist to say I get things done because of my looks. What would your mother say?'

He laughed. 'Touché.'

'In any case, I thought you had googled me and knew everything worth knowing about me already.'

'That only told me the basics. Not the real, true, private you.' He looked at her so intently that she felt her face flush. 'Tell me, how on earth did you manage to do all those things and bring up three kids as well?'

'I'm no domestic goddess, to be honest. There were two of us. And we had quite a lot of hired help at home. A cleaning firm came in and cleaned the whole house from top to bottom once a week. Then we had a part-time nanny, plus a housekeeper who spent a few hours every day doing the nitty-gritty of everyday chores like laundry and stuff like that. It all ran like clockwork and everyone was happy. No live-in staff so we were on our own in the evenings to bath the kids and read them stories and later do homework with them. That's my dirty secret. Thought I'd tell you in case you thought I was one of those superwomen.'

'Sounds perfect. All planned by you, no doubt.'

She nodded and wiped her mouth again for possible remnants of cream. 'Yes. If you're organised you can do more.'

'And how do you see the rest of your life now that you're free to pick and choose? I bet that's on some kind of list, too.'

'No.' Roisin picked a few crumbs from the table and put them on her plate. 'Right now I'm just trying to get the house ready for the summer season. I'm taking a break the coming week for the boys but then I'll get going again. So much to do, you know.'

'Of course.'

'But what about you?' she asked in order to direct the spotlight back on him. 'What are you up to professionally? You never talk about your writing. You're working on something exciting?'

'Oh, but I thought you had googled me.'

'No, but my sister did. Not much there except what you've told me yourself. Age forty-six, three marriages, the son of Derval O'Mahony, an illustrious career in journalism until that hard-hitting series of articles made you famous but also unemployed.'

'I prefer to call it freelance. Much better, actually. And better paid. At the moment I'm writing about successful women and their problems with sexism in the workplace from a male point of view. Watch out for a hot debate in the press in a couple of weeks.'

She looked at him with interest. 'Really? Sexism in the workplace, huh? From a male point of view? That should be fascinating.' Her eyes narrowed. 'Or are you having me on?'

'Not at all. It's true.' He studied her for a moment. 'What about you and sexism? Have you experienced that in the workplace? With your looks, I wouldn't be surprised.'

She sighed theatrically. 'I'm having a sexism moment right now, actually. This guy keeps talking about my looks and doesn't see me as a person, just some bit of skirt he's chatting up in a way he thinks is clever but oh-so-obvious.'

Declan threw his head back and laughed. 'Yeah. You're right. I'm being the typical male here.' He held up his hands. 'Okay, so I'm guilty. But it's just that I love spending time with a beautiful, intelligent woman.'

'That shows a remarkable lack of imagination,' she quipped, taken aback by this new way he looked at her. What had happened to the big brother image she had come to like?

'I know. But back to my first question.'

'Did I experience this in the workplace?' She shook her head. 'No, never. I worked with my husband, remember. We kept our private life very private. In the office, we were partners and concentrated on our business. I worked hard and looks never came into it at all.' She shrugged. 'Generally, it's perhaps too unrealistic to expect the chemistry between men and women to disappear even in the workplace. But I think there is a code of behaviour and respect that has to be maintained at all times. And men abuse that a lot more than women. I think men often blackmail women into sleeping with them for promotions and other things. Showbusiness is probably the worst affected. And men play on the fact that women want to look pretty and often like being complimented. You can put that in your article if you like.'

He nodded. 'I think you're right. Very good point. Thank you. I'm sorry if I came on a bit strong there. It just happened by accident. Won't do it again, I swear. To any woman I meet.'

Roisin giggled. 'Not even to Olga?'

'Especially not her.'

'I wonder how she'd react if you started flirting with her.'

'I wouldn't dare. She'd probably sock me in the jaw. Not that I don't find her very sexy, of course.'

Roisin stared at him. 'Really? Olga? You find her sexy?'

'I'd love to ask her out but I don't know how to go about it. I have a feeling she is very hard to please. What do you think?'

'Me?' Roisin laughed. 'I have no idea. We haven't talked much about men except when she told me she clobbered her husband when she found him cheating on her. Apart from that it's just been chats about Ireland and her work and so on. But I could find out for you without mentioning your name.'

Declan beamed while he finished his tea. 'That would be terrific. Thank you.'

Roisin looked at him and started to laugh. 'Oh, yeah? You're having me on, aren't you?'

He let out a chuckle. 'Had you going there for a while though.'

'Just for half a second. Olga is a very attractive woman and fantastic at her job. But maybe not your type?'

'She's fun, but no. Not my type in any way.' Declan got up. 'I'd better go and check in to my room at Sheen Falls. See you there later. The ceremony starts at six.'

Roisin checked her watch. 'Oh my God, it's nearly five already. I have to make a few calls and then change in the ladies' loo here.'

'You'd better get your skates on, then. I'll let you pay for tea in the name of equality. See you at the venue.'

'Yeah, see ya,' Roisin said and picked up her phone. She wondered if she should try to get Cian, even though she knew he might be out of range. But just as she scrolled through her contact list, her phone rang and Cian's name came up.

Her heart beating, she pressed the button to reply. 'Hi! I was just going to call you. Where are you?'

'Arranmore Island. It's beautiful here. Andrew wanted to go to Tory, but we couldn't take Rita there, so now we're on this one instead. It's absolutely stunning. Have you seen my Insta pics?'

'No,' Roisin said, blinking away tears at the sound of his voice. She realised how much she missed him, despite enjoying her freedom and independence. 'I didn't even know you had an account.'

'I'll text you the link.'

'Great. So how are you coping?'

'Coping?' He laughed. 'I'm loving it. You have no idea how liberated I feel. I should thank you for letting me come on this trip. I feel ten years younger. You probably wouldn't be able to hack it. But the two of us are managing fine. We eat and sleep when we want and go where we want to go. Haven't shaved since I left, so I look a little woolly. But it's great to relax and not have to think of appearances. If we want company, we just wander into a pub and meet the locals. Great bunch of people here in the north. We've hooked up with some people in another campervan. They're from Germany. We're teaching them Irish as this area is nearly all Irish-speaking.'

'Sounds like fun. I'm in Kenmare and I'm going to a party with… a friend.'

'Good. I'm sure you'll enjoy it.' There was whining sound and a crackle and Cian's voice disappeared, then came back. 'Very windy. Signal getting weak. I'll call you soon. Bye, Roz.' He hung up.

Roisin stared at her phone, tears welling up in her eyes. He had prattled on about himself and never once asked how she was or how things were going with the house or the boys. He didn't say anything about missing her or that he loved her. He hadn't even been listening when she told him what she was doing. That made her feel sad and slightly worried. What was happening to them?

'Me, me, me,' she muttered, looking for Johnny's name in the contact list. She found it and pressed call.

'Yeah? Johnny here,' he grunted.

'Hi, Johnny, it's Roisin Mor— McKenna. I'm just calling to see when you can start on the floor in the downstairs rooms? If you've finished Declan's roof, of course.'

'Just about done here,' he replied. 'The material for the flooring has arrived and we'll be over in the morning to take a look and then we'll get it started. I have hired two more lads and they'll do that job so I can get back to the big house.'

'Brilliant,' Roisin chortled. 'Thanks a million, Johnny.'

'Okay.' Johnny hung up.

Roisin's phone pinged as she paid the waitress for two high teas. Cian had sent her the link for his Instagram account. She clicked on the link which took her to an account called 'Cian's adventure', which already had a lot of photos. She looked at each one and stared at the photos of Cian posing beside the van, Cian in a wetsuit holding a surfboard, Cian climbing on a rock at some seashore, all against the backdrop of stunning views of mountains and ocean. There were indoor shots too, of quaint pubs, of Andrew holding up a pint of Guinness, grinning into the camera. They both sported full beards and their clothes were a mixture of designer chic and chain-store dowdiness. All wrinkly with mud stains, as if they had slept fully clothed, which they probably had, she thought with a shudder, imagining what life in a campervan must be like.

Roisin peered closely at a bearded Cian. He looked so different to the neat, nearly obsessively tidy man she was used to. She couldn't help smiling. Talk about casting off. She saw he was being followed by her sons and also Andrew. She clicked on Andrew's name and his photos came up on a grid. She clicked on each of them in turn but saw they were nearly the same as Cian's, except for a shot of a big white van with German number plates. Must be their new friends. Then she came to the latest shots and blinked as she saw the occupants of the German van. Not two other bearded men, but tall, blonde women. And Cian had his arm around one of them, the prettiest one with her hair in plaits. Her name appeared to be Greta and she smiled at Cian with her perfect teeth, pressing her ample chest against him. Roisin felt a surge of jealousy. It wasn't so much that Cian was posing with a pretty woman. It was the expression in his eyes as he looked at her. Outraged, Roisin tapped in a text on her phone. *Who is Greta?*

But there was no reply. Maybe the signal was still too weak, or… he was refusing to answer.

Chapter Thirteen

Fuelled by a smouldering anger, Roisin was now more determined than ever to enjoy the party. She applied full war-paint in the form of smoky eyes and red lipstick, put on the skirt and silk top and threw on her black winter coat. She drove the short distance to Sheen Falls Hotel, her mind churning, teetering between rage and jealousy. Cian had never, during the twenty years they'd been together, as much as glanced at another woman. Roisin wouldn't have minded had he occasionally said he found someone else attractive or even flirted a bit but he never did. Roisin was everything he ever wanted, he said. And he was usually quite shy around women, looking awkward if one of them came on to him at a party, which used to make Roisin laugh. So why was he breaking out now, flirting with some German floozy? Was he going through some kind of mid-life crisis, or was it Andrew's influence? Roisin couldn't figure it out and decided to leave the problem alone until she could speak to him again. But she was certain of one thing. She needn't feel guilty any more about going to a party with an attractive man like Declan.

Roisin forgot all her worries as she arrived at Sheen Falls Hotel. The former hunting lodge of the Marquess of Lansdowne, dating from the eighteenth century, was lovely. The pillared entrance, the pale-yellow façade and the original sash windows spoke of former glories and were beautifully maintained. This was a house that had been rebuilt and added to through the centuries but still kept its period feel. As she drew up in front of the entrance, the massive front door opened and a young parking attendant in hotel uniform appeared, opening the door for her. 'Welcome to Sheen Falls Hotel,' he said. 'If you hand me the key, I'll park the car for you. Do you have any luggage you wish me to take care of?'

Roisin got out and smiled at him. 'No, I'm only here for the evening.' She handed him the car key and slipped him a five-euro bill, which earned her a smile and a thank you. Very gracious of him, she thought, as five euros was probably not as much he usually got. But it was all she had in her wallet.

Roisin watched the car drive off, wondering how she would find it again. But there had to be a clever system so she forgot about it and walked into the hotel lobby, nearly gasping as she looked around. This was possibly the most beautiful hotel she had ever been in. Not so luxurious as to be intimidating, it had a discreet elegance that whispered class and money. The silk shaded lamps cast a golden light on the polished oak floors with its colourful rugs. Two enormous yellow sofas flanked the fireplace where logs blazed, and the coffee table was stacked with glossy magazines. Roisin immediately felt she wanted to sink into one of the sofas and stretch out with a magazine and a glass of wine. But the receptionist behind the mahogany counter smiled at her in a way that required some kind of explanation. 'Not staying,' Roisin said, 'I'm here for the award ceremony.'

'Of course,' the girl said and pointed at a door at the other end of the lobby. 'In the dining room. But it hasn't started yet, so maybe you'd like to relax by the fire?' Her smile widened. 'That way you can watch everyone arriving. There'll be some big names.' She leaned forward. 'Even the Mayor of Kenmare, I believe.'

'Oh? Does he play golf?' Roisin asked, confused.

'No but he's a great friend of Alan Sheehy. Alan knows *everybody*.'

'Of course.' Roisin went back to the sofas and settled in the corner of one, picking up a copy of *Vanity Fair*. She jumped as a waiter glided across the floor towards her with a glass of champagne on a tray. 'Eh… I didn't order that,' she protested when he placed the glass in front of her.

'Compliments of the management,' the waiter mumbled and disappeared as soundlessly as he had arrived. How did he do that? Roisin wondered, taking a sip without thinking. Then she put down the glass. 'I'm driving,' she said to the girl at the counter, but, busy with a phone call, she didn't appear to have heard. Ah well, it would be hours before she got in the car again. She'd have plenty of time to digest it.

She sipped the champagne and leafed through the magazine, stopping to read an article about the ten top businessmen in the US, discovering that the majority of them had, despite humble backgrounds, managed to amass huge fortunes by applying various techniques and selling skills and of course working nearly twenty-four hours a day. Roisin nodded to herself. Oh, yes, that's what it took. A hard slog for years and years and years. And here she was, sipping champagne in a five-star hotel, not missing the hard slog at all any more. The house restoring had been a challenge and fun to tackle and she would row that boat ashore within months even if it took a lot of arguments with builders and contractors. Then what? Running the guesthouse with Phil would be a low-key affair that would give her a lot of free time to spend with Cian. It would be lovely to end up in Sandy Cove and settle in to a permanent life there with both Maeve and Phil so close. And she would be there when Maeve's baby arrived and would be able to help out. A life with a more gentle pace in a beautiful part of Ireland, what could be better? She took another sip of champagne, feeling hopeful about the future.

If only she hadn't seen that Instagram photo, things would be even better. But she had and it had stuck a painful thorn into her otherwise rosy plans for the future. She took another sip of champagne and pushed her worries aside. She was here and she was going to enjoy the evening and not think about Cian and that woman. She'd worry about that later.

Then the door opened to admit a group of elegant people who were obviously there for the award ceremony and the party afterwards. Roisin stared at them and hoped her outfit was dressy enough. She jumped as someone sat down beside her.

'You look great,' he whispered in her ear. Roisin turned and discovered Declan, in a white shirt and dark blue blazer, beaming from ear to ear. 'Elegant bunch, don't you think?'

'Oh, yes.' Roisin glanced at her silk top. 'I didn't expect it to be this glamorous. I hope this is dressy enough.'

'You look perfect. That was some high-profile businessmen and their wives.'

'I know. I thought I saw the head of Ryanair. And the minister for enterprise. I had no idea there would be so many important people here.'

'Alan Sheehy has a lot of fans among the top business people in Ireland. All keen golfers, too.'

'That's amazing. I mean, Alan came from quite a poor family, who had to scratch for a living.'

'Most of these people came from very humble backgrounds, too,' Declan remarked. 'Being born in a stable doesn't mean you're a horse, as Wellington so famously said.'

Roisin giggled. 'That was about being born in Ireland. And I doubt he even said that.'

'Who knows? Do you want more champagne?'

Roisin looked at her empty glass in dismay. 'Oh! I didn't mean to drink it all. I have to be careful as I'm driving.'

'Of course.' He got up. 'We should go into the dining room anyway. I think Alan is arriving soon and then the ceremony will start and then we can party.'

Roisin struggled to get out of the embrace of the deep sofa. She held up a hand. 'Help me up. This is like being buried in a snowdrift.'

Declan helped her up and when she got to her feet, pulled her close and looked at her with ill-disguised admiration. 'You really do look lovely tonight.'

Blushing, she stepped back and smoothed her skirt. 'Thank you. I borrowed the whole thing from Maeve and the shoes are vintage Chanel I nicked from Phil's collection. You have no idea what an amazing wardrobe she has. All the designer stuff from the sixties and seventies.'

'Looks fantastic. And she must be a very interesting woman, being an author and everything.'

'She's fabulous. You'd love her. I'll introduce you when she comes back.'

'Looking forward to meeting her. Maybe she'd agree to an interview? Her story seems fascinating.'

'Oh, yes,' Roisin replied. 'She's had an amazing life. I'm sure she'd be happy for you to interview her. I'm sure she'll love to be interviewed by a handsome journalist.'

'It's a date, then.' He pulled at her hand. 'Come on, let's go inside while there's still room. I want you to meet Alan before he's swallowed up by the crowd.'

'Okay,' Roisin said as the Mayor of Kenmare walked in the door. She smiled at him and nearly fainted as he smiled back. 'Look there's—'

'Yeah, okay. Let's go in,' Declan urged, putting his hand in the small of her back, giving her a little shove.

The dining room with its view of the waterfall, wood panelling, the white tablecloths on the round tables and the flower decorations was so lovely that Roisin felt she was walking into a fairy tale. Someone thrust a glass of champagne at her and she took a few sips to steady her nerves. All around her, the guests greeted and air-kissed each other and there was din of chatter and laughter. The air smelled of expensive perfume and delicious food. Cameras clicked and flashed and some people took selfies. Roisin wondered if the mayor would agree to do a selfie with her but lost her nerve at the last moment.

'There's Alan,' Declan said and propelled Roisin through the crowd, pushing and shoving until they reached the man, who on closer inspection looked older and more tired than the photos in the press.

He glanced up from the script. 'Declan! Great to see you.'

'Wouldn't miss this for anything,' Declan said and clapped Alan on the back. 'Congratulations on the award. You deserve it. I'll do a feature for the *Irish Independent* about it next week.'

'That would be great.' Alan beamed a thousand-watt smile at Roisin, making him instantly look both younger and more glamorous. 'And who's the lovely lady?'

'This is my friend Roisin Moriarty,' Declan said before Roisin had a chance to open her mouth. 'She's a hot-shot businesswoman with brains to burn.'

'And other things, too, I bet,' Alan said and took her cold hand in a warm handshake. Then he bent his head and kissed it. 'Lovely and smart, what a combination. Maybe this is the one after all the trial runs, eh, Declan?'

'God no,' Roisin exclaimed a little louder than necessary, making several people turn and stare. 'I mean,' she said, lowering her voice, 'Declan is just a friend. I'm married, you know.'

Alan took a step back. 'Oh, I'm sorry. I assumed…' He scanned the crowd. 'Is your husband here?'

'No he's… away,' she replied.

'On business?'

'Uh, no. Just… We're…'

'Oh.' He nodded. 'I see. Sorry. I was just making conversation.'

'Of course,' Roisin replied, feeling foolish for having overreacted. 'Very happy to meet you and seeing you receive the award. Congratulations.'

Alan smiled and nodded. 'Thank you.' He turned his attention the script in his hand. 'My thank you speech,' he explained. 'I think the mayor might be ready.'

Declan stepped away. 'We'll leave you to it, then. I have been asked to say a few words after the presentation.'

'You're making a speech?' Roisin asked, surprised that it wasn't any one of the prominent business people in the room.

'Yup.' Declan adjusted the collar of his shirt and pulled at the cuffs. 'Alan wanted someone with connections in the media to say a few words. The fact that I'm not exactly flavour of the month didn't worry him.' Declan gestured at a camera crew that had just arrived. 'And look, RTE is here in force to record the event for the evening news. Just like the old days. Except they might not want me in the picture.' He smiled as the cameras started to roll and pulled Roisin closer. 'Try to look cheerful and less like a rabbit caught in the headlights,' he muttered in her ear.

Roisin smiled at the camera, wondering if anyone she knew was watching. Pity Cian was on a remote island in the north and couldn't see her at this event. Then the mayor went to stand beside Alan and cleared his throat, launching into a short speech that ended with: 'I hereby declare Alan Sheehy Kerry person of the year. Congratulations, Alan. We're all so proud of you.' He handed Alan a box with something that looked like a medal. They shook hands while the cameras flashed and everyone in the room applauded and cheered.

When the applause had died down, Declan cleared his throat and delivered his speech. 'Ladies and gentlemen, as you know we're here to celebrate Alan Sheehy's award for Kerry person of the year. I know you are all so proud of this son of Kerry who has always stayed true to himself despite fame and fortune.' Declan held up his glass. 'I would like to propose a toast to Alan and wish him the very best of luck with his future career. *Slainte*, Alan, and *go néirigh an t-ádh leat*, which means good luck to you in Irish, for those of you who slept through Irish class at school.'

'*Slainte!*' everyone shouted and downed their drinks.

Alan laughed and bowed. 'Thank you, dear friends. And thank you, Declan.' He looked at the script and laughed, tossing it behind him. 'I was going to make a long speech but I think I'll just tell you how happy I am to be here and how honoured I am to be named Kerry person of the year. Thank you all for coming and for your support. Many thanks to the people of Kerry for bestowing me with this honour. And now, I hope you all enjoy the party.'

There was more applause and a rush of people wanting to shake Alan's hand. He then mingled with his guests and the waiters served more champagne and some delicious finger food to which Roisin liberally helped herself, hoping it would mop up all the champagne she had drunk without thinking. But she was beginning to wonder if she should really attempt the long drive to Sandy Cove in the dark. She would have to find accommodation either in the hotel or in Kenmare and then go back in the early morning, but that shouldn't be too much of a problem. Having given up all plans of driving, she accepted yet another glass from a passing waiter and proceeded to enjoy the party, putting off the problem of a bed for the night until later. She looked around and noticed that most of the top people were slipping away, leaving the remaining guests to continue the party.

Alan and Declan were chatting animatedly with two of the journalists from the Irish press and appeared to have forgotten all about Roisin, who helped herself to more of the delicious finger food and glasses of champagne that kept being pushed under her nose. She was at the 'what the hell' stage when a buffet was laid out and

Irish music played through the sound system. It was turning into a typical Irish party. Roisin joined the queue at the buffet where she discovered platters of shrimp, mussels and oysters, salads, a whole ham, a side of beef, potato salad and even Irish stew in a big pot on a heating tray and a huge basket with fresh bread rolls and Irish soda bread. Everyone dug in as if they hadn't seen food for days and Roisin was astonished to see some of the skinny women heap huge amounts of food on their plates, while others nibbled on a bread roll and a lettuce leaf.

Declan suddenly appeared at her side and handed her a plate. 'Here. I took the liberty of getting some food for you before it all disappears.'

Roisin took the plate. 'Thanks. I'm starving actually, even though I've been nibbling on the finger food.' She looked around the room for a place to sit down but all the tables were occupied. 'I'll just have to eat it standing up though.'

'No, it's okay. Look, some people are leaving. I saw the limos lined up outside. I think they're going on to the Parknasilla resort near Sneem where most of them are staying. Alan is too. They're having some sort of charity golf tournament there tomorrow. Hang on, I'll get myself some food and we'll squash in somewhere.'

'Okay.' Roisin sipped some more champagne while she waited. She knew she was drinking too much but vintage champagne was too lovely to resist. It didn't seem to make her drunk but simply gave her a nice buzz and a happy feeling inside that made her momentarily forget about Cian and the young woman cosying up to him in that Instagram photo. She was hugely enjoying the party and the beautiful surroundings and didn't want the evening to end. She chatted to people about Kerry and mentioned Willow House and the guesthouse that would be opened in early June. They all asked her questions and said they would be happy to recommend it to any visitors to the area and handed her their cards so she could email them the website address once it was up and running and taking bookings. The problem of a bed for the night was far from her mind, and when Declan came back with a heaped plate, she was so happy to see him she planted a big kiss on his cheek. 'Hi there, where have you been?'

'Trying to get somewhere for us to sit,' he replied with a laugh. 'But I think we'll have to give up and sit in the lobby instead. Hope you don't mind.'

'Of course not,' Roisin chortled and followed him out of the dining room and into the relative quiet of the lobby, where Declan steered her to the sofas and she plopped down, narrowly missing dropping her plate. She steadied herself and started to eat, spilling a little stew onto her silk top. She squinted at her chest. 'Oops, I seem to have made a mess of Maeve's blouse. I hope she won't be cross with me. But I think she might be too big to wear it now anyway.' She waved her empty glass at Declan. 'More champagne, please.'

He took the glass from her. 'I think you've had enough.'

'Have I?' Roisin peered at him. 'Says who?'

'I do.'

'Oh.' Roisin nodded, feeling quite tipsy as she realised she had drunk quite a lot of champagne. 'You're right. I think I'd better get home now. Where's my car?'

'You can't drive after all that champagne.'

'Maybe not,' Roisin agreed. 'That would not be very sensible.' She rummaged around in her bag for her phone. 'I'll see if I can book a room somewhere. Maybe here?'

'I think they're fully booked tonight.'

'Oh.' Roisin giggled and put her head on one of the sofa cushions. 'Then I'll have to sleep on this comfy sofa, won't I?'

'I don't think that would work.' Declan picked up his phone. 'I'll see if I can get you a room at the Lansdowne. Then I'll put you in a taxi and you can come back to collect your car in the morning. How's that?'

Roisin beamed at him. 'Fabuloso, my friend. You're terrific, do you know that?'

'Of course.' Declan punched in a number on his phone. 'The line's busy. I'll try again in a minute.'

Roisin nodded, the full force of too many glasses of champagne suddenly hitting her. 'That's a good idea. You're a good friend. You're my only friend, you know.'

He looked at her with a frown. 'Are you feeling all right?'

'Sure, I am.' Roisin hiccupped and put her empty plate on the table. 'But now I feel a little sad,' she said and burst into tears.

Declan moved closer and put his arm around her. 'Why are you sad?'

'Because,' she sobbed, leaning her head on his shoulder. 'Everything is overwhelming. I don't know what I'm doing any more – who I am – who my husband is. He's so far away. That was his dream all his life, he said, to go off without me.'

'Really?'

'Yes, it's true. He told me before he went off. He tried to make me come with him but I hate camping and he hates staying stuck in one place and we sent the boys off to boarding school and sold our business and now I have nothing to do.' Roisin had a vague feeling she was rambling but she was off on a roll and all her pent-up sorrows welled to the surface. 'It was the money that started it all, you know. Cian's uncle died and left him a lot of money and we thought we'd have a ball. But we didn't. I tried and tried to be one of those girls who shop and lunch and go to yoga but it was so boooring. And just this afternoon I saw a photo of him on Instagram with another woman – a pretty German girl.' Roisin grabbed a paper napkin and dabbed her eyes. She blew her nose noisily. 'And then,' she continued, 'there's Rita.'

He raised an eyebrow. 'There are two women?'

'No, no, that's the van. He called it after his first girlfriend. What do you think that means?'

'I have no idea.'

'Neither do I.' She blew her nose on the napkin. 'Sorry about being such a drag. You can leave now, if you want.'

'No, it's okay.' Declan glanced around the lobby and smiled at the receptionist, who was staring at them. 'We're leaving now,' he called to her.

'Are we?' Roisin asked. 'Where are we going?' She yawned. 'God I'm tired. I don't think I can get up.' She put her head back on his shoulder and closed her eyes. 'I'll just have a little nap.' She was so tired she felt partly paralysed and floppy, like a big rag doll. Half-asleep, she was vaguely aware of someone pulling her up and making her walk to the lift. She opened her eyes for a second but that made her so dizzy she closed them again and then everything disappeared in a black cloud of drunken sleep.

Chapter Fourteen

A shaft of early morning sunlight pierced through the darkness of the room like a surgeon's knife. Roisin moaned and screwed her eyes shut. 'Put out the light,' she groaned.

'You have to wake up,' a voice said beside her. A man's voice.

'Cian?' Roisin croaked. 'Is it time to get the boys up for school?'

'No, it's Declan.' The man put his hand on her shoulder. 'Roisin, wake up. You have to get home. Didn't you say your boys were coming today?'

'Today?' She tried to focus her eyes. 'Where am I? Who are you?' She tried to concentrate but the throbbing in her head made it impossible. Then vague images entered her befuddled brain and she started to remember. The party, the hotel. The champagne… Declan. She looked around in the dim light. A strange room. She was in a hotel room. With Declan. How had that happened? And *what* had happened? The boys arriving by bus this morning… 'Oh, nooo,' she wailed. 'What time is it?' She tried to get up but the pain in her head was so bad, she had to lie down again. She turned and stared at Declan, lying fully clothed on top of the bedclothes in the vast bed. 'Where are we? In your room?'

'Yes.'

She recoiled in horror. 'What? We… No, please don't tell me that…' She pulled the sheet up to her chin. 'I don't remember how I got here or what we did.' Gripped by a wave of panic, she started to shake. 'I can't believe I did that.'

'Did what?' Declan laughed and got up. 'Don't worry. We didn't do anything. You were positively comatose after all the champagne we drank. I managed to get you up here by throwing you over my shoulder in a fireman's lift. Then I put you in bed and covered you up.'

Roisin glanced under the covers and discovered she was still wearing her party outfit, which looked decidedly wrinkly. But at least she still had her clothes on, so it wasn't as bad as she thought. But oh God why did she drink so much champagne? She hadn't planned to spend the night with any man, least of all Declan. 'Was that really necessary?'

'Yes. What else could I do?'

'So you carried me in here, dumped me on the bed and covered me up? That was all that happened?'

'Absolutely. I swear.'

'But you slept in this bed, too?'

'Yes. Fully clothed on top of the bedclothes. Couldn't have been more chaste even if I were a monk. I like my women conscious if there's to be any, ahem, action,' he added, his voice full of laughter.

'Stop laughing,' Roisin groaned. 'This is not funny. How do you think I feel?'

'After all that champagne? Like shit, I would imagine. Don't feel so hot myself, to be honest.'

'Yeah, right. But I'm a happily married woman and I spent the night in a hotel room with a man who's not my husband.'

'And your husband is having some kind of fling with a German girl called Greta, you told me last night. In a campervan. Some happy marriage.'

The image of Cian and that girl floated into Roisin's befuddled brain, increasing the pain in her head. 'Oh, God,' she moaned. 'Did you have to remind me?'

'Sorry.'

'I hope nobody saw us when you carried me in here. What time is it?'

'Nine o'clock. You've been asleep since ten last night.'

'Shit,' Roisin exclaimed. 'The boys are arriving in Cahersiveen in an hour. I'll never make it.'

'That's for sure. It's at least three hours' drive away from here.'

Roisin wrung her hands. 'What am I going to do? I can't call Maeve, she'll kill me.'

'Why don't you call your friend Nuala and ask her to pick them up while I have a shower?' Declan suggested.

'Oh, yes. That's a great idea,' Roisin said with a relieved sigh. 'Where's my phone?'

'In your bag.' Declan picked it up from the floor. 'Here. I'll go and have that shower. And I'll check and see if there's anything for a headache in the bathroom.'

'Thanks.' Roisin winced as he switched on the bedside lamp. Declan disappeared into the bathroom and she could hear him turn on the shower. She picked up her phone and peered at it, discovering several missed calls from Maeve and a text:

I saw you on the evening news, hope you got home all right, please call.

Roisin felt a surge of guilt. Maeve must have been so worried when she got no reply. But first she had to get Nuala to help out with the boys.

Nuala picked up straight away. 'Hi, Roisin. Gee, that was some party you were at last night! You looked terrific.'

'Thank you. Yes it was an amazing evening.'

'I'd say. I saw you chatting with the handsome mayor. I nearly died of jealousy.'

'Did I? I can't remember much, actually. Lots of champagne. Vintage,' she added as if that made it more acceptable.

'How fabulous. But you'd better call Maeve. She was having kittens last night when you didn't answer your phone. Too busy chatting up the mayor of Kenmare, I told her. It must have been amazing to see all those people in the flesh.'

'It was. I'll tell you about it later. But I have a bit of a problem and thought you might help me out.'

'Sure, what can I do for you?'

Roisin lay back against the pillows. Sitting up was too painful. 'I wasn't able to get back last night, so I'm still in Kenmare. Couldn't drive after all that bubbly. But the boys are arriving by bus in Cahersiveen in an hour, so I thought you might…'

'Of course, darlin',' Nuala interrupted. 'I'll get my eldest, Olwyn, to pick them up. She just got her licence so she'll be delighted to go and meet three handsome boys and bring them home.'

'Oh, fantastic,' Roisin whispered. 'Thank you so much.'

'You sound a little ropey, love. Did you catch cold?'

'Yeah, something like that,' Roisin replied, trying to clear her throat. 'But I'll be okay.'

'I'll keep the lads until you get back. I'll feed them too. Knowing boys, they'll be hungry. Don't worry about a thing.'

Roisin sighed. 'Thank you so much, Nuala. You're a saint.'

'The nuns in my school wouldn't agree, but thanks, pet. What are friends for, eh? But call Maeve right away, she was worried sick last night.'

'I will. See you later, Nuala, and thanks again.' Roisin hung up and quickly called Maeve, who picked up at the first ring.

'Roisin! Where the hell are you? I've been calling and calling. Did you get back late? I saw you on the news last night with all the celebrities. It must have been a fantastic party. Pity you couldn't stay. I realised that you must have gone to bed straight away when you got back. The drive must have been tiring. Are you off to get the boys now?'

'Er… no,' Roisin started. 'I'm still in Kenmare. I… couldn't get back last night so…'

'Oh.' Maeve paused. 'I see,' she said in a pinched voice. 'You were with Declan?'

'No!' Roisin exclaimed. She closed her eyes as a wave of pain hit her. 'I didn't spend the night with him. Not the way you think anyway.' Shit, why had she said that? 'It's a long story and nothing happened so don't get any ideas, okay?'

'I'll try. You can tell me about it when you get back. But what about the boys? Have you forgotten all about them with all your partying?' Maeve suddenly sounded like the reverend mother in their old school.

'It's all fixed,' Roisin replied. 'Nuala is picking them up and they'll stay there until I get back.'

'That's good. See you later then.' Maeve hung up.

Roisin turned off her phone with a sigh. Maeve obviously thought the worst. How was she going to be convinced that the whole thing had been a stupid accident and Roisin hadn't done anything wrong? She sighed deeply as Declan came out of the bathroom wearing a bathrobe with his clothes and the robe's twin draped over his arm and a bottle of water. He handed Roisin two tablets. 'Here, take these.'

She stared at the tablets. 'What are they?'

'LSD. Should make you feel wonderful instantly.' He laughed and shook his head at her horrified expression. 'Nah, they're paracetamol. I found them on a shelf in a little packet with two bottles of water.'

'Very funny.' Roisin rolled her eyes and swallowed the tablets, chasing them down with a huge gulp of water. 'Thanks.'

He handed her the robe. 'Go and have a shower. I just had mine and it made me feel a lot better.'

'Okay.' Roisin took the robe. 'But I need the clothes I wore yesterday. They're in a bag in my car.'

'I'll go and get them as soon as I'm dressed. I suppose the valet guy has the keys?'

'Yes.'

'Great. Won't be long. I'll get them to send you up some breakfast.'

'I don't know if I can eat anything.'

'You have to try. Coffee and toast at least. Otherwise you might go to sleep at the wheel.'

'I suppose,' Roisin said without enthusiasm.

Roisin went into the bathroom, wincing as she caught sight of herself in the mirror. Her face was ashen and the sexy smoky eye make-up had turned into panda eyes with streaks down her cheeks, making her look like something from a horror movie. She stripped off her party outfit and rifled through the toiletries in a cute little basket beside the sink and found a face wash, eye make-up removal, moisturiser from Chanel, a mini-toothbrush and toothpaste in a tiny tube. Thank God for luxury hotels. Pity there wasn't time for a session in the spa. But after a hot shower and a mini-facial with the skin care products, she both felt and looked nearly human. She was back in the bedroom drying her hair with the hairdryer when there was a knock on the door and a maid appeared with a breakfast tray. Roisin asked her to put the tray on the table by the window and thanked her.

When the maid had left, Roisin pulled back the curtains, wincing as the bright sunshine hit her sore eyes. But the headache was better and she even found the smell of coffee and fresh bread rolls quite enticing. She tightened the belt of the bathrobe and sat down, picking up the copy of the *Irish Independent*. She'd flick through it while she had her breakfast.

As the headache eased, she gazed at the stunning view of the famous waterfalls of the Sheen river from which the hotel got its name. It must have been wonderful in the old days when the Marquess of Lansdowne set out with the lords and ladies to hunt deer and pheasant. Not that she approved of hunting, but it would have been quite amazing all the same.

Roisin poured herself a cup of coffee, smeared apricot jam on a roll and picked up the newspaper. The front page had the story of the award ceremony at the bottom with a nice photo of Alan Sheehy. *Award ceremony for Kerry person of the year*, the headline said. Then a little piece about Alan Sheehy and his life and career then: *more photos on page three*. Roisin sipped coffee and took a bite of her roll and turned to page three, where there was an array of photos of all the high-profile business people. She was startled to discover a photo of herself with Declan, his arm around her, both looking happy and relaxed, Roisin smiling broadly at him. Then she read the caption and nearly choked, dropping her full cup of coffee on the pristine cream carpet.

Chapter Fifteen

When Declan came back with Roisin's bag, she was on her hands and knees dabbing at the carpet with her napkin.

He dumped the bag on the bed. 'What are you doing?'

She looked up, her face red. 'I dropped my coffee cup on the carpet and now look at it! It's all your fault.'

'What?'

She gestured at the newspaper on the floor beside it. 'Just take a look at the item on page three.'

He picked up the paper, flicked to the page and stared at the feature. 'Oh, I see. That photo.'

'And the caption. Lovely, don't you think?'

'*Declan O'Mahony with his latest squeeze, businesswoman Roisin Moriarty,*' he read out loud. 'Oh God, I am so sorry, Roisin.' He took her by the elbow. 'Get up, willya. It's just a coffee stain. The hotel staff will deal with it. I'm sure they're used to it.'

'I suppose.' Roisin sat down again and poured herself a fresh cup of coffee. 'What will we do?'

'Do?' Declan sat down on the other chair and picked up a cup from the tray. 'About that?'

Roisin pointed at the crumpled newspaper on the table. 'Yes, of course. What else would I mean? What are we going to do about it?'

'Nothing,' he replied with a sigh. 'I realise it's upsetting to you. They didn't have to put it like that and make it look as if... Well, you know. That's really low of them. But journalists sometimes hint at things just for fun, which is truly disgusting. But it's better to ignore it and do nothing and then it usually dies very quickly.'

'What do you mean?' she exclaimed. 'They print those lies and we do *nothing*? You have to send them a disclaimer or something.'

He poured himself some coffee. 'The more you deny it, the more they'll believe it's true. If you keep quiet it will be yesterday's news very quickly. We'll just carry on, keep the same low profile as before and it will all disappear. Except if...'

'Except if – what?'

He avoided her eyes. 'Nothing. Forget it.' He gulped down the coffee and reached for a roll. 'Let's enjoy this nice breakfast and then you'll be on your way and I'll stay here for a bit. I was planning to do some hiking around here as the weather is nice and I won't be able to move into my house for another couple of days.'

'Good idea.' Roisin gathered up her clothes from the bag and went into the bathroom to change into her jeans, shirt and sweater. That done, she went back into the room and carefully packed her party clothes and was then ready to go. She stood in the doorway, looking at Declan who, unperturbed, was reading the political section of the newspaper. 'I'm off now,' she announced.

He looked up. 'Okay. You look a lot better.'

'I feel fine apart from a bit of a headache. Thanks for rescuing me last night.' She hesitated, trying to think of something to explain her behaviour the night before. 'I don't usually drink myself into a stupor, you know.'

'Of course. That kind of thing can happen by accident. And you were upset, so you reached for the booze. Quite natural under the circumstances.'

Roisin dropped her bag and stared at him. 'What circumstances?'

'Your husband and that German girl on Instagram. And him going off on his own for an adventure or something.'

'I don't remember telling you about that.'

'Well, it might have slipped your mind as you were a little sloshed, to put it mildly.'

'So I told you everything?'

'Pretty much, yeah.'

Roisin looked up at the ceiling and closed her eyes as if in pain. 'Oh, noooo. I didn't want anyone to know. Can't believe I blabbed all that to you. Please forget it.'

'I already did.'

Roisin picked up her bag again and was about to leave, but one question still nagged her. 'Just one thing before I go.'

He lifted an eyebrow. 'Yes?'

'What was that you were about to say? About it all disappearing if we keep a low profile – except if… Then you clammed up. Except if – what? It seemed serious.'

He shrugged. 'Nah, just a thought. Won't happen. We're small potatoes.'

'What won't happen?' Roisin insisted. 'If it won't happen, why can't you tell me what it was?'

He sighed. 'You're such a stubborn woman.'

'Yes. And I'm not leaving until you tell me.'

'Okay then.' He put down the newspaper. 'Nothing will happen, except if…'

'You're driving me nuts on purpose. Except if bloody what!?' she shouted.

'If the tabloids pick it up.'

The drive back was a lot less pleasant than the previous day's journey. All the events of the night before – those she could remember – played like a bad movie through Roisin's mind. She swept past gorgeous scenic spots and cute little thatched cottages with donkeys grazing in the green fields, ignored the deep blue ocean, the sweep of the coastline and the seabirds gliding around in the blue sky. All she could think of was that photo, the caption underneath and the horrible threat of the tabloids getting a hold of the story. Then the shit would truly hit the fan. She dreaded the thought of Maeve even seeing that picture in the *Independent*, which was a distinct possibility. But the tabloids might blow it up out of all proportion, not because of her, but because Declan was a high-profile reporter with an interesting past. And what about the boys? They weren't likely to tear themselves away from their phones, but it might float past them on some social media site. She shuddered at the thought of how she would explain why she was cuddling up to a stranger at a party in a posh hotel while their dad was off on an adventure in his campervan. And what about Cian? Would that drive him further into the arms of another woman?

Roisin blinked away tears of frustration as she drove, not stopping until she pulled up outside Willow House. The new windows at the front gleamed in the late afternoon sunshine. Johnny's lads must have put them in yesterday after she had left. She looked up at the house and felt a dart of pleasure. She hadn't seen the full impact of the repairs that had been done during the past month until now. It looked terrific. The render of the façade had been repaired and painted its original pale pink, the stucco decorations around the windows white. The front door with its fanlight was the same sage green as before, the brass knocker polished. She stepped inside and breathed in the smell of new wood and fresh paint, walking through the rooms where the floorboards had yet to be done but the beams had been replaced. The house was nearly ready. Some things still to do but it wasn't the wreck she had found when she arrived over a month ago. They would be ready for guests as scheduled in early June. What a relief.

Except... where would the boys stay on their future breaks when the guesthouse was up and running? She'd have to see if that house she had seen was still available. With its well-appointed kitchen, big living room and large bedrooms, it had looked great in the photos on the website but it might be a different story in real life. Still, it was a possibility. She'd get on to that as soon as she could. But first she had to see Maeve, a meeting she didn't look forward to. Maeve had been worried about Roisin getting too close to Declan. This would make her suspect something was going on and then she'd jump to all the wrong conclusions. But hopefully neither Maeve nor Paschal would have seen the photo and the caption, but that was like whistling in the dark as they read the *Independent* from cover to cover every day.

She checked her watch. The boys would have been picked up by Nuala's daughter by now and probably getting to know the other teenagers in the house. She'd have time to pop into Maeve's before she picked them up. Better get it over with. Like a lamb to slaughter, Roisin walked slowly along the path to the cottage, stopping for the moment to look out over the ocean, noticing black clouds on the horizon. The storm that had been promised for days would finally arrive. She hoped she'd get the shopping done and the boys settled before it hit. But now she was facing a different storm: Maeve's reaction to her night with Declan and that photo. It wasn't going to be a pleasant encounter.

The cottage was deserted. Roisin looked into the kitchen and found the back door open. Maybe they were walking on the beach? She spotted the copy of the *Independent* on the table and wondered if Maeve had got to page three yet. Then she heard voices and laughter outside. Roisin peered out and discovered Paschal carrying a cardboard box full of fish and Maeve following behind him, laughing, Esmeralda weaving between their legs.

'Hi,' Roisin said. 'Have you been fishing?'

'Yeah,' Paschal replied. 'And I got lucky. The approaching storm chased a whole shoal of sea bass into the bay.' He shoved the box at her. 'You want some?'

'Yes, please. I can bake them for the boys' supper. They love fish.' Roisin peered at Maeve, trying to gauge her mood. 'Hi, Maeve.'

'Hi,' Maeve said in a curt tone. 'So you're back.'

'As you can see.'

'Good.'

Paschal put the box of fish on the rough table outside the door. 'I'll just clean these if you want to… talk.'

'We'll make tea,' Roisin suggested.

He nodded. 'Good idea. I'll leave you alone so.'

'There's a fish knife in the shed,' Maeve said and picked up Esmeralda. 'And old newspapers.'

'I know.' Paschal winked at Roisin behind Maeve's back. Roisin returned his smile, relived that Paschal didn't seem to judge her. But maybe he hadn't read the paper yet?

Maeve had read it in any case. Once inside the kitchen she put Esmeralda on the floor and faced Roisin. 'So… that photo on page three… Can you explain what that's all about?'

'There's nothing to explain,' Roisin said hotly. 'I just happened to stand there when they took the shot.'

'And he just happened to put his arm around you, and you just happened to look at him as if he was the greatest thing since sliced bread?'

'I didn't think he was – is. It was the champagne.' Roisin pulled out a chair at the kitchen table and sat down, her legs suddenly weak. 'It's not the way it looks, I swear.'

'Are you having an affair with Declan?' Maeve asked with concern in her green eyes.

'No!' Roisin shouted. 'Absolutely not. I was standing beside him and smiling when someone took a photo. So what? I stood beside the mayor of Kenmare as well. Do you think I'm having an affair with him, too?'

'Don't be ridiculous.' Maeve turned on the kettle on the kitchen counter.

'*You're* being ridiculous,' Roisin countered. 'Why on earth do you suddenly think I'm having an affair?'

Maeve turned around and looked at Roisin with concern. 'I'm sorry. I didn't mean to accuse you or judge you. If you and Cian are having problems, I'm really sorry. I do believe you when you say that you and Declan are just friends. But you have to realise that you have been seen with him a *lot* ever since you arrived, and there's no sign of your husband. People are talking and suggesting things that may or may not be true. And now, with that photo and the text underneath, they'll talk even more. I'm worried about you, but even more about the boys. How are they going to feel when they hear all the rumours?'

'I'm sure they won't believe them. I'll explain that Declan and I are just friends and that…'

'That what? Where is Cian in all of this? What's he up to with that camping trip and the going on a break stuff?'

'I don't know.' Roisin's eyes suddenly filled with tears. Maeve was right. The boys might not believe the rumours about her but how was she going to explain what was going on with their dad? 'I don't know what's going on with Cian myself. He's been very short with me on the phone lately and I have a feeling we're somehow drifting apart. This break or whatever it is might not have been such a good idea after all. I got upset when he didn't seem interested in what I was doing and then I saw a photo on Andrew's Insta page with him and a girl called Greta very up close and personal.'

'Him, meaning Cian?'

'Yes.' Roisin fiddled with the tablecloth. 'There were only photos of landscapes and houses and the campervan and the guys drinking beer on Cian's page, but then I looked at Andrew's and there it was.'

'Show me the photo.'

Roisin got her phone from her bag and clicked to the Instagram app. It didn't take her long to find Andrew's account and that photo. She flinched as she looked at it and held out the phone for Maeve to see. 'Here. What does that look like? A complete accident?'

Maeve looked at the photo. 'Hmm. Yes, looks weird all right. But she looks more interested than him. And he's still wearing his wedding ring. She must know he's married.'

'Ha.' Roisin turned off her phone. 'I'm sure that doesn't mean a thing to a woman like her.'

'Like what? You don't know anything about her. She might be a nun on holidays for all you know. Just being friendly.'

'Yeah, right. She looks just like a nun,' Roisin scoffed.

The kettle boiled and Maeve busied herself with the tea. 'Have you asked him what's going on?' she asked over her shoulder.

'Yes. I texted him. But I got no reply. I think they're out of range on that island. And now the storm is coming and I don't know where he is.' Roisin's eyes filled with tears. 'What a mess.'

Maeve put two mugs on the table and sat down beside Roisin and put her arm around her. 'I'm sure he's all right. And that girl was just a silly photo. You know yourself how that can happen, don't you?'

'Yes, but… Oh, it's so complicated.' Roisin buried her face in her hands. 'I've just realised how much I miss him. I didn't think of him much when I was busy, but now I just want him to come back. I have to look after the boys on my own now. I always thought I did everything, but now that Cian isn't here, I realise how much he did with them. Homework, football. I was the one who provided comfort and clean clothes and food and a shoulder to cry on. Not to mention discipline that Cian was really bad at. But he did all that boys' stuff. Oh, God.' She looked at Maeve through her tears, suddenly gripped by panic. 'I said *was*, didn't I? As if…'

Maeve squeezed her tight against her. 'Shh. Don't get yourself into a state. The boys are with Nuala. Go and get them and then you have to try not to worry about Cian. I'm sure he's fine and will contact you when he can. You've been a terrific mum and wife all through the years. I'm sure Cian appreciates it and wants to get back to you as soon as he can. Remember how you said this would be good for you and you'd be stronger than ever? You'll see that you were right. He's just taking a little me-time just as you have. Once you're together again, you'll be happier than ever. Cheer up, sweetheart, and go and give those boys a big hug.'

Roisin nodded and sniffed, calmed as usual by Maeve's comforting words and her sensible approach. Maeve was always so caring and so good at cheering anyone up. 'I will. Thank you.' She kissed Maeve on the cheek. 'I feel better now.'

'Good.' Maeve handed her a piece of kitchen paper. 'Here. Blow your nose.'

'Yes, big sister.' Roisin laughed and blew her nose so loudly Esmeralda jumped up from her cushion by the stove. All the problems seemed minimal except for Cian's whereabouts. But as Maeve said, he was probably fine, just tucked up in that campervan in the shelter of some rocks or something, secretly enjoying the whiff of danger. He loved taking risks now and then, always diving from the high cliffs or skiing down steep slopes, going off-piste, as he used to say. Well he was off-piste now, that's for sure. Roisin smiled as she thought of him and his mad adventures and hoped he'd get it out of his system and come to his senses. Then they could settle into a new life together.

Chapter Sixteen

Nuala lived with her family in a big two-storey house just off the main street. The lawn in the front garden was a mess of bikes, footballs and hurley sticks and the front door was half-open. Roisin pulled up outside and tooted the horn to announce her arrival. The door flew open as she got out and Nuala stuck her head out. 'Come in, willya. I'll put the kettle on.'

Roisin made her way up the garden path and opened the door, giving a little yelp as big black dog hurled himself at her.

'Don't mind Benny,' Nuala called from the kitchen. 'He just wants to say hello.'

'Okay,' Roisin panted, pushing the dog away. 'Good boy. Please get off me.'

'Down, Benny!' Nuala yelled. 'Come here and behave yourself or I'll lock you in the shed.'

The dog stopped jumping and slunk in through the kitchen door. Roisin followed and stepped into the bright kitchen with a big table in the middle. Nuala was taking a tray of muffins out of the oven and talking on the phone at the same time. She gestured for Roisin to sit down and finished her call. 'Hi,' she said, putting the tray on the counter. 'The lads are in the TV room, except your youngest and our Brendan, who are playing some weird game on the Xbox upstairs. Great kids, I have to say.'

'Thank you. And thanks for rescuing me. I don't know what I would have done if your daughter hadn't been able to pick them up.'

'No problem,' Nuala laughed. 'Olwyn was delighted to get the chance to show off her driving skills.'

'That's great. Where's the TV room?'

'Down the corridor. Last door on the left. Sure you don't want a cup of tea?'

'Maybe later,' Roisin said and hurried down the corridor and in through the half-open door, from where she could hear murmurs and laughter. She stopped and smiled as she discovered Darragh and Rory and two girls hunched together over an iPad, looking at something that obviously had them all highly entertained. Both girls were dark with their mother's eyes and their father's strong features. The older girl had long hair with pink streaks; the other one, her hair short and her ears bristling with earrings, was the chubbier of the two. They both looked up and smiled as Roisin entered but the boys were too absorbed by the screen to notice.

'Hi, lads,' Roisin called and held out her arms.

They all looked up. 'Hi, Mum,' Darragh said.

'How about a hug for your old mum?' Roisin suggested, her heart melting as his likeness to Cian struck her.

Darragh straightened his tall frame and gave his mother a quick, awkward hug before he returned to the sofa and the iPad.

Rory hesitated, looking self-conscious. 'Hi, Mum,' he said without getting up.

'Ah, go on,' the older girl said and pushed at Rory. 'Go and hug your mammy.'

Rory shuffled forward and gave Roisin a peck on the cheek. 'Hi.'

Roisin wrapped her arms around him despite his obvious reluctance and smoothed his tousled brown hair. 'You okay? Sorry I wasn't there to meet you. I was at a party in Kenmare last night. I had a little champagne, so I thought it would be better not to drive.'

Rory shrugged and pulled away from her embrace. 'No problem. It's great to be here and meet these guys.'

'We saw the photo of you in the paper,' Darragh said. 'Cool party, Mum.'

'It was. I'll tell you about it later.'

The older girl stepped forward. 'Hi. Sorry, I should have said hello earlier. My name's Olwyn and that's my sister Sorcha.'

Roisin shook Olwyn's hand. 'Hello, Olwyn. Nice to meet you. Hope the boys are behaving themselves.'

'So far, yes.' She grinned. 'For spoiled Dublin brats, they're not too bad. We'll knock them into shape when we get down to the surfing on Monday.'

'If there's anything left of the beach after the storm,' Sorcha cut in. 'Hi, Mrs Moriarty. I love your jacket. Is it from North Face?'

'Yes. Thank you. I wasn't sure about the bright turquoise, but…'

'It's fab,' Olwyn said. 'And I love the top you wore in that picture. Did you really get to meet the mayor of Kenmare?'

'I just smiled at him and said hello,' Roisin confessed. 'He said hello back but that was all. He looks even more handsome in real life.'

'But sure he's ancient,' Olwyn said. 'Must be at least fifty.'

'I think he's nearly sixty, actually,' Roisin replied.

Olwyn's eyes widened. 'Sixty? Gee, that's old. Was he able to walk without a cane?'

Roisin laughed. 'Very much so. Seemed very fit and healthy. Sixty is hardly ancient, though. But I suppose it is to you.'

'Nearly dead,' Darragh mumbled.

Roisin laughed and looked around the room for luggage and pointed at the pile of bags near the door. 'Are these yours?'

'Yeah,' Rory replied, his eyes on the screen of the iPad.

'Could you please get your stuff together, then,' Roisin ordered. 'We have to get to Willow House before the storm hits. Then we might be stuck there until it blows through. But don't worry, there's plenty of food. I stocked the freezer before I went to Kenmare and we'll get more supplies in the grocery shop on the way home.'

Darragh got up. 'Okay. I'll take care of the bags. Rory, go and get Seamus so we can get going.'

'I'll get him,' Sorcha volunteered and jumped up. 'Then Rory can help with the bags.'

Nuala stuck her head in the door. 'Roisin, how about that quick cuppa while the lads get their stuff?'

'Thanks. Just a quick one, though.' Roisin followed Nuala into the kitchen, where a steaming mug on the table waited for her.

Nuala took a carton of milk out of the fridge. 'How do you take your tea? Milk? Sugar?'

'Milk, no sugar.'

'Okay.' Nuala glanced at Roisin over her shoulder. 'Hey, I thought I'd tell you, before you leave with the kids. There's an item about you and yer man in the paper.'

Roisin stopped in her tracks. 'Oh, no. Which paper?'

'One of the tabloids. The *Mirror*, I think it was.'

'The *Mirror*?' Roisin asked, appalled. 'Oh, dear God, no. Cian is sure to see that somewhere. He always takes a look at those just for a laugh. Please tell me you're joking.'

Nuala put the jug on the table. 'Afraid not. Sean Óg happened to see it when he was having his hair cut. I think there was something in the *Evening Herald* too. A picture of the two of you together he said. Looking cosy on a sofa.'

'On the front page?'

'Yes, the *Mirror* has it as their top story. There must be a real news drought as the royals are behaving themselves and no real celebrity has been caught with drugs or having it off with someone other than their partner. Except you.'

'Me?' Roisin spluttered and choked on her tea. 'I haven't… And I'm not a celebrity.'

'No but *he* is. That O'Mahony fella. I'd say some of his journalist colleagues are after his blood since that shit storm he stirred up, exposing everyone.'

'But that was years ago,' Roisin argued.

Nuala sat down and waggled her eyebrows. 'Those people have long memories. And some of those press guys are in the politicians' pockets.'

'Shit.' Roisin's stomach churned. This was bad. The tabloids were obviously short of stories so they had to pick up something small and turn it into some kind of sleazy scandal. 'On a sofa?' she asked. 'We were sitting together in the hotel lobby but there was nobody around. Oh,' she added, as it dawned on her. 'The hotel receptionist. She might have snapped us with her phone.'

'Could be. Maybe she does that regularly to make a bit of extra cash. That hotel is always packed with celebrities.' Nuala piled the muffins on a plate and pushed it at Roisin. 'Here, have one. Might make you feel better. I made them for the kids but have one before they're all gone.'

Roisin looked at the muffins, nausea rising in her throat. 'No thanks. I don't feel like eating right now.'

'Of course. Lucky you. I usually feel like stuffing my face when I'm stressed,' Nuala said and helped herself to a muffin. 'But everyone's different.'

Roisin gulped down some tea and got up. 'I'll take the boys home now. It's nearly four o'clock. It'll be dark in an hour. We'd better get organised before the storm hits. It's forecast to be the worst one for a long time. Could be a near hurricane. And…' she paused, 'I have to think of something to tell them about this new picture in the *Mirror* in case they see it. What should I do?'

'Don't say anything until you have to. They might never see it if it isn't picked up anywhere else. Just lie low and then the story will disappear. They probably had nothing to write about right now. We'll just have to hope that someone more important dirties their bib.' Nuala took a plastic box out of one of the cupboards. 'I'll put some muffins in this for your boys for later. I know how they eat. Mine never stop.'

Roisin laughed and took the box when Nuala had filled it. 'That's for sure. Thanks for this.' She glanced out the window as raindrops hit the glass. 'Got to go. Thanks a million for helping out this morning.'

'No problem at all. It was great to have them. The girls usually spend all day bickering, so the boys were a great distraction. Haven't seen them so well behaved in months.'

'But they're lovely girls.'

'When they're in the mood.'

'I know what you mean.' Roisin smiled and nodded. 'Bye for now. I'll see you on Monday at the surfing school.'

'Take care. Oh, and don't worry if the power goes during the storm, that usually happens. Just make sure the phones and laptops are charged. And that you have flashlights and candles and the Aga going full blast. Lucky you have a new roof. The old one leaked like a sieve, Maeve said.'

'I know. I'm glad we have the new roof and the new windows. Johnny has been amazing lately too, not to mention Olga. Thanks for the muffins. You take care, too. Bye for now.'

The boys were already in the car when she came out, the bags piled into the boot. Roisin handed Darragh the box. 'Here. Some of Nuala's excellent muffins. But don't touch them until we get home, okay?' She was interrupted by her phone ringing. She took it out of her bag thinking it was Maeve checking if she was all right. But the ID showed an unknown number.

'Hello?' Roisin said, easing into the driver's seat.

'Roisin Moriarty?' a female voice asked in a heavy Dublin accent.

'Eh, yes?'

'Ellen Murphy here from the *Herald*. I just wanted to ask about your relationship with Declan O'Mahony. And how things are between you and your husband? Are you separated or…?'

'No comment,' Roisin said and turned off her phone.

'Who was that?' Rory asked.

'Nobody. Nobody at all.'

Chapter Seventeen

The rain had turned torrential by the time they reached Willow House. Roisin was surprised to see Olga's van parked beside the front steps. There was a bit still to do in the new bathrooms but she thought Olga would take the day off because of the storm. Yet there she was, holding the door open, waving at them. 'Get inside before you all blow away,' she yelled as a gust of wind tore at the door of the car as the boys got out.

'She's right,' Roisin shouted. 'Get your stuff and get inside, and the bags of food. I'll just park the car away from the trees.'

They quickly bundled everything inside and Roisin managed to park the car in relative shelter and ran hell for leather across the gravel, managing to get inside and push the door against the hurricane-force wind that had just started to blow. 'Oh my God,' she panted, leaning against the door. 'They weren't joking when they said it'd be bad.'

Olga nodded. 'Yes, it's bad. They say it's dangerous to be out. It's okay for me to stay, yes?'

'Of course.' Roisin gestured at the boys, who were still standing in the hall staring at Olga. 'Boys, this is Olga, the plumber who's fixed the bathrooms. Wait till you see them. They're amazing. Olga, this is Darragh, my eldest,' she added, pulling at Darragh, willing him to come out of his shell and at least be polite.

Olga held out her hand. 'Hi there, Darragh. You're nice and tall.'

'Hi,' Darragh mumbled, darting a look at Roisin. She sighed. He was obviously not going to make an effort. She knew he was shy and she wasn't expecting him to kiss Olga's hand, but she had hoped he could be a little more vocal. But he was a real introvert so it might be too much to expect.

'And Rory and Seamus,' Roisin continued and pushed her two youngest forward.

'Hi,' they said in unison, shuffling their feet.

'Hi, boys.' Olga smiled at them. 'Nice to meet you.'

'Are you really a plumber?' Seamus asked.

'Of course,' Olga replied. 'It's not a job just for men, you know.'

'Cool,' Seamus said. 'You must be really strong.'

'But why are you here?' Roisin asked. 'I thought you might take the day off because of the storm.'

Olga shrugged. 'Yes, I did too, but then it didn't look so bad so I came here to finish the taps and a few little things that were left to do. I thought I'd get home before the storm arrived.' She glanced out the window. 'But now it looks like the end of the world out there.'

Rory looked around the newly painted hall and the gleaming new floor. 'This looks amazing, Mum. The hall is like new.'

'Wait till you see the new bedrooms,' Roisin replied. 'And the living room and Phil's bedroom and sitting room.'

Her words were accompanied by a loud crash somewhere outside. 'There goes the beech tree by the gate,' Roisin shouted and ran to the window. But it was too dark to see anything, as the wind howled and the rain hammered against the windows. 'Okay, it looks like it's coming from the north-west. Go and close the shutters in the dining room, Darragh, just in case the windows should break. Rory, check the windows upstairs and close any that are open. Seamus, come with me to the kitchen. We'll light the Aga so we have something to cook on if there's a power cut. And we have to find candles and a flashlight in case the power goes.'

'What do you want me to do?' Olga asked.

'Uh, nothing for the moment,' Roisin replied. 'Maybe you could help Darragh with the shutters and secure all doors and windows down here.'

'Good. Come on, handsome boy,' Olga said to a blushing Darragh and disappeared down the corridor. Darragh shuffled after her, darting a look of pure venom at his giggling brothers.

'Stop laughing and get going,' Roisin ordered. 'I just heard on the radio that it's an orange storm warning, which means near hurricane-force winds. This is not a video game, this is real life and real danger.'

'What about Dad?' Rory asked. 'He's in Donegal. I heard the storm would hit the hardest there. I checked the weather map on my phone. It looks incredible over the north-west.'

'He sent me a text when we were at that lady's house,' Seamus piped up. 'Said he was all right and anchored down with another campervan in a safe place. Not to worry, he said and sent his love to everyone. He'll call after the storm.'

'Oh,' Roisin said, feeling a mixture of relief and anger. Anchored down? With that woman, no doubt. And he hadn't bothered to send a message to her, just a general greeting through his youngest son. Did this mean he didn't care about her? A cold hand gripped her heart but then she brushed away any kind of feeling. This was no time to worry about emotions. They had to ride out the storm and get back to life later. Thank God the boys were with her and not in school. She felt like a mother hen with all her chicks under her wings, and it felt good. Her marriage might be in question but her children were safe and sound and here with her.

Seamus had run ahead to the kitchen. 'Loads of wood for the stove here, Mum. With a note from Maeve that says there's a flashlight and candles in the cupboard under the sink and that they're all right and not to worry.'

'I know they'll be fine. Their house is in a very sheltered spot with no trees around them and the dunes to protect them from the worst. We're more exposed here on the top of the hill.' She glanced at the window as there was crashing and banging in the yard. 'Buckets and stuff flying around. I should have secured it all. I hope there won't be too much damage. We'll lose a few slates off the shed, I'm sure, but that's a minor matter.' She opened the stove and put a match to the wood piled inside. 'Paschal must have put this in here, bless him.'

'Auntie Maeve is having a baby,' Seamus said out of the blue. 'Dad told us.'

Roisin patted his cheek. 'Yes, and you will have a little cousin.'

'Cool. Hey, Mum, maybe you could make dinner before the power goes? I'm sure the guys are hungry.'

Roisin closed the door of the Aga. 'Absolutely. Better to be in the dark on a full stomach, right?'

'Can we have pizza?'

'Should be easy to organise. Get them out of the freezer and I'll put a few in the oven of the electric cooker and then you can call everybody while I set the table.'

'Does Olga like pizza?'

'I'm sure she loves it.'

'She's nice.'

Roisin smiled at him. 'She's terrific.' She went to the freezer and took out the boxes of pizza. 'I have three large ones here. I hope that's enough.'

'Should be fine for now.'

Roisin put the pizzas beside the Aga. 'I'll wait for the oven to heat up. So, sweetheart, how's school?'

Seamus sat down at the table. 'Great. I like it anyway. We do a lot of sports. Mostly rugby, though.'

'And are Darragh and Rory looking after you?'

Seamus made a face. 'No, Mum. They don't have to. I'm not a kid. I can look after myself. I don't need my big brothers to check up on me.' He suddenly grinned. 'I check up on them, though.'

Roisin laughed. 'I see. So do you have anything to tell me about them? Are they behaving themselves?'

'Darragh is. He's good at sports but he's doing extra study, too. Weird, huh?'

'Not weird at all,' Roisin replied. 'I'm happy to hear it. He is in fifth year after all and will be doing his finals next year. What about Rory?'

Seamus shrugged. 'He's normal. He loves rugby and is trying for the A team.'

Roisin sighed. 'Oh, God, I hope he won't make it. I'm always worried he'll get hurt the way he throws himself around doing that awful tackling and gets into the scrums or whatever it's called.'

'But he's a strong lad, the coach said. So is Darragh. I'm a bit of a titch really, but I'll grow, he said.' Seamus looked at Roisin with his big blue eyes. 'What does that mean, really?'

'I think I will have a word with that coach,' Roisin muttered. She ruffled Seamus' hair. 'Don't worry about it. It doesn't mean anything.'

Her phoned pinged and she took it out of her pocket, hoping it would be Cian. But it was a message from Maeve.

Candles on shelf in the larder. Another flashlight in the small sitting room on the bookshelf. Light the Aga and the fire in the sitting room. Stay safe. We're okay. I don't believe that stuff in the Herald. Maeve xx

Good. At least Maeve wasn't cross with her any more. But what was 'that stuff in the *Herald*' all about? Was there something worse about her and Declan there? She shrugged. That could wait until after the storm. Right now she had to look after her children and stay warm and get them fed.

The pizza was cooked, the table set and everybody was digging in around the table when the lights blacked out. 'There it went,' Roisin said and lit the candles in the candlestick she had put on the table. She looked at her three sons eating as if they hadn't seen food for a week and smiled. How lovely to have them all here together around the table, just like the old days. She wished Cian could have been here, too and she said a silent prayer that he would ride out the storm in relative safety. 'Turn on the radio, someone,' she ordered. 'I want to hear the latest report.'

'It's windy and dark, what else do you want to know?' Rory muttered, his mouth full of pizza.

'Don't be smart, young man,' Roisin snapped and got up, trying to get her bearings in the dim light. Outside, the wind howled with renewed force and she thought she could see something big flying past the window. 'There goes the wheelbarrow,' she exclaimed as a loud crash followed. 'Must have hit the greenhouse.' She found the small radio and turned it on, hoping the batteries weren't too old. 'Shh,' she said when the news started.

'Storm Deirdre has been upgraded to hurricane force and has caused enormous damage in the north-west. It is now moving further south, where the winds are already strong, but nothing like what they will be in the next hour or so. The general public is warned that it is extremely dangerous to go outside and the security forces urge everyone to stay indoors until the wind has dropped. Later tonight, the winds will ease somewhat but the risk of falling trees is still high. So far there has been no loss of life but—'

'Mum, there's someone outside,' Rory shouted and pointed at the window.

Roisin forgot about the news as she directed the big flashlight at the window and saw the outline of a man, his face white, his eyes like black holes and his hair plastered to his head. He looked like something from a horror movie.

Olga screamed. 'Don't open the door! It's a banshee. I've heard of them. They howl with the wind and come to take your soul.'

'Don't be silly.' Roisin undid the latch of the door, pushing it open with all her might against the wind. 'Come inside but hurry up before the door blows off,' she shouted into the storm. A wet hand grabbed the door and then a man heaved himself in and crashed onto the kitchen floor. Roisin managed to heave the door shut again and turn the lock. She stared at the man on the floor and gasped. 'Holy shit, what are *you* doing here?'

Chapter Eighteen

Nobody moved or spoke. The man lay on the floor, his eyes shut, his breathing laboured. His face was covered in scratches and his hands were turning blue. 'I… I…' he croaked.

Roisin fell on her knees. 'Don't try to talk. Olga, get me some cotton wool and a bowl of warm water. There's some stuff in the first-aid box on the shelf by the window. Then we have to get these wet clothes off and get him warm. Boys, you might help me with that. But we'll see to these scratches first. And someone put some more wood in the stove.'

The man half-opened his eyes. 'Always the sergeant major,' he mumbled with a wan smile.

Seamus tiptoed across the floor, holding a candle high. He stared at the man on the floor. 'Who is he?' he asked.

The man opened his eyes fully. 'Declan O'Mahony at your service, young sir.'

'Oh.' Seamus crouched down and peered at Declan. 'Hi. I'm Seamus. You were at that party with Mum.'

'So I was,' Declan agreed, looking a little brighter. 'Hello there, Seamus.'

'I've seen your photo in the newspaper,' Seamus said and got up. 'But what happened to you? Why are you here all scratched and beaten up?'

Roisin took the bowl and cotton wool Olga handed her. 'Shh, leave him alone. We can talk later.' She started to clean his face and dab at the scratches.

Declan pushed away her hands and sat up. 'I'm okay. Stop fussing. I'm just a little shaken and stirred, like a James Bond martini. I was on my way home but then I saw that stuff in the papers when I stopped at a café, and thought I'd drop in and apologise for—' He looked at the boys. 'Well, I'll tell you later perhaps. But anyway, just as I came to the gate, that huge tree fell on my car. I managed to duck my head and escape being killed.'

Roisin clapped her hand to her mouth. 'Oh my God. I heard the crash. I had no idea someone was under it. It's a miracle you're still alive.'

Declan nodded. 'You can say that again. But there I was, nearly flattened, so I had to crawl out through the window. It was broken and the branches… Well, you can imagine. It all cut me to ribbons as you can see. Took me a while to get through it, too. And then I made my way to the back door. Your front door is actually covered in broken branches and debris, so you will have a job taking that away tomorrow. I went around the house to the back, trying to dodge all the stuff that was blowing around, including a wheelbarrow that could have killed me stone dead. It's now in what was your greenhouse, by the way.'

'Nearly killed again,' Olga chortled behind Roisin. 'Your guardian angel must be very busy.'

'That's for sure,' Declan said. 'Hi, Olga. Didn't know you were here.'

'It's the best place to be in such bad weather,' Olga said, peering at him. 'Silly to drive in this storm. All that effort just to say hi to Roisin.'

'I wanted to say a bit more than that,' Declan replied. He led out his hand. 'Come on, boys, help me up. I'll go and take these wet things off if you can find me a blanket or something.'

Darragh got up from the table and went to help Declan. 'I'm Darragh,' he said as he took Declan's arm and pulled him up in one easy movement.

'You're a strong lad, Darragh,' Declan remarked as he was finally upright, his legs a little unsteady. 'You play rugby, right?'

Darragh nodded. 'Yeah. I'm a hooker but hoping to be in the forwards if I train and put on a bit of weight.'

Declan put a hand on Darragh's shoulder. 'I think you're on the way, my boy. Strong muscles there.'

'Why don't you go to the new sitting room through that door,' Roisin interrupted. 'It should be quite warm from the Aga and you can take your clothes off and the boys will lend you something dry to wear. Then come in here and sit in front of the stove and I'll heat up some soup or something.'

Declan sniffed the air. 'Any pizza left?'

'There's some margherita here,' Rory called from the table. 'We can stick it in the Aga while you change.'

'Perfect.' Declan smiled at him. 'You must be Rory.'

'I am. Nice to meet you, Mr…'

'O'Mahony. But you can call me Declan.'

'Are you a friend of Mum's?' Seamus asked, studying Declan intently.

'Yes, and mine,' Olga said as she washed her hands by the sink. 'He's everyone's friend, you know,' she said with a wink at Roisin.

'That's it.' Declan laughed. 'Never been anyone's friend until I got here. This village is the best place for making friends.'

'Except if they decide to hate you,' Olga said. 'Then you might as well just leave.'

'Who hates you?' Roisin asked, putting what was left of the pizza into the oven.

Olga shrugged and sat down beside Rory. 'Nobody here. They're all really nice. But in Stockholm, they didn't like me very much. Thought I was a spy, or at least a reporter working under the covers to say bad things about Sweden in Russia.'

'You mean undercover,' Declan corrected. 'Under the covers would mean something else.'

Olga looked confused. 'What?' She waved her hand at him. 'Oh, maybe. My English slips sometimes. Very difficult language. What was I saying?'

'That the Swedes hate you,' Rory filled in. 'They thought you're a spy who's working undercover as a reporter.'

Olga nodded. 'Not really like that. But they thought I was someone who was there to make trouble. Russians are not liked over there. But I understand them. I don't like Russia myself.' Olga's face turned scornful. 'Bad regime right now. They just want to make trouble in Europe.'

'Why?' Seamus asked.

'Power,' Olga said.

'That's what it's all about in the world of politics. And everywhere else.' Declan undid the zip of his jacket. 'I'd better get out of these wet things.' He peered across the room in the dim light. 'The sitting room is over there? That door next to the window?'

'Yes,' Roisin replied. 'I'll come in and light the fire there when you're ready and then we'll take your clothes and dry them in front of it.'

'Thank God for Agas,' Declan declared. 'What would we do without them? When Armageddon finally arrives, we'll survive thanks to the good old Aga.'

'Invented in Sweden,' Olga cut in. 'Those Swedes are mean but good at some things.'

'A lot of things,' Declan agreed and took a candle from the table and disappeared through the sitting-room door.

Rory pushed his plate away. 'Great pizza, Mum. What's for dinner?'

'You want dinner too?' Olga exclaimed.

'Of course.' Roisin laughed. 'Pizza is just a snack to them. They'll have a big dinner and then ask for a sandwich before going to bed.'

'But you're so skinny,' Olga said to Rory. 'All of you. Where do you put the food?'

'We burn it up thinking,' Seamus cut in. 'We think a lot.'

'What do you think about?' Olga enquired.

'Food. And girls,' Seamus said. 'At least those two do. I haven't started thinking about girls yet. They give me a headache.'

'You're onto something there, my friend,' Declan declared. 'Girls give me a big headache too. What do you think about then?'

'Rugby and food and surfing. And then I play video games and that uses up a lot of thinking,' Seamus replied.

Olga laughed and ruffled Seamus' hair. 'You're a funny boy.'

'Darragh, go and get some dry clothes for Declan to wear,' Roisin interjected. 'A sweater and some jeans or tracksuit pants and socks.'

'Okay, Mum.' Darragh went to get his bag, returning minutes later with a pair of jeans, a hoodie and socks, which he brought to the little sitting room for Declan.

Roisin busied herself with hanging up Declan's clothes and the warmed-up pizza, putting it on a plate and taking it to the sitting room, peeking in to see if Declan was ready. 'You okay? I have two slices of pizza here.'

'I'll come into the kitchen,' he replied. Wearing Darragh's clothes, he was soon settled at the table, eating pizza and chatting to the boys, regaling them with stories of his career as a political reporter, the boys hanging on his every word as he told them how he had discovered corruption in the world of both politics and business and blown the whistle on all of them. Then he explained how it had all gone a little pear-shaped and he had got into hot water as some of the people involved threatened the newspaper with lawsuits which had resulted in him being sacked. 'I think it all went to my head for a bit,' he confessed. 'So I went too far and I was the one who had to take the flak.'

'That's very unfair,' Rory exclaimed.

Declan smiled and shrugged. 'Life's unfair, my friend. I got a little trigger happy and overdid it. But hey, that's the way the cookie crumbles, as they say. I'm enjoying this new phase in my life. You have to take the rough with the smooth and know when to stop.'

'Boys, would you go and unpack your stuff and settle in upstairs?' Roisin instructed. 'Could you give them a hand with the bags,

Olga? Then I'll make tea and see how I can sort out the sleeping arrangements down here. Maybe you could light the fire in the sitting room, Declan? I think the sofa's quite comfortable for you to sleep on. You will probably have to stay the night if the storm gets worse.'

When Olga and the boys had gone upstairs, Declan lit the fire in the small sitting room and sat down on the sofa. 'Nice room,' he said as Roisin came in and sat down on the little rug by the hearth.

'Yes. It was part of the kitchen, which was huge, so this was sectioned off to make a sitting room for Phil. She'll love it. Maeve has done such a good job.'

'Excellent, what I can see of it.'

'Yes.' Roisin sat back on her heels, enjoying the warmth of the fire. She looked at Declan over her shoulder. He was reclining in the sofa looking tired. She could see his eyes glinting and she remembered how those grey eyes had looked at her when they met on the beach. 'Not the kind of woman I usually go for,' he had said later, which had lulled her into a false sense of security, thinking they could be friends and nothing more. But now she was feeling that something more than friendship was going on...

'Are you okay?' she asked to stop her thoughts drifting into dangerous waters. 'I hung your clothes on the drying rack and pulled it up over the Aga.'

'You still have one of those drying racks? I thought they'd all been replaced by tumble driers these days.'

'We still have one.'

'Good for you. Hey, come over here, so I can see you. I need to talk to you.'

'I'm fine right here.' Roisin turned around, still sitting on the rug in front of the fire. 'What was that you wanted to say? We can talk now. The boys are still upstairs with Olga to make beds and put their things away.'

'Oh. Okay.' He sat up, leaning forward, looking serious. 'I don't know if you saw that stuff in the *Herald* with that photo... And the text.' He put his head in his hands. 'Oh, shit, I'm so sorry.'

'What?' Roisin asked, alarmed. 'I saw the one in the *Independent*, but I haven't seen the *Herald*. I just heard bit and pieces, but I'm guessing it's not good.'

Declan looked up. 'You bet it isn't.' He sighed. 'I shouldn't have said anything, but...'

'But what?'

'But I made the mistake of saying there was nothing between us, when this reporter called me.'

'So? Why was that so bad? You were telling the truth.'

'Hell, yeah. Of course I was. But they used it to make it seem sleazy. You have no idea how journalists can turn an innocent statement into something else. They published a photo of the two of us going into the lift. You might not remember, but I had to practically carry you. Then the caption was a quote of what I had said and then something like, "as you can see there was very little between Declan and his new girlfriend Roisin Moriarty last night, and possibly even less once they got to his room at the Sheen Falls Hotel."'

Roisin gulped and stared at him, suddenly cold despite the warmth of the fire. 'Oh my God,' she whispered. 'That's horrible.'

'I know. And there's worse. They've hinted that you stayed the night in my room. Just a hint, as they had no proof, but you were seen leaving the hotel the next morning and they somehow found out that you were not booked in, so you must have stayed in someone's room, they concluded. Who that someone was, they left to the reader's possibly very lively imagination. Clever, huh?'

'Oh, feck.' Roisin's eye filled with tears of frustration and shock. 'But how did they find that out? Hotels don't usually reveal guests' names, do they?'

He shrugged. 'No, I don't think they do. But maybe they think differently about saying who wasn't a guest.'

'A woman called me just as we arrived home. Ellen something from the *Herald*. Asked me about the nature of my relationship with you and if I and Cian were separated. I said "no comment" and hung up.'

'Good. That's what I should have done, but I was caught off guard and didn't think straight after all the booze last night.' He sighed deeply. 'I'm really sorry. I was so stupid. Should have known better than to say anything at all.'

'You told me that that was what we should do.'

Declan let out a sigh. 'And then I went and slipped up like that. What a stupid thing to do. But I thought as a fellow journalist, she'd behave correctly.'

Roisin got up. 'There's no honour amongst thieves, they say.'

He laughed bitterly. 'Yeah. Very apt in this case. And very true.' He looked up at her. 'I wish I could undo it. But now the snowball is rolling down the hill and will get bigger and bigger.'

'And all we can do is say nothing?'

'I'm afraid it is.'

Roisin took his plate. 'How on earth did they get my number?'

'No idea. But they have ways. Especially the ones writing the gossips.'

'But they seemed to know about me and Cian having marriage problems, and I haven't told anyone about it except a few close friends.'

'That's weird. Maybe they talked to Cian?'

'That's not very likely.'

'No, of course not.' Declan sighed.

'But if she wanted to know more, that must mean they're planning to publish something else about us.'

'That's very possible. I feel awful about this.'

'Not your fault,' Roisin said, touched by the regret in Declan's voice. 'I shouldn't have drunk so much. And I should have driven home last night instead of staggering out of your room the morning after. You were kind enough to help me.'

'I could have kept an eye on you and reminded you…'

'It's my own fault, not yours at all.' She paused for a moment. 'Can I get you anything else? I could boil some water on the Aga and make tea.'

'Only if anyone else wants some. Don't make it especially for me.'

'I could do with a cuppa. And I'm sure Olga would like one, too.' Roisin went to the door and stopped. 'Do you think this will go on and on? The stuff in the tabloids, I mean.'

'I hope it won't. I'd say it'll die down when they have someone else to hound.'

'Sounds like wishful thinking to me. I only hope Cian won't see that stuff in the *Herald*. Or even the *Indo*.'

'Where is he now?'

'Somewhere in Donegal.'

'I hope he's all right. The storm has hit there with a vengeance. Half the country is without power and…'

Roisin shivered. 'Please. I don't even want to think about what might happen to him. But he sent the boys a message to say he was okay and staying put in a safe place. So, hopefully, by the time he gets to the mainland, all copies of today's newspapers will be in most people's garbage bins.' She gave a start and let out a yelp as Olga appeared by her side like a ghost.

'Sorry,' Olga said. 'Didn't mean to scare you. We're all organised upstairs. I found sheets and duvets in the hot cupboard, or whatever it's called around here.'

'Hot press,' Roisin corrected. 'Or airing cupboard as they say in England. Don't know what they say in Sweden or Russia.'

'They don't have those kinds of things there,' Olga replied. 'Only in Ireland do they use a water heater and put in a cupboard for keeping sheets and towels warm. A big problem for plumbers when there's a leak. Installing them is a bad dream, too.'

'You mean nightmare,' Declan cut in.

'Do I?' Olga sighed. 'I'll never speak this language correctly.'

'Does it matter?' Declan asked. 'As long as you can make yourself understood, you don't have to worry.'

'I suppose,' Olga said without conviction. 'Thank you anyway. You Irish are very nice. Wild but kind, a bit like Russians. And like us you like to laugh. And to cry.'

There was suddenly sounds of scuffling and shouting from upstairs. Roisin looked at the ceiling. 'What's that racket?'

Olga laughed. 'They're playing hockey on the new floor of the landing. They thought it was slippery after it had been polished and then I said they could play ice hockey like in Russia and they found some hurling sticks in a cupboard and a tennis ball, so…'

'Oh, God,' Roisin exclaimed. 'If they break the new windows, I'll kill them. How can they manage that in the dark anyway?'

'They found two flashlights up there and put them on the table.' Olga started to move away. 'I'll go and tell them to stop. Sorry I started it.'

Declan laughed as moments later they heard Olga shout and give out a loud whistle and then all was quiet, except for the storm raging with renewed force outside. 'Kids, eh?'

'Boys,' Roisin said with a sigh. 'I'll go and sort them. I know they'll be bored now that they can't use their phones or play video games. How on earth will I entertain them until we get the power back?'

'Haven't a clue. When I was a kid, my mum used to give me chores if I had nothing to do. That made me stick to my books like glue. The threat of any kind of work is a great incentive.'

'I bet,' Roisin said and left to tidy up and put a saucepan of water on the stove and put some more wood into it. She looked at the pile of wood in the basket and wondered what they would do when it ran out. She stood there for a while and listened to the wind. Stuck in an old house with no power and three teenagers, a Russian woman and last but not least a man who was now rumoured to be her lover, how weird was that? And where was her husband? Was he safe? And if he was, how long would it take before he saw the newspapers? *You were looking for something to change your life,* she said to herself. *Be careful what you wish for, they say… Be very, very careful…*

Chapter Nineteen

The wind had dropped the following morning and the rain eased to a light drizzle before the sun poked through the clouds. Roisin woke up just as the skies cleared and a weak ray of sunshine peeked through the curtains. It was freezing cold in her room and she hoped the boys were all right. She put on Uncle Joe's wool dressing gown she had found last night among Phil's things downstairs, pulled on her socks and padded out across the landing and down the corridor to the bedrooms, peeking in, finding the boys still asleep under heaps of duvets and blankets. Olga had slept in Phil's bed downstairs and Declan had stayed on the sofa in the sitting room, promising to keep the fires going. She found them both asleep when she went downstairs and the fires had gone out.

Last night had been a hoot. They had found an old version of Trivial Pursuit in a cupboard and decided to play despite protestations from the boys that it would be boring and that this version was from the last century and nobody would know the answers. But it had turned out to be untrue, as the adults were good at the entertainment and sports questions, while the boys were masters at geography, science and history. Darragh had won followed by Declan in second place. Roisin had made pancakes on the Aga and then they had toasted marshmallows over the fire in the new sitting room. The evening had ended with ghost stories, and real-life experiences of ghostly moments told by Olga and Declan, who tried their best to scare each other, making everyone laugh. There had been no arguments about going to bed as the house grew cold and the wind kept howling outside. Roisin was grateful Olga and Declan had been there to provide company and fun.

When she had lit the stove with the wood that remained in the large basket, Roisin looked out the kitchen window at the debris and broken slates from the shed, at the shattered glass from the greenhouse, where the wheelbarrow was sitting, wedged into what was left of one of the walls. There was an eerie silence and a strange stillness out there, as if the world had stopped turning and time stood still. Roisin stood there staring out at the devastation, wondering what kind of calamity had happened elsewhere. The storm had gone through like an express train, leaving destruction in its wake and now the mopping up had to begin.

They had been lucky, she thought, the roof had held and none of the windows had shattered. The only major damage was the beech tree that had flattened Declan's car. Roisin turned on the small radio on the shelf by the window, and soon she was listening to reports about the storm and the havoc it had wreaked all the way up the west coast, Donegal being the worst hit. She shivered as she listened, thinking that if it had been worse up there in the north-west than here, how had Cian survived? Just as the thought struck her, there was a pinging sound from her pocket and she pulled out her phone that she had put there last night. There was a text message from Cian's number that said:

I'm okay, I hope you and the boys are too. Please let me know.
I saw some weird stuff about you in one of the papers but we
will talk about that later when the weather improves.

End of message, the first one since before the storm, without even
a kiss like they always put in their messages to each other. Come to
think of it, she hadn't been putting kisses in her messages to him lately
either, ever since she had spotted that picture on Andrew's Instagram
page. 'You bet we'll talk,' she muttered as she went to fill a saucepan
with water to make tea, thinking that at least she knew he was alive
and well. Had he been cuddling Greta during the storm and forgotten
he had a wife and children? Or was that German woman just a friend?
She was suddenly dying to know and eager to talk to him and sort out
how they felt about each other and this strange break they were on.
Freedom for a while, they had said. But at what cost? And for how long?

'Hello?' Declan, fully clothed in dry but wrinkly jeans and
sweater, stuck his head in through the door of the sitting room.
'Are you okay?'

Roisin shrugged. 'Yeah, sure. As okay as you can be in a freezing cold house without electricity and three teenagers who will be
looking for a gargantuan breakfast in a little while. On top of that
a husband demanding to know what is going on and…'

'And two houseguests, one of whom is implicated with you in
some kind of liaison dreamed up by newspapers who seem to be
short of anything better to write about. But good morning, anyway.
Did you sleep well?'

Roisin managed a smile despite her bad mood. Declan had a
way of disarming even the grumpiest person. 'Good morning. Sorry

about the moan. Yes, I slept well despite the storm. I suppose I was tired after all that happened yesterday. A major hangover didn't help either. I think I'll give up the booze from now on.'

'So says many a hungover person after a night out.' He shot her a glance that made her tighten the belt of the dressing gown. 'Nice – whatever that thing you're wearing is.'

'My late uncle's wool dressing gown from 1972. Warm as toast but hideous.'

'On you it looks very nice. But then, anything would.'

Roisin pinched her mouth and looked at him sternly, feeling she needed to put some boundaries between them. He was getting far too flirty which felt both uncomfortable and dangerous. How could their relationship suddenly change from friendship to – whatever this was turning into? 'Let's not get mawkish, okay?' she snapped. 'Let's just get through this and then try to avoid each other for a bit.'

He leaned nonchalantly against the door jamb. 'I don't think that's going to be possible in this small village. I think people will talk even more if we avoid each other. We're friends who have nothing to hide.'

Roisin nodded and opened the fridge. 'Okay. Probably the best idea. And I hope I can get Cian to come down soon too. That'd be a good way to dispel the rumours.'

'Do you think he will?'

'No idea.' Roisin examined the contents of the fridge. 'Milk, butter, ham, eggs, bacon, black pudding, tomatoes,' she muttered, trying to hide her confusion. His new way of looking at her made her feel awkward and slightly flustered. She closed the fridge again. 'Better not have this open while we have no power. And I dread to think what'll happen to all the food in the freezer if this goes on. Thousands of people are cut off in this area, they said on the radio. Could be days before we're connected.'

'I'll go home later, though.'

Roisin turned and stared at him. 'How? Your car is under the beech tree, flat as a pancake. I just looked at it through the front window. Completely crushed with the windows all broken. I'm sure many of the roads are blocked by fallen trees, anyway. And it's still risky to go outside, they said on the news.'

'I'll walk.'

'You'd be in for a long walk.'

'Only just forty-five minutes or so. I'm used to walking.'

'I suppose. And I have to confess I feel it would be better if you left. It's a bit awkward to have you here under the circumstances.' Roisin put two teabags into the teapot on the sink.

'What circumstances?' he asked, looking the picture of innocence.

'Please. Don't pretend you don't know what I mean.' Roisin turned as she heard a hissing sound. The water was boiling over. She went to take the saucepan off and pour the water into the teapot. 'Have a cup of tea and toast… there's bread in the breadbin and you can help yourself to marmalade and butter and whatever else you fancy. I'm going upstairs to get dressed.'

'Have a cup of tea first,' Declan suggested. 'That'll make you feel better.'

'I feel fine, thank you.' Roisin bristled, suddenly irritated by him standing there looking cool while she was flustered and confused, troubled by what had happened yesterday and now having her sons to look after and keep amused until they could go outside. And then there was something else, something in his eyes that made her feel that the vibes between them were suddenly something more than just friendship. He was an attractive man with enormous charm and empathy. He had that free spirit that spoke to her wild side she had suppressed for so long while she and Cian worked so hard. With Declan she had allowed herself to be irresponsible and free from her role as a mother and wife. It had been liberating but maybe a little risky spending time with someone who seemed to be a kindred spirit. Someone she'd love to get to know better. Someone she'd be ready to fall in love with if she wasn't married. *Stop it*, she told herself while she avoided his eyes, moving away as he approached. She needed to get away from him and concentrate. And she needed to save her marriage. If it wasn't already too late.

She walked away, tightening her dressing gown again. 'Yes. I think it would be best if you left. You have to check on your house and see if there was any damage.'

He poured tea into a mug, glancing at her. 'I'll be gone when you come back. Thank you for helping me last night.'

'I think I owed you that one.'

'Maybe. But in that case, we're quits. Nobody owes anyone anything, okay?'

'Okay,' she whispered as their eyes met across the room. Then she turned on her heel and fled. She had to get away from him. Away from her own feelings.

Chapter Twenty

Declan had left by the time Roisin came back downstairs. She had managed a quick wash in freezing cold water and put on as many layers as possible in order to keep warm. She found Olga in the kitchen frying bacon and eggs in a big cast-iron pan. She turned as Roisin entered. 'Morning. I put more wood in the stove.' She gestured at the frying pan. 'I'm making breakfast for the boys. And me. I like a big breakfast. Is that okay?'

'Brilliant. I think I heard the boys moving around so they should be down soon. The smell of cooking never fails to get them out of bed.'

'Okay. I hope we can get that tree at the gate cut up soon. I got more than ten calls asking me to go and help with leaks in houses and some flooded basements. I have two pumps and I need to get them and go and help out. I could walk, but I need to use my van to get to these people with my equipment. I've checked with the guys who work for me and they're waiting for me at my place.'

'I'll ring Maeve and Paschal. I think they might have a chainsaw we could borrow.'

'Great.' Olga pointed at the frying pan. 'I found this in the cupboard under the sink. Must be very old.'

'There's a lot of stuff there from when the house was built. I thought we should throw them out and get more modern saucepans, but these cast-iron pans are great for cooking up a real old-fashioned breakfast. I'm sure people who come to stay here will like it.'

'Good for using on the Aga,' Olga agreed and expertly flipped over the bacon. 'But maybe not so good for the modern stove with induction hob.'

'Hmm. That's true.' Roisin felt the teapot. 'Still hot enough. I'm dying for a cup of tea.'

'Declan made fresh tea for you before he left.' Olga paused, spatula in her hand. 'He is very fond of you. Maybe... too fond?'

Roisin was about to tell Olga it was none of her business, but the real concern in Olga's eyes stopped her. 'Maybe he is,' she mumbled as she poured tea into a mug.

'And you?'

Roisin shrugged. 'I like him and I wish we could be friends. But I also wish there wasn't that... *feeling* between us. But how can I stop it?'

'How do you feel about your husband?' Olga went back to her task.

Roisin sighed and took a sip of tea. 'I'm angry with him.'

'For going away?' Olga asked, looking at Roisin over her shoulder.

'Yes, and for not being interested in what I'm doing. He seems to have become hooked on living in that campervan and being free from all responsibilities. I do understand him in a way, because coming here has made me appreciate the little things in life and that constantly working and having projects isn't really what makes you happy. But...' she sighed. 'I wish he'd communicate with me. He seems to be ignoring me lately. And then there was that picture on Instagram of him cuddling a sexy German girl. It made me both angry and hurt.'

'Maybe it didn't mean anything?' Olga suggested. 'Maybe it was the girl cuddling and him being polite?'

Roisin let out a snort. 'He didn't look polite, he looked…'

'What?'

'I don't know. Delighted? Highly attracted? Something that is not okay for a married man.'

'And you having feelings for Declan is okay for a married woman?'

'No. Not at all. But it's not the same.' Roisin looked out the window and thought for a moment. 'It's just that Declan is an attractive, interesting, nice man. And very kind. We have become close friends during the time I've been here. He's such a good listener. Funny, but when I've been with him, it's been a little like speaking to myself. I've been able to resolve a lot of my problems while simply talking to him. It's been such a great help to be with someone who has no prejudices and takes everyone as they come. I can't help being fond of him. How do you feel about him?'

'Declan?' Olga laughed. 'He's very, uh, sexy. And I like him. But any woman would. If I was in your place, I would not worry about how you feel about a man like that. Of course you would be fond of someone who takes an interest in you. It's normal. If you did not, you would not be a real woman. And he's famous so that could be a reason you find yourself – you know – more attracted.' Olga turned and looked at Roisin. 'You understand what I mean?'

'Yes.' Roisin cut a slice off the loaf of soda bread and spread some butter on it. 'Thank you. Makes me feel a little less guilty.

And better about Cian and the German girl. Could be the same for him.'

'She is famous?'

Roisin giggled. 'No. But she's cute. She might be a good listener, too. It could be that we both need to talk to someone who isn't part of our life. Maybe that's all?'

Olga pulled the frying pan off the heat. 'I haven't seen the picture so I couldn't tell you.'

Roisin pulled out her phone and quickly located the picture on Instagram, wincing as she saw it again. She held it out to Olga. 'There. What do you think? How does he look to you?'

Olga studied the screen. 'Hmm. Like a little boy opening a Christmas present. But it's just a photo, a frozen moment. He could have looked annoyed a minute later.'

Roisin turned off her phone. 'I bet he didn't.'

'No.' Olga looked at Roisin with pity. 'I'm sorry you had to see that. But then there was that photo of you and Declan in the *Herald*...'

'You saw that, too?'

'Yes. They were selling it in the newspaper shop. Everyone was asking for it, so I had to have a look to see what was so interesting.'

'Everyone?' Roisin asked, her voice hoarse.

Olga nodded. 'Yes. It's out there now, I'm afraid.'

'Shit. And the fact that the McKennas are so well-known around here adds to the interest,' Roisin said glumly. 'All the gossip-mongers will love this.'

'I know. It's very bad.'

'Mum?' Rory wandered into the kitchen, his hair on end, wearing a thick wool sweater over his pyjamas. 'What's wrong?'

Roisin pulled herself together. 'Uh, nothing. Just a lot of damage out there. We have to work hard to clear up today. I hope Paschal can give us a hand.'

'Is there anything to eat?' Rory asked.

'Breakfast,' Olga interrupted. 'I burned the bacon a little bit but it looks fine to eat anyway.'

Rory sniffed. 'Smells good.'

Olga put the contents of the frying pan on a platter. 'Here. Take a plate and—'

'No,' Roisin cut in and took a stack of plates from the cupboard. 'I'll dole it all out. If you let them help themselves, they'll scoff the lot and there'll be nothing left. Rory, get some glasses and put them on the table and then fill a pitcher with water. Your brothers should be down soon. I'll make more tea and Olga, please cut up some bread.'

'Yes, Captain,' Olga chortled.

The other boys shuffled into the kitchen and soon breakfast was in full swing. Roisin kept busy cooking more bacon and eggs, feeding the stove with wood and planning the day and the clearing up. Occupying herself helped her push her problems to the back of her mind. After breakfast, Roisin ordered the boys upstairs to get dressed and Olga started to tidy up the kitchen.

While the boys and Olga were busy, Roisin picked her way through the debris of branches and driftwood thrown up by the waves along the path to Maeve's house. Here she could see across the bay that the swell in the aftermath of the storm was enormous. If it continued, the boys would have some great surfing during the week. The air smelled of salt and seaweed and everything looked newly washed, including the flagstones of the path leading up to the front door. The cottage had been spared any damage apart from bits of thatch that had blown onto the bushes. The smell of turf smoke coming out of the chimney reminded Roisin of days gone by when every house had been burning hand-cut turf from the bogs in the mountains. These days the turf was mainly shop-bought briquettes, but they had the same tangy smell.

Roisin knocked on the door and opened it, calling for Maeve.

'Come in,' Maeve replied from the kitchen, where Roisin found her at the little wood stove stirring something in a pot, Esmeralda winding herself around her legs, meowing loudly. 'Irish stew,' Maeve said as Roisin entered. 'I made it before the power went out, but this little stove is a great back-up. How did you manage last night?'

Roisin sat down at the table by the window. 'It was a bit of a challenge, what with the boys and then Olga having to stay and then Declan falling in through the door, having been nearly flattened by the beech tree at the gate. He was nearly killed and his car is a total wreck.'

Maeve's eyes widened. 'Oh, God, that's terrible.'

'Awful. He walked home this morning, despite being still quite shaken up by what happened.'

'This morning?' Maeve asked. 'You mean he stayed the night?'

'Yes, what else could he do? It was dangerous to go outside.' Roisin laughed. 'Don't worry, we had plenty of chaperones with the kids and Olga. We ended up playing Trivial Pursuit by candlelight.'

'Oh.' Maeve put a lid on the pot and pulled it to the side. 'Do you want a cup of tea? It takes a while to boil the water, though.'

'I'd love a cup. Olga is tidying up and the boys are getting dressed. I was hoping Paschal might come with the chainsaw to cut up the tree so Olga can get out. She's had a lot of calls from people who had damaged pipes and leaks as a result of the storm. The amount of rain last night was incredible. Thank God for the new roof and windows.'

Maeve put a kettle on the stove. 'Oh, yes. If that hadn't been done the house would have been damaged. Paschal is outside in the shed getting the chainsaw. He said you might need it. We heard the crash last night, so we thought it might be one of the trees, but we didn't know which one.' Maeve turned around and folded her arms, looking at Roisin with concern. 'The storm gave everyone something else to think about. But when the mopping up is over, it'll still be out there and it won't go away.'

'It?' Roisin asked, even though she knew the answer.

'You know. You and – him and all that stuff.'

'And what can I do about it?' Roisin stared at Maeve, trying to gauge her mood. 'I have a feeling you believe the worst.'

'The worst being – what?'

'That I'm somehow cheating on Cian with Declan. But it wasn't like that at *all*.' Roisin got up and started to pace around the small kitchen. 'Look, what happened was an accident and it was all my fault. I had too much to drink and couldn't drive home. And then I accidentally had a little more and was completely legless, so Declan helped me upstairs to his room so I could sleep it off. That's all that went on, nothing else.'

'Where did he sleep?' Maeve inquired.

'In the same bed. But nothing happened, I swear to God.'

'Hmm,' Maeve said, looking doubtful.

'For God's sake, Maeve,' Roisin exclaimed. 'That bed was the size of a field. He might as well have been in the next county, that's how far apart we were. We only slept – at least I did. No idea what he did but he didn't come near me, that's all I know,' Roisin declared. 'He doesn't fancy me in the slightest anyway. I'm not at all his type. He's told me so many times.'

Maeve's eyebrows shot up. 'Really? He told you that? And you believed him?'

'Yes, yes, you must know that he usually goes for the dark, skinny, sultry type. The Morticia Addams clones, judging by his ex-wives. They all look like they've never been out in daylight or eaten a proper meal. And look at me – short, chubby and blonde, the complete opposite. I'd say Olga would be more to his liking than me.'

'What are you talking about? You're very attractive. But what about him? Is he your type at all?'

'No, I...' Roisin stopped and glared at Maeve. 'What is this? The Inquisition? Could you please stop grilling me and try to see it from my point of view?'

'Your point of view? As far as I can tell, you had a crush on him for years. And then he turns up here in our village, all hero-like and handsome and even better than on the telly.'

'How do you know he's better than on the telly? You said you didn't even know who he was as you were out of the country during his glory days.'

'I saw some old clips the other night when they ran that documentary he presented. He's better looking in real life.' Maeve suddenly laughed. 'Gee, Roisin, what a shock it must have been to meet him there on the beach that day. I saw how starstruck you were and I could nearly hear the "Halleluiah Chorus" playing from the clouds. Woohoo, your hero right in front of you, it must have been like a dream come true.'

Roisin couldn't help laughing, too. 'Yeah. I thought it was some kind of mirage at first. And then we became such close friends during the past month, when we were both struggling with the builders and I tried to help him. But…' she paused for a moment, 'please believe me, it was nothing more than friendship right from the start. It never will be anything else. Even if—'

'Even if you now find yourself more drawn to him than you should be?'

Roisin shrugged without replying, feeling her face grow hot.

'That's not good,' Maeve said sternly. 'You have to—' She gasped, putting her hands on her stomach. 'Oh my God.'

'What!?' Roisin exclaimed, alarmed, getting up and running to Maeve's side. 'Is something wrong? Are you in pain? Will I get Paschal?'

Maeve shook her head, letting out a sound halfway between a sob and a laugh. 'No, nothing wrong. The baby moved, that's all. It's the first time I've felt it like this.'

'Oh.' Roisin let out a relieved sigh and put her arms around Maeve. 'That's an amazing moment, isn't it? How many weeks is it?'

'Nearly four months. The doctor said I'd begin to feel real kicks around this time. It's incredible.' Maeve leaned her head against Roisin. 'I've felt some kind of flutter before but this was a real kick. Like a little message from him or her.'

'I know. It's lovely. That's when you start bonding with the baby.'

'Yes,' Maeve whispered, her hands on her stomach. 'Oooh, there it is again.'

'When is it due exactly?'

'Late July. Can't wait.'

'Neither can I. How are you feeling? All the nausea gone?'

'Oh, yes,' Maeve replied with a happy sigh. 'Such a relief. Now I just feel hungry all the time.'

'Oh, great. Eat whatever takes your fancy. As healthily as possible, of course. July is only five months away. We should be all together by then. Cian and me and the boys. I'm thinking of renting that house up the road from Willow House and then I'm going to help Phil run the guesthouse. Cian will… Well, he'll take a break and be with the boys during their summer holidays. We didn't really make a definite plan when we parted, but now I think this is what would be best.'

'It's all decided then?'

'Yes,' Roisin said with more conviction than she felt. 'Absolutely.'

'You have it down on paper? With bullet points?' Maeve asked with more than a touch of irony in her voice. 'I mean, you wouldn't want to do anything without a proper plan and loads of lists, would you?'

'No. Nothing is written down yet. I haven't even got a plan. Just a lot of wishful thinking.' Roisin let her arms fall and sank down on the chair next to Maeve. 'I wish it were. I wish I had it all on paper and Cian's approval. But that's very far away right now. I don't even know if this is what he'll want to do.' She put her head in her hands. 'It's such a mess, isn't it? What am I going to do?'

Maeve sighed and shook her head. 'I don't know.' She put her arms around Roisin. 'I'm sorry you're feeling so bad. But I'm sure it will all work out in the end. You and Cian were so happy together, you were such a great team. And you will be again, once he has had enough of his adventure. Try not to worry. Everything will be fine.'

Roisin looked at Maeve. 'You think so?'

'Of course it will.' She kissed Roisin on the cheek and got up. 'I think I'll go back to bed for a while. Nothing much to do until we have power. Oh, and Phil was in touch yesterday before the storm. She wants to chat on Skype with both of us. But we have to wait until we have electricity and a better signal. She said she had something amazing to tell us.'

'Really? I hope it's some kind of good news.' Roisin was interrupted by her phone ringing in her pocket. Without thinking, she pulled it out and replied. 'Hello?'

'Hi, Roisin, this is Ellen Murphy again. From the *Herald*? Just to ask about you and your husband and your relationship with—'

Roisin felt a surge of rage at the woman's voice. Forgetting her pact with Declan to say nothing, she took a deep breath. 'Listen, Eileen, or whatever your name is, stop hounding me like this, fishing for some juicy gossip you are hoping to publish in that rag you call a newspaper. There's nothing wrong with my marriage. My husband and I are just not together for the moment, as we are taking a break from work and stress and he's on holiday in Donegal. I'm here in Kerry to help my sister with the rebuilding of our aunt's house. Declan O'Mahony just happens to live nearby and he's just a friend, nothing more.'

'So you're just friends?' Ellen asked, her voice dripping with irony. 'How sweet.'

Roisin gritted her teeth. 'Have you never been friends with a man,' she snapped, 'or does that not happen in your sleazy little world? Write whatever you want, but if you tell lies, I'll sue your fat arse to kingdom come. Got that?'

'Uh, yes,' Ellen replied.

'Good!' Roisin hung up and glared at Maeve, who was having hysterics. 'What's the matter with you?'

Maeve couldn't stop laughing. 'I know I should tell you that was a very bad idea, but it's so funny. How do you know she has a fat arse?'

'She sounds as if she does.' Roisin threw her phone on the table. 'Oh, God, what have I done? Now they'll print something worse about me and Declan.'

'She won't if she doesn't want her fat arse sued,' Maeve said with a giggle.

'I'm sure she'll think of something. And me losing it will have made her more determined to keep going with this.'

'You could be right,' Maeve said, looking more sober. 'But I don't blame you. I think I'd have let it rip, too.'

'Well, whatever.' Roisin glanced out the window. 'I hear the chainsaw. I'd better go and make sure no one gets hurt. The boys love to play with machinery.'

'Just one thing.' Maeve frowned as she looked at Roisin. 'How did the *Herald* get all the stuff about you? I mean where Cian is and all that? It wasn't in the *Independent*. And the stuff about you selling the business and about the campervan?'

Roisin looked back at Maeve. 'That is really what's bugging me the most. I have no idea. Someone must have talked. But who? Not

Declan, of course. And I haven't told anyone else—' She stopped. 'Except Nuala, but I didn't tell her that much.' Roisin stiffened. 'Shit, I did tell someone else. In great detail.'

'Who? Spit it out, willya,' Maeve urged. 'Don't just stand there staring at me. Who else did you tell?'

'Olga.'

Chapter Twenty-One

Nothing was published about Declan and Roisin in the following two days. All the newspapers were full of the drama of the storm and the havoc it had wreaked along the coast. Photos of wrecked houses with torn-off roofs, cars blown into rivers and trees ripped up by the roots dominated the front pages of most papers, including the *Evening Herald* and the *Sun*. Roisin, thinking her own personal storm had also blown over, felt more relaxed. She felt like she could concentrate on the clearing up and getting the boys to and from the surfing camp on the main beach and keeping them amused and fed in the evenings. She met Nuala on the beach one blustery morning while the boys got into their wetsuits in the shed that had been erected by the surf club.

Roisin looked out over the beach where the waves were crashing onto the sand, throwing a salty spray high into the air. Seagulls glided above, letting out plaintive cries and black-and-white oystercatchers tripped around the rocks, picking at shells, their red beaks and legs brilliant in the morning sun. The air was fresh and clean. It was the kind of day when it was good to be alive.

'Lovely day,' someone said.

Roisin turned around and smiled at Nuala. 'Really nice. Such a relief after that awful storm.'

'And we got the power back yesterday. That was a true miracle. I was saying novenas every half hour. Stuck in the house with teenagers and no electricity. What a total nightmare. I thought I'd end up killing one of them. It was moan, moan every ten minutes. And Sean Óg was no help either. But he had an excuse. The kitchen in the pub was flooded when the high tide hit, so it was all hands on deck. Olga gave him one of her pumps, so that was a huge help. Thank God we have a generator that he could use.'

'And now, with this gorgeous day, it's hard to believe there was such a bad storm.'

Nuala shivered and pulled the collar of her jacket closer around her neck. 'It's cold, though. How about a coffee at The Two Marys'? They've opened for half-term.'

'Sounds great. I don't think the boys want their mammy hanging around.'

'Absolutely not. Let them get on with it. My kids hate me hovering over them when they're with their friends. And the surf instructors are really experienced. No need to worry about a thing. And this will exhaust them so much they'll be too tired to cause trouble.'

'Brilliant.'

Nuala started to walk along the beach. 'We can get to the café on the path over there. No need to get into our cars.'

Roisin followed Nuala, breaking into a half-run to keep up with her brisk pace. 'Hey, wait, I have only got short little legs,' she panted.

Nuala slowed down, laughing. 'Sorry, pet. I'm always in a hurry, it seems.'

They walked up a path that wound up around the dunes and onto a grassy plot where a small thatched cottage stood, its windows overlooking the ocean. Nuala pulled open the back door and walked in, calling a cheery, 'Hello.'

Inside the small café with its rustic tables and chairs and flagstone floor, a fire glowed in the open fireplace and the smell of turf mingled with coffee and freshly baked cakes. A chubby woman behind the counter smiled as they came in. 'Hi, Nuala. Lovely day, isn't it?'

'Gorgeous,' Nuala replied, pulling out a chair at a table by the window. 'Mary, this is Roisin, Maeve's sister.'

'I know,' the woman said. 'I've seen her picture in the papers. Hello, Roisin. Nice to meet you. That party must have been a wee bit of craic.'

'Yeah, a bit too much for my liking,' Roisin replied.

'Ah sure, them journalists would make up anything to sell a few copies,' Mary soothed. 'Don't take any notice, darlin'. They'll forget all about you soon enough. What can I get you, girls?'

'Coffee and a slice of that lemon sponge you just took out of the oven,' Nuala said, sitting down.

'And you, Roisin?' Mary asked.

'The same for me.'

'I'll bring it over to you,' Mary said.

'Where's the other Mary?' Nuala asked.

'Gone out for supplies,' Mary replied. 'But I'll tell her you were asking for her. And don't you worry, Roisin, we won't let anyone gossip about you around here.'

Roisin sat down opposite Nuala and took off her jacket. 'That's a relief,' she said to Nuala. 'If the rest of the village think like Mary, I'll stop worrying.'

Nuala shrugged. 'Ah, some will talk and make up even more stories. But…' She looked thoughtfully at Roisin. 'I had an idea this morning. How you can fight back and get that husband of yours to come to his senses.'

Intrigued, Roisin looked at Nuala. 'Go on.'

'Well, it was just a thought. But this morning I got a call from Mick O'Dowd, who's a fisherman and also works as a guide on Skellig Michael in the summer. He said that the sea will be dead calm tomorrow, according to the shipping forecast, so there will be no surfing. He offered to take us all out to Skellig Michael, the kids and you and me, I mean. The tourist boats don't run in the winter, so the place will be deserted. I thought it might be fun for the kids, what with the last *Star Wars* movie having been shot there and everything. We can get them to learn a bit of history on the sly that way.'

'Skellig Michael?' Roisin asked, glancing out at the craggy outline of the island in the distance. 'That would be amazing. I've never been there, strangely enough. Every time we planned to go the sea was too wild. Of course we would all love to go. But what does that have to do with me and all that stuff in the tabloids?'

They were interrupted by Mary arriving with a laden tray. Nuala got up and took it, placing it on the table. 'Put it all on my tab, please, Mary.'

'Will do,' Mary said. 'I hope you like the cake.'

'I'm sure we will,' Roisin said, breathing in the citrusy smell of the moist cake.

Nuala handed her a mug of coffee. 'I thought that if we take lovely shots of you and the kids on Skellig Michael and post them on Facebook and Instagram and whatever, we could give Cian a jolt, reminding him what a gorgeous family he has. And send the pictures to him, too, of course. And the newspapers. They want news about you? We'll show them what a lovely family you have and what a great mum you are, taking the boys on this lovely trip. The best news ever.'

Roisin smiled, touched by Nuala's concern for her. 'Oh, yes, that's a fabulous idea. Thank you.'

'No need to thank me. It's just a bit of fun for me, too. Happy to help.'

'I hope whoever leaked stuff about me and Cian to the press will pick it up, too.'

Nuala's eyebrows shot up. 'Someone blabbed all that stuff about you? To those awful newspapers?'

'Only the *Evening Herald*, as far as I know. But yeah, some stuff was printed that I only told a few people. Declan and Maeve for a start, but also – Olga.' Roisin paused. 'I don't know her that well, but do you think she could have—?'

Nuala looked thoughtful. 'I wouldn't have thought so. She's such a nice, straight person. Very honest. But I know she's had to take a loan to start her business, so if she needed a bit of cash…'

'I hate to talk like this,' Roisin said. 'It makes me feel awful. But I also have to think of me and my family. And my marriage. If this stuff goes on, God knows what's going to happen. It could create a lot of problems for me.'

'Well, the best thing to do is to be careful about what you say to people. Not me and Maeve, but anyone else, including Olga.' Nuala waved her hand in the air. 'I know, she is probably innocent, but it might just be safer.'

'Yes, I suppose it is. It makes me sad because she was so great during the storm and helped out with the boys. She was really such a brick during it all.'

Nuala helped herself to her slice of cake. 'That doesn't mean we can't be friends with her. Just that you can't tell her anything you don't want to see in the papers.'

'Yes, I think you're right.' Roisin drank her coffee and looked out across the ocean at the Skellig Islands and felt a dart of excitement at the thought of their outing. It would be an amazing day. And Nuala's idea was excellent. Not that the newspapers would be interested in writing about what a wonderful mother she was, but it might get Cian to wake up, and even send a signal to Declan, who was getting a little too cosy for comfort. He might protest that she wasn't his type, but the way he had looked at her that morning after the storm told a different story. And she needed a wake-up call herself, she thought with a dart of guilt. She had had a crush on him during his glory days, the way one would have on a handsome film star and then he had appeared as if by magic on the beach that day, looking, as Maeve had remarked, even better in real life. It had been like meeting Brad Pitt in the flesh. Starstruck was the only word to describe how she had felt. The friendship that later sparked up between them had been amazing, but if it was developing into something else she didn't know how to handle it.

Nuala pointed out the window at the view of the beach. 'Look. The kids are surfing. Your Seamus is the best of them all. And my girls aren't bad either.'

Roisin followed her gaze and looked at the wetsuit-clad figures riding the waves or wading out to catch the best ones. She spotted Darragh paddling out to meet the swell and Rory just coming back, grinning at his brother. 'They're having a great time.'

'Long may it last,' Nuala said. 'Hey, you know what? We could go to the shop while they're out there and get some stuff for a picnic lunch tomorrow. The grocery shop in the village, I mean. Just to get some ham and sausage and bread for sandwiches. We'll have an early start tomorrow, so there will be no time to buy anything. We'll be back in plenty of time to pick the kids up when the surfing lessons are over.'

'Great idea. Then I can make the picnic tonight and be ready tomorrow morning.'

They finished their coffees, said goodbye to Mary and walked out the front, up the lane and into the village where the shop was situated at the end of the main street. There were only a few customers browsing among the shelves, chatting to each other, catching up on the latest news. Nuala and Roisin grabbed a basket each and started to fill them with ham and sausages and various treats, consulting each other on what to bring. Roisin was examining the pile of bananas, when someone touched her arm.

'Roisin Moriarty, isn't it?' a woman with short greying hair and mean little eyes asked.

'Eh, yes?' Roisin replied, trying to remember if she had met this woman before.

'I've seen you in the papers. Don't blame your husband for looking for comfort somewhere else.'

'What?' Roisin asked, confused.

'It's in the early edition of the *Herald*,' the woman said with a nasty glint in her eyes. 'Him and another woman, cosying up to each other.'

'What?' Roisin said again. 'Who are you?' She looked around for Nuala, who was picking at the apples displayed in a big bowl.

Nuala looked around and spotted what was going on. She threw some apples into her basket and marched down the narrow aisle. 'What kind of dirt are you spreading today, Orla O'Dea? Leave my friend alone. She's done nothing wrong.'

Orla backed away. 'You might say that, Nuala, but what she's been up to was all over the papers for all to see. Carousing with another man in that hotel and now her poor children have to witness their mam being exposed. Marriage is a sacrament, you know,' she declared, glaring at Roisin.

'And slandering people without proof is a crime,' Nuala remarked. 'How about being informed instead of just opinionated, Orla? Maybe take what you see in the gutter press with a pinch of salt? It's all a lot of fake news published by journalists who have nothing better to do than trying to hurt innocent people.'

'Ha,' Orla said with a snort. 'That's fine talk from someone who overcharges their customers.'

'We don't, and you know it,' Nuala retorted. 'I'd get that husband of yours to spend a little more time at home instead of bending his elbow at the pub every night of the week. But maybe he is looking for a little comfort elsewhere? I can't say I blame him.'

Orla glared at Nuala, her nostrils flaring. Her mouth opened, then closed again before she flounced out of the shop, banging the door behind her. There was a brief silence and then a communal titter, as the women in the shop started to giggle. 'Well done, Nuala,' a woman called from the deli counter. 'That Orla O'Dea needed to be told off.'

'Yes, she did,' another woman declared. 'I know she's a devout Catholic but that doesn't give her licence to judge other people and to spread gossip about them. And Roisin, darlin', nobody takes a blind bit of notice of that rubbish in the papers. We know the McKenna girls have too much class to be involved in anything like that. It's all lies by that rag to sell more copies.'

'Thank you,' Roisin said, feeling near to tears at the kind words.

The women nodded and went back to their shopping, some of them patting Roisin's arm as they passed on their way out. Nuala and Roisin paid for their purchases and went out into the bright sunshine, carrying their bags. They were about to double back to the beach, when Nuala stopped. 'Hang on, I'll pop into the newsagent's for a copy of the *Herald*. We need to see what's up with them.'

Roisin took Nuala's bag. 'Yes, of course. Good idea. I'll wait here.'

Nuala came back moments later brandishing the paper. 'It's not too bad,' she called. 'At least it's not on the front page. But who found that photo?'

Roisin dropped the bags and tore the papers from Nuala. 'What is it?' She flicked to the next page, where, at the bottom, she discovered the photo of Declan and Greta and the caption:

A happy marriage heading for the rocks, as Roisin Moriarty's husband finds a pretty shoulder to cry on.

She had looked at the picture a hundred times, so it didn't shock her any more and the caption made her snort. How ridiculous. 'No big deal,' she said with a shrug. 'Only…' She stared at Nuala. 'How did they know about it? I only showed it to you and Declan and…'

'Olga?' Nuala said.

Chapter Twenty-Two

The next morning turned out to be as lovely as Nuala had promised. It was 'a pet of a day', as they say in Kerry about a beautiful day in the middle of winter, with clear blue skies, bright sunshine, a warm breeze and calm seas. She had no problem getting the boys up early as they were excited about the excursion to the '*Star Wars* island' and the climb to the top to see the beehive cells the monks had built over a thousand years ago. The lecture about safety precautions from Mick during the boat trip only made them even more excited and they listened with rapt attention, promising to climb at a steady pace, stay on the path and not do anything that might be dangerous. They had all dressed in warm clothes and walking boots, carrying rucksacks with spare clothes and enough food for a whole day, including bottles of water and thermos flasks with tea. It felt like a polar expedition, having to be prepared for a sudden change in the weather and a possible prolonged stay on the island. Mick's friend and colleague was driving the boat as it was impossible to dock at the steep cliffs.

The island rose above them as they approached, its pinnacles pointing dramatically up to the clear blue sky. Slightly queasy, Roisin held on to the side of the boat as it swayed in the mild swell and she was happy to follow the boys ashore, jumping onto the quay and grabbing

Mick's hands as she nearly slipped into the dark water. She caught her breath and steadied herself, looking up at the steep slope ahead, where steps had been hewn out of the rock more than a thousand years ago.

'Six hundred steps to the top,' Nuala announced. 'Take it nice and easy, gang, and rest if you need to. No fooling around or pushing and shoving, is that understood?'

Everyone nodded, intimidated by the stark surroundings, the line of steps going up the nearly perpendicular slope and the feeling of being touched by something otherworldly, as the light wind whispered around them. The feeling of peace and tranquillity silenced even the usually chatty Seamus. 'We'll be good,' he said, looking around as if to appease the spirits that might still be on the island.

Mick nodded and hitched his rucksack higher on his back. 'Let's go, then. It's a tough climb. We'll take a break halfway up.'

They followed Mick up the steps in silence as the stunning views of the ocean and the birds gliding above them took their breath away. Seamus took Roisin's hand, and she squeezed it tight, smiling at him, thinking of Cian and how he loved this kind of thing. Seamus looked back at her with his lovely hazel eyes, so like Cian's, his freckly snub-nosed face full of wonder at the sights and sounds of this rock in the middle of the Atlantic. 'It's like being in a story,' he said. 'A story about castaways long ago. Lucky we have food and water, Mum, don't you think?'

'Oh, yes,' she agreed. 'And Mick's a very good guide. He'll make sure we're safe as long as we do what he says.'

'Yeah, he seems okay,' Seamus replied. 'But if Dad was here, he'd be even better. Do you think he'll come and see us soon? I mean, while we're here on this break?'

'I hope so,' Roisin said, promising herself to do everything she could to get Cian to get to Sandy Cove before the end of the week. They had never made any concrete plans but she had been sure he would get tired of living in the campervan in a few weeks. But so far he hadn't showed any signs of wanting to get back to civilisation. 'It's only Wednesday. He'll have plenty of time to get here from Donegal by the weekend.'

'Are you sure?'

'Absolutely.'

'Great.' Seamus let go of her hand and grabbed a hold of the security chain that ran along the rock. 'I'll catch up with the lads up there now. See you at the top, Mum.'

'Be careful,' Roisin warned. But her fears disappeared as she watched him climb steadily up the steps ahead of her, keeping as close to the cliff face as he could. He was as steady on his feet as a mountain goat and as supple as a cat. *My darling little boy*, she thought, *how can I make your dad see that we need to be a family again?* Her recent adventures suddenly seemed so sordid and selfish. She looked up at the green slopes and the outline of the beehive monks' cells above and said a silent prayer to the spirits that might be floating around that Nuala's idea would work and that the photos they were planning to take would have the desired effect and get Cian to see what a lovely family he had. And, she now knew in her heart, that she wanted him back with her. The freedom she had craved suddenly seemed lonely and empty and she longed to see him again.

There was an eerie silence at the top, where, on a kind of platform, the monks' beehive cells stood like silent sentinels, looking out over the infinite ocean. It was an eerie place with a stark beauty, the grassy platform sheltered from the storms by these strange, round little cells, where the monks would have slept, wrapped in their robes. A wisp of cloud clung to the top of the pinnacle above, making it look like a volcano about to erupt, but it floated away and the rock was again outlined sharply against the clear blue sky. A cold breeze played with Roisin's hair and ruffled the grass. The boys walked around the cells, touching the rough stones, marvelling at the perfect round shapes and the symmetry of the small buildings. It was strange to think that over a thousand years ago, the monks had lived and prayed here, living a life of complete abstinence, at one with God and nature.

'Isn't it awesome to think they made *Star Wars* here,' Darragh remarked, his voice breaking the contemplative silence. 'I wonder what the monks would have thought of that?'

'They wouldn't have allowed it,' Nuala replied, peering up at the pinnacles above them. 'Look, there's a little platform at the top for praying in solitude, as if living down here wasn't hard enough. Those monks were incredibly self-disciplined.' She put her rucksack on the ground and took out a camera. 'Okay, Roisin, you and the boys strike a pose.'

Roisin put her arms around the boys and they all smiled at the camera, squinting against the sun. With the rough wall and the glittering ocean stretching to the horizon behind them, it would make a wonderful photo, Roisin thought. They proceeded to walk around the cells and into the ruins of the little church, examining rough stone crosses and looking in through holes in the ground and pointing upwards while Nuala snapped away, obviously happy with her subjects. Then they all sat down in the shelter of the rock and had their picnic, devouring the sandwiches, cold sausages, chicken legs and the various buns and cakes Nuala and Roisin had bought. Nuala showed them the photos she had taken which were all amazing. The light, the sunshine and the happy faces could be from a tourist brochure.

'I might even send them to the Kerry Tourist Board and see if they want to use them,' Nuala said, looking proud of her photographic skills.

While they finished their picnic, Mick entertained the boys with stories of his adventures as a guide and how he had had to rescue people who had either fallen from the boat as they tried to get ashore in high seas, or slipped off the steps in wet weather, nearly plunging to their deaths down the cliff face.

Roisin only half-listened, lying back against the grassy slope, her face turned to the warm sunshine. It had been a wonderful idea to come here. It was a welcome break from all the hassles and stress. She sat up and looked out over the ocean and felt as if she was at the end of the world and that the water stretched to infinity with no land beyond it, just this immense tract of water meeting the sky. She wished she could fly like a bird and sail away, floating over the water and watch all the marine wildlife she knew was down there.

But then a cloud floated across the sun and the light changed. Mick looked up and announced it was time to leave, as the weather looked like it would change, as it often did in these parts. There wouldn't be a storm but the stronger winds would mean high waves which would make it difficult for a boat to dock. The spell was broken and they made their way down the steps while a cold wind started to blow and more clouds rolled in from the sea. When they had finally managed to get down the steps and into the boat that was now rolling and pitching on the waves, Roisin hung on to the side and looked up at the dark cliffs and the beehive cells towering high above them with a feeling of foreboding. Something told her things would get a lot worse before they got better.

Chapter Twenty-Three

That feeling stayed with her all through the evening, until the boys went to bed without a quibble and she was left alone in the little sitting room with a glass of wine, trying to concentrate on the late evening news. There had been no messages from Cian for days, which hurt her more than if he had been hurling abuse at her. Where was he? What was going through his head? How could he be so cold-hearted? All those questions continued to plague her while she tried to listen to news about political conflicts, the state of the stock market and other facts that used to catch her attention but no longer seemed relevant.

Roisin's phone pinged with a message from Nuala, saying that she had uploaded the photos on to her Facebook page as soon as she got home, telling Roisin to do the same. She looked at them again and had to agree, the photos were indeed wonderful. She shared them to her own Facebook profile and Instagram account, hoping Cian would find them. Her phone pinged again, this time with a text message from Maeve, who was wondering if she could come over as Phil would be on Skype and wanted to talk to them both. Peeping in on the boys, Roisin found Rory and Seamus asleep and Darragh in bed, flicking through his phone.

'What are you up to?' Roisin asked.

'Nothing, Mum. Just chatting with a friend.' He yawned. 'But I'll go to sleep soon. That was a hell of a climb and a hell of a day, wasn't it?'

Roisin smiled and ruffled his hair. 'It sure was, pet. I posted the photos on Facebook, if you want to take a look. I'm popping over to Maeve's for a bit. Will you be okay?'

Darragh rolled his eyes. 'I'm seventeen, not five. And the guys aren't babies either. We'll be fine. You go on. I'll call you if the monsters attack or someone wets their bed.'

Roisin laughed. 'Okay. I keep forgetting you're all grown men. I wish you were still cute babies. I'll see you in the morning. The surf will be up again, I think.'

'Cool,' Darragh grunted and went back to his phone.

Roisin walked carefully along the path to Maeve's house carrying a torch. But she found she didn't really need it, as the stars shining from the dark sky provided plenty of light. She stopped for a moment and looked up at the heavens and all the constellations, and the Milky Way stretching across the sky like a shimmering pathway to heaven. The skies here were always spectacular on a clear night, especially in winter, when the stars sparkled even more clearly. The air was cool and the strong wind tore at her clothes and hair. She shivered and pulled her jacket tighter, resuming her walk, looking forward to the warmth and peace of Maeve's cottage.

Paschal opened the door. 'Hi there, Roisin. Wild night, isn't it?'

'Yes, but compared to the storm the other night, it's like a summer breeze.'

He stood aside to let her in. 'That's for sure. Sorry about the beech tree. It's been there forever and now it's gone. Seems like the end of an era or something.'

Roisin hung her jacket on a peg in the tiny hall. 'That sounds a little gloomy, Paschal.'

He laughed and pushed his unruly black hair from his forehead. 'Just a little Irish gloom and doom, darlin'. How was your outing to Skellig Michael?'

'Amazing. But who told you we were there? I didn't get a chance to tell Maeve.'

He shrugged. 'I think someone in the grocery shop said something when I went to get a few things for Maeve. Can't remember. But you know how it goes in this village. You blink and everyone knows about it at once.'

'That's for sure,' Roisin said with a sigh, thinking about how her own little secrets had been spread to the press. Not from the villagers, but the story had been out there in a flash once it was published.

'Go on in,' Paschal said. 'Maeve has the laptop all ready. I'm cleaning up after dinner. I'll get you a cup of tea and a slice of soda bread when you're done.'

Roisin smiled at her tall, handsome brother-in-law. 'Thanks, Paschal. That sounds great.' She walked into the living room where Maeve had put the laptop on the coffee table. Roisin joined her on the sofa in front of it. 'Hi. Is Phil ready?'

Just as she finished her question, Phil's face popped up on the screen. 'Hello, darlings,' she chortled. 'Looks like a cosy winter's evening by the fire over there. Wish I could join you. This constant sunshine is getting monotonous.'

Roisin smiled at her aunt, who looked tanned and happy, her silver grey hair cut into a becoming short bob. 'Hi, Auntie Phil,' she said. 'You look good. The grey hair suits you. You look like one of those grey panther ladies, or whatever they're called.'

'I prefer to call myself a silver swan,' Phil replied, patting her hair. 'We decided on the colour because it would be good for my older-woman-with-attitude look. It was all Cordelia's idea. I was tired of dyeing it anyway.'

'Cordelia?' Maeve asked, waving at the screen. 'Hi, Phil. You look so glamorous.'

'Thank you, pet. The reason I wanted to speak to you is to tell you about Cordelia. She'll be here in a minute when she's finished laying out my outfit for my book talk in Miami today. It's a lovely navy kaftan with silver embroidery. I'll send you photos later.'

Phil sat up straighter and folded her hands in her lap. 'Cordelia is, believe it or not, related to me – and you too. She's the daughter of my first cousin Frances who went to America about forty years ago as a young girl. Then – poof – she disappeared. Nobody in the family heard from her for years. We thought she had died. She was my mother's only sister's daughter. Wild and naughty and badly behaved.' Phil leaned closer to the screen. 'A bit of a tart, really,' she said under her breath, glancing over her shoulder. 'But anyway, it appears she wasn't dead at all but married and living right here, in Miami. Isn't that extraordinary?'

'Amazing,' Maeve said. 'How did you find her?'

'I didn't find *her*. I found her daughter, Cordelia. Or she found me, to be precise.' Phil's eyes sparkled. 'Imagine, just after I had appeared on a local daytime TV show and talked about my life and told them how I was a McKenna from Kerry, and that my mother was called Brennan before she married, and that I wrote under a pseudonym, Cordelia got in touch with my publisher and asked to meet me. And then she told me.'

'Told you what?' Roisin asked.

'That she was poor Fran's daughter,' Phil said, beaming. 'Her mother sadly died two years ago, she said. And she had heard stories about Kerry and the house all through her childhood but had never been to visit. Fran never wanted to have anything to do with her family. She felt they had treated her badly and there was a lot of bad blood between them. Cordelia didn't know how to get in touch with any of us either, but when she saw me on TV, she felt it was meant to happen. So she did. Get in touch, I mean. And now, to cut a long story short, she's my stylist.' Phil laughed. 'Okay, maybe not quite, but she's helping me out with my outfits for the book signings and interviews on local TV. Only cable, but still quite exciting. Cordelia is more like a personal assistant. She does everything. Such a relief.'

'Oh.' Maeve glanced at Roisin. 'That's, eh, quite a story.'

'And here she is now,' Phil announced, pulling at someone beside her. 'Cordelia, meet your cousins.'

A young woman with a pretty face, dark curly hair and blue eyes appeared on the screen. 'Hi, cousins. Maeve and Roisin, I've heard so much about you. Which is which?'

'The red-haired beauty is Maeve,' Phil explained. 'And the cute blonde is Roisin.' She waggled her fingers at them. 'Say hi to Cordelia.'

'Hi, Cordelia,' Maeve and Roisin said in unison.

'You'll meet her when she comes to visit us at Willow House.'

'That'll be lovely, Phil,' Maeve replied. 'When are you coming home?'

'In May as planned.' Phil paused and winked. 'Well, first I have promised a certain gentleman that I'd visit him in London, you see.'

'Oliver!' Maeve exclaimed. 'Your handsome gentleman friend. I was going to ask if he'd been in touch.'

'More than that,' Phil replied with a happy smile. 'He's been here to visit me twice already.'

'Oooh,' Roisin cooed. 'How romantic. So... are you getting serious?'

Phil sighed. 'Not it the way you might think. He's a dear friend, that's all. Very dear. But we have been talking and decided to keep it the way it is. Our lives are so different and neither of us is prepared to live away from our families – or our countries. I know I would never be happy in London, and he couldn't possibly move to Ireland. So we'll just enjoy our friendship and keep in touch and take turns to go and see each other. It's my turn to visit him. And then, next time, he'll come to Sandy Cove. I have promised him the best room, the one with views of the ocean. I hope that's all right?'

'Of course,' Roisin promised. 'I understand how you feel. You couldn't possibly feel the same for anyone as you did for Uncle Joe. But it's so nice that you have this friendship. Maybe better than anything else.'

Phil nodded. 'Oh, yes. We're still both grieving for the love of our lives. We understand each other like nobody else could. I'm so grateful that I have him in my life.' She grinned. 'And the fact that he's very wealthy and lives in the best part of London has nothing to do with it, of course.'

'I bet you're putting together your wardrobe for that London trip already,' Roisin teased.

Phil laughed. 'Of course I am. Cordelia is helping me with a brand-new look. I'll model it all for you when I get back home. I'm looking forward to the trip very much. But the best part of it will be having Oliver take me around London. He's such a dear man.'

'I adore him,' Maeve said. 'You will, too, Roisin.'

'I'm sure I will.' Roisin smiled at Phil. 'Can't wait to welcome him to the new guesthouse.

Phil smiled and nodded. 'Neither can I. I hope the house repairs are finished by now?'

'Nearly done,' Roisin assured her.

'Oh, good,' Phil said with a happy sigh. 'I can't wait to see it. Florida is nice, but I have to confess I'm homesick for my lovely house. I'm so grateful to you, Roisin, for picking up the reins now that Maeve has to take it easier. How are you feeling, Maeve, darling?'

'I feel great,' Maeve replied. 'The baby is growing and kicking like mad. Roisin is a great help both with the house renovations and advice about pregnancy and what to expect afterwards.'

'I'm an old pro when it comes to babies,' Roisin cut in.

'Of course you are,' Phil remarked with a chuckle. 'How are the boys? Enjoying school?'

'They love it,' Roisin said, laughing. 'They're here right now on their February break and out surfing.'

'And Cian?' Phil asked. 'How is he? Still off on that skite in the campervan?'

'Yes.' Roisin sighed. 'He seems hooked on it. I hope he'll manage to get here before the boys go back to school, though.'

'I'm sure he will,' Phil said reassuringly. 'He just needs to get it out of his system. Joe sometimes went off like that with his pals. Fishing in Mayo and living in some kind of hut. Came home filthy and smelly and glowing. Boys will be boys, you know.'

'I know,' Roisin replied, feeling suddenly better about everything. Good old Phil, always looking on the bright side.

'How long are you staying at Willow House?' Phil asked. 'I hope you'll be there when I get back.'

'Yes, I will,' Roisn replied. 'I'm going to stay on here for a while to help out. At least until Maeve's baby is born anyway, but maybe even longer. I'm looking forward to running the guesthouse with you.'

'That's wonderful,' Phil said.

'Time to go, Phil,' Cordelia's voice cut in. 'We have to look our best for the talk, don't we?'

Phil nodded. 'Yes, Cordelia,' she said obediently. 'Bye, girls. Talk soon. Lots of love.' She blew a kiss and then the screen went blank.

Roisin and Maeve looked at each other in astonished silence.

'Cousin Fran?' Maeve mumbled. 'The one who ran away. I have a vague memory of her. How about you?'

Roisin thought for a moment. 'Yes, I remember hearing about her years ago. She's that cousin Dad talked about. The one who was a real rebel and then ran off to America. Her family cut her out of their will and everything. But that branch of the family was always a bit weird, Dad said. And they're all dead now, except this Cordelia woman. How amazing that Phil found her – or she found Phil.'

Maeve turned off her laptop. 'Nice for Phil, too. She seemed a little bossy, though.'

'Yes, maybe. But you know Phil, she needs someone to organise her. Could be a great help.'

'I'm sure it is.' Roisin looked up as Paschal came in carrying a tray with tea and slices of buttered soda bread. 'Just what we need.'

Paschal put the tray on the table and sat down opposite them. 'I saw the photos on your Facebook page, Roisin. They're lovely. I shared some of them just because they were so stunning and everyone looks so happy. Great shots of the ocean, too. Hope you don't mind.'

Roisin smiled at him. 'Of course not. I put them there for all to see.'

'Especially Cian, I bet,' Maeve remarked. 'About time he had a look at his gorgeous sons.' She poured tea into a cup and handed it to Paschal. 'Here you are, sweetheart. Thank you for cleaning up and all the tea and TLC.'

Paschal smiled back at Maeve with such love in his eyes it made Roisin feel tears well up. What a lovely couple they were. Cian used to look at her like that when she was pregnant. It was a long time since they had been that close. Would they ever get back the love and complete understanding they had lost? She smiled at Maeve as she handed Roisin a cup and sat back against the sofa, sipping tea and enjoying the home-made bread, chatting idly about this and that until Roisin began to feel sleepy. It was time to go home and get some sleep. She was about to get up when her phone rang. She picked it up, wondering who was calling at that late hour. The caller ID said 'Darragh'.

'Darragh?' Roisin asked. 'What's up?'

'Mum,' Darragh's voice said in a hoarse whisper. 'There's someone outside the house, trying to get in.'

Chapter Twenty-Four

Roisin followed Paschal as he walked ahead towards Willow House. He had called Sean Óg, who was on his way. 'No use calling the police,' he had said before they set off. 'The nearest Garda station is either in Waterville or Portmagee. It'd take them more than half an hour to get here. We'll sort this out ourselves.'

'Yes, fine. We have to hurry,' Roisin half-sobbed, throwing on her jacket. 'Come on, then.'

Paschal nodded, grabbed a torch and a hurling stick and ran out the door, walking swiftly along the path. 'I won't turn on the torch,' he told Roisin in a soft voice over his shoulder. 'It's bright enough to see and it'll alert the burglar trying to get in. Don't worry, Sean Óg will be here in a minute. We'll deal with the bastard.'

'Okay,' Roisin replied, her throat dry with fear. She walked behind Paschal, her legs like jelly, trying not to imagine the worst; someone breaking in and threatening the boys – or hurting them. *Dear God in heaven*, she prayed silently. *Let them be safe. Don't let anyone hurt them. Holy Mary mother of God…*

She halted suddenly at the wrecked greenhouse, bumping into Paschal, who stood stock-still, listening, hardly breathing. 'He's at the back door,' he whispered in her ear. 'Trying to break the lock.'

Roisin gasped, but Paschal put his hand over her mouth. 'Shh. Stay here while I…' He began to move towards the back door, where in the dim light of the stars Roisin could see the outline of a man.

'Be care—' she started, but Paschal made a sign for her to be quiet and to go to the front of the house. Probably to see if Sean Óg had arrived, she thought and walked silently across the grass around the side of the house, where she spotted something inside the gate. A large van. Thank God. Sean Óg must just have arrived. She looked at the white shape that was oddly familiar. Then it dawned on her who was there. She ran back around the house to the back door, where Paschal was struggling with someone, both of men grunting and swearing.

'Take that, you bastard,' Paschal shouted. There was a sickening thud of a blow against a jaw. The other man struggled and ducked as another blow just missed his head.

'*No!*' Roisin yelled and grabbed one of them by the jacket. 'Paschal, stop hitting him! It's Cian!'

'What?' Paschal let go of the other man so suddenly he crashed to the ground. 'Cian? Is that you?'

'Yeah,' Cian grunted from below. 'It's me. Stop attacking me, ya bastard.'

'Oh.' Paschal backed away and stared at Cian. 'Why didn't you tell me?'

'You didn't give me a chance,' Cian muttered. 'Why don't you ask before you start beating people up?' He held out his hand. 'Help me up, please.'

'Let's go inside.' Roisin went to get the key to the back door from the hiding place under a brick.

'Oh, so that's where it is,' Cian said as Paschal pulled him to his feet. 'Wish I had known. Could have saved me a lot of pain.' He rubbed his jaw. 'You throw quite a punch there, mate.'

'I'm sorry.' Paschal patted Cian on the shoulder. 'Great to see it wasn't a burglar.'

'You scared Darragh witless,' Roisin said angrily. 'He phoned me to say there was someone outside trying to get in. He was terrified.'

'Oh, God,' Cian mumbled. 'That's terrible. I never meant to—'

'What's going on here?' a voice said from the shadows of the house and the shape of a man approached.

'Nothing, Sean Óg,' Paschal replied. 'A bit of a mix-up, that's all. We thought it was a burglar but it was Cian, Roisin's husband, and he couldn't find the key.'

'And then he hit me on the jaw,' Cian complained, wincing as he carefully touched his face.

Sean Óg laughed. 'Bad luck, Cian. I remember you. We met at the wedding, didn't we?'

'That's right,' Cian replied, massaging his jaw.

'Come inside and I'll light up the Aga.' Roisin opened the back door. 'It's freezing and Cian's in pain.'

Sean Óg backed away. 'No thanks. It's late, so I'll get back home. Glad nobody's hurt or anything.'

'Except me,' Cian grunted. 'But I'll live.'

'You have a hard bloody gob,' Paschal said and rubbed his knuckles. 'But no harm done, I hope.'

'Nah, it's okay.' Cian followed Roisin.

'I'll be off then,' Paschal announced. 'See you in the morning.'

'Thanks for helping me,' Roisin said and touched his shoulder.

'You're welcome. Sorry again, Cian.'

'Never mind,' Cian muttered. 'I know it was an accident.'

They said good night to Paschal and went inside, where Roisin put on the lights and ran upstairs to tell Darragh what was going on. She bumped into him as he came down the stairs. 'It's okay, sweetheart,' she soothed. 'It wasn't a burglar, it was—'

'Dad!' Darragh exclaimed, hugging his father, who had just appeared at the foot of the stairs. 'It was you! Why didn't you phone me to say you were outside?'

'I did, but there was no reply,' Cian said. 'And I knocked but nobody came. So then I had to try to break in to see if you were all all right. Should have known you'd be fast asleep.'

'Oh.' Darragh looked at his father and blinked. 'I put my phone on silent because I wanted to sleep. Sorry.' He peered at Cian's jaw. 'What happened to you?'

'Paschal beat me up because he thought I was a burglar. I'm glad to see you have such a watchdog nearby.' Cian sighed and smiled at his son. Despite looking tired, he seemed fit and healthy. Thinner, Roisin thought, and his hair was longer. The beard was gone which was a relief and she realised that the month of outdoor living had rejuvenated him. He looked much more like the Cian she had fallen in love with all those years ago and she realised, at that moment, how much she loved him. Absence really did make the heart grow fonder. In this case anyway.

'Bad luck, Dad.' Darragh yawned and rubbed his eyes. 'But I'm really happy to see you. The guys will be too when they wake up. We missed you. The surfing here is brilliant. Do you want to come and watch us?'

'Of course I do,' Cian replied. 'Missed you too, Darragh. I'll drive you to surfing tomorrow and watch you.'

Darragh smiled and yawned at the same time. 'Great. I'll go back to bed.' He hugged his dad again. 'Nice to see you, Dad. We'll catch up in the morning.'

'Goodnight, Darragh,' Cian said. 'See you at breakfast.'

Back in the kitchen, Roisin stoked the fire in the Aga and turned on the kettle. 'Sit down,' she ordered. 'I'll have a look at your jaw. Maybe you need ice on it?'

Cian remained standing at a distance away from her and they looked at each other for a loaded minute before he spoke. 'I'm grand,' he said. 'Just get me somewhere to sleep.'

Roisin bristled at his short tone. Why was he so cold and angry? 'Can't you sleep in the campervan?' she asked, only just managing to avoid sounding sarcastic.

'I could, but a bed would be more comfortable.'

She turned around and stared at him. 'Why are you so angry? Shouldn't I be the one to—'

'To what?' he cut in. 'I saw all that stuff about you and O'Mahony in the tabloids. You didn't mention that you'd met him in any of your messages. I didn't even know he was here. Can you even begin to imagine how I felt when I saw all that stuff?'

'Oh.' Roisin felt faint as she took it all in. He had read everything and come to all the wrong conclusions. 'It's not at all the way it looks,' she started, knowing how lame it sounded.

He raised an eyebrow. 'Isn't it? You at a party in that posh hotel with that man you've been swooning over when he was on TV. Don't tell me that was some kind of photoshopped picture. And then all the rest of it in the *Herald*.'

'Some of it happened,' she started. 'But not the way…'

'Please. Can we stop it right here?' He looked at her in silence for a moment before he spoke again. 'I drove all the way from Donegal without stopping, so I'm exhausted. I don't need tea or sympathy or anything from you, just a bed for the night.'

'Okay,' Roisin mumbled. 'But tomorrow, we have to talk. I'm not the only one who has some explaining to do, you know. I'm glad you're here though,' she ended, throwing in an olive branch. 'Thanks for driving all that way to get here.' She felt a small dart of happiness as she looked at him, despite his anger and her own feelings of resentment. It was wonderful to see him again, even if it felt awkward.

'I came here mainly to see the boys,' he said. 'You too, of course. But I suppose we do have to talk at some stage.'

'Yes. We do,' Roisin said, her heart breaking at the coldness in his voice and the harsh words. 'You can sleep in Phil's room. I'll make up the bed for you.'

'Thank you. I'll wait here, in front of the Aga.'

'You shaved off your beard,' she said. 'Makes you look nice,' she added.

His eyes softened, but he looked away as if he was afraid to show it. 'Yeah. Thanks. Get me some bedclothes, please. I'm exhausted. And…' He sighed. 'I didn't mean to be quite so rude. I meant to tell you I was on my way back. We should have made some kind of plan, but we were both in such a hurry to do our own thing. Can we just sleep on it and talk tomorrow?'

'Of course.' Roisin went upstairs to get sheets and a duvet and quickly made up the bed downstairs. Cian waited in silence in the kitchen and when she told him the bed was ready, nodded and went into the bedroom, closing the door. She heard him moving around and wished she could open the door and make everything better. But it was no use. He had seen all that rubbish in the tabloids, which explained his bad mood. From the outside, it must look quite believable, even for Cian, who had trusted her completely before. But now that trust was gone. What had broken between them couldn't be fixed with a few words or even a long explanation from her. They needed to talk for a long time before they could carry on in one way or another. She knew they would never get back what they once had. And it was all her fault.

Roisin woke with a start. The sun shone in through the windows as she had been too tired to pull the curtains last night. Despite her exhaustion, it had taken her a long time to go to sleep and she had lain there, staring out into the dark night, wondering what was going to happen to her marriage. The worst-case scenario went through her mind with horrible clarity. If Cian still didn't believe her even after she had told him her side of the story, she supposed he would want them to split up and then he'd go back to Dublin while she stayed behind in Sandy Cove, running the guesthouse with Phil. The boys would go back to school and spend some of their holidays with her and the rest with Cian… That was what it would be like after the eventual… divorce. She flinched at the word. She couldn't imagine that it would ever happen to them. Would it? How horrible, how utterly devastating. All because of her own stupidity. Tears spilled onto the pillow as she continued to imagine a bleak future without Cian and having to share custody of the boys with him. Then, somehow, she had finally drifted off and woken up late.

She glanced at the little clock on her bedside table. Ten o'clock, and the house was so silent. Where was everybody? She dragged herself out of bed and put on Uncle Joe's dressing gown. It felt comforting, like a pair of arms hugging her, protecting her from harm. She shrugged at the silly thought and went downstairs, where she found the remains of a huge breakfast having been cooked and all the dishes and the frying pan dumped in the sink. There was a note on the table that said:

Went to the surf school with the lads. Back soon. C.

Comforted by the thought that he was looking after their sons, Roisin pushed up the sleeves of the dressing gown and started tidying up, turning on the kettle as she worked. At least Cian was considering the boys, which had to be the priority for them both. That at least was something positive. She put the dishes in the dishwasher, turned it on and made herself a cup of tea and buttered a slice of soda bread. She might as well have something to eat before the fair and frank discussion with Cian. There would be a lot to talk about and she wasn't going to shrink away from the cold, hard facts of what they had both been up to during their separation. Cian might think he was the injured party, but he had a lot of explaining to do himself. She sat down at the table with the tea and chewed on the bread while she planned what she was going to say.

A sound of someone moving outside made her look at the back window. Was Cian back already? But whoever it was didn't come in. She got up and opened the door.

'Oh,' she exclaimed as she came face to face with Declan. 'What are you doing here?'

'I just popped in to say…' He stopped. 'What's the matter?'

She backed inside. 'Nothing. Just… my husband arrived last night.'

He looked surprised. 'Your husband? From Donegal?'

'Yes. He drove all the way yesterday.'

Declan stared at her. 'All the way from Donegal in one day in that camper-yoke?' He winked. 'Did he bring Greta?'

Roisin bristled. 'It's not funny.'

Declan's face took on a more sober look. 'What's up? He wasn't happy to see you?'

'No, he wasn't.' Tears of frustration welled up in Roisin's eyes. 'He was very upset and angry.'

'Why?'

'Why do you think? He's seen all that rubbish about us. All of it.'

'Oh.' Declan frowned. 'He read the papers? The tabloids, I mean.'

'Yes.' Roisin backed away from the door. 'He read them all, it appears.'

'So he's a little upset?'

'To say the least.' Roisin glared at him. 'Use your imagination, Declan. How do you think he feels after all that stuff in the papers about us? And that picture of him and the German girl someone leaked to the press? It made me feel awful to see how hurt he was and realise what it's doing to our marriage.'

Declan stepped inside and closed the door behind him. 'Yeah, but what about his picture? I think he needs to tell you what his relationship is with her.'

'I'm sure it's quite innocent,' Roisin said, trying to sound confident. 'And there's nothing between you and me either, no matter how it looks, which I will explain to Cian when he gets back from the surf school.'

Declan looked at her in silence. 'Nothing?' he asked. 'Nothing at all? I mean, between you and me and the wall, I think there's quite something going on, even if you try to deny it.'

Roisin looked away from his probing eyes. 'Well, yeah, maybe. But nothing has happened, has it?'

'Yet.' Declan moved closer and took her hand. 'Roisin, I…' He hesitated. 'Okay. I suppose it's not the right time.'

She snatched her hand away. 'There will never be a right time.' She looked at him squarely trying to sort out her feelings for him. 'I can't deny that I was… am attracted to you. But whatever there is, or could be, it can't happen. I love my husband and I want to get my marriage back to what it was. But maybe I never will.' Tears welled up in her eyes. 'We were happy, you know. Really, really happy. And then we felt we needed a little space so we took a break from each other. And then… things happened and—' She wiped her nose on the sleeve of the dressing gown. 'Shit, I'm such a mess. Please go away. I can't think straight when you look at me like that.'

He smiled tenderly. 'Oh, Roisin, how can I leave you like this, all mussed up and sad and snotty and totally adorable?'

'Stop it. I'm married, Declan,' she exclaimed. 'Hasn't that ever entered your head?'

'Yes, but…' He laughed. 'Don't tell me you take that marriage lark seriously?'

Roisin stuck out her chin. 'Yes, as a matter of fact I do. When you stand in front of a priest and a church full of friends and family and promise to love someone till death do you part, you have to stick to that. I know that must sound so nineteen fifties, but that's how I feel.'

He shrugged. 'I never saw it that way. My first marriage was a huge mistake. My second worked for a while but then she found someone else, and my third…' He smiled and shook his head. 'That was just a bit of fun. We flew to Las Vegas when I had a bit of money and got drunk and stumbled into something called the Chapel of Love. It was just for the craic really. We annulled the whole thing when we got home. So, no, marriage isn't really number one on my list of priorities.' He smiled tenderly at her. 'But being with you is. At first it was just friendship and meeting someone who was on my wavelength, but then it became something more. You must have realised how much I fancied you.'

'No, I didn't. You said I wasn't your type.'

'I lied. I don't have a type.' He stepped closer still and tried to put his arms around her.

Roisin backed away. 'Please. Leave me alone,' she begged. 'Just go.'

He sighed and let his arms fall. 'Okay. I'll go. We'll talk about this later.'

'No we won't.'

'Maybe later. When you've sorted everything.' Declan walked to the door and opened it. Then he stopped and turned around and glared at her. 'Take this from someone who's been married a few times.'

'What?'

'Happily married people don't go on bloody breaks!' The walls shook as he banged the door behind him.

Chapter Twenty-Five

Cian came back an hour later as Roisin came downstairs after her shower. 'Hi,' she said shyly.

He looked at her blankly. 'Hi.'

'Boys okay?'

'Fine. Seamus is surfing like a pro. We might have a future world champion.'

She smiled. 'Yeah. He's amazing.'

Cian walked into the sitting room and sat down on the couch. 'We have to talk. This is our only chance. We have to get the boys back in a few hours and Nuala has invited us over tonight with Maeve and Paschal. The kids seem to have become great friends, so she thought it would be fun to have us all together. I think she wants to help get us back together or something. But nobody can do that, can they?'

'No. Only we can.' Roisin sat down in the armchair opposite the couch.

'If we want.'

'Yes.'

'O'Mahony was here earlier, I heard when I was at the petrol station.'

Roisin sighed. 'Jaysus, the people in this village are psychic. They seem to read your thoughts as well. It's scary.'

'Nah, just that gossiping old bat, whatever her name is, saw his car in the drive. Then it was all out in a flash. Just small village life, really.'

'I suppose.' Roisin met his eyes, then looked away, feeling oddly shy and awkward. She didn't know what to say, didn't even know how she felt at that moment. She had wished for Cian to come back for days but now that he was here, she felt confused.

Cian cleared his throat noisily. 'So,' he started. 'Declan O'Mahony.'

'And Greta the German girl,' Roisin countered, looking at him coldly. 'If there is anything between you and her, I need to know.'

'Likewise, sweetheart,' Cian snapped. 'I think you need to go first.'

Roisin swallowed, her throat so dry she found it hard to speak. 'Okay,' she croaked and coughed. Then she sat up. 'Cian, I…' She didn't know how to go on. Then she suddenly found the courage to speak. 'It all started with that stupid campervan you bought without consulting me. Then you called it after your first girlfriend and said you would go off on your own on that mad trip.'

'You told me I should,' Cian argued. 'And you even told me to invite Andrew to come with me.'

'I know, but I thought you'd get tired of the whole thing very soon. But you didn't. I didn't hear from you for ages, and then I saw that photo of you and Fraulein Boobsy on Instagram. How do you think that made me feel? And then you didn't seem to want to be with us for half-term. The boys were waiting and waiting, but you didn't come.'

'I wanted to stay away to punish you.'

Roisin shot up from the chair. 'Did you have to punish them too?'

'I'm here now.'

'Only because you saw the photos.'

'Okay, yeah. I admit those pictures from your outing on Skellig Michael gave me a jolt. I realised I was being a mean bastard to the kids and they don't deserve that.'

'Did you show them to *her?*'

'No. Sit down. I'll tell you.'

Roisin sat down. 'Okay. Go ahead.'

'And then you have to tell me about you and – your man O'Mahony and that evening at Sheen Falls and the photos and all the rest of the crap I've been reading.'

'I will. But go on.'

'Okay. I'll wind the film back a bit to before I took off in Ri— the campervan. Way before, actually. To when we sold the business and all that. It was all your idea.'

'But you agreed,' Roisin interrupted. 'You never said that you didn't want to do it.'

'How could I? It was such a good plan. But you know what? This is what it's been like all our married life. You have called all the shots and drawn up plans and proved your point before anyone has had a chance to say what they thought. You were the boss in the office and at home too. It all worked like clockwork, that's true. I don't think we could have managed so well without your plans and lists. Putting part of my inheritance into trust funds for the boys and investing the rest was also the best solution. Your idea but my money. I could have blown it all on a yacht and a luxury villa in the

south of France, but that would have been stupid. So I can't argue
with what you decided. But…'

He stopped for a moment and ran his hand through his unruly
brown hair. 'I always felt I was second best, second to you and a
very poor second to the boys. And then, when we were suddenly
free, I wanted to… To make my own decisions, live my own life.
You didn't want to come with me, and that was a relief in a way.
I needed to be on my own away from you for a bit.' He looked at
her with a sad expression in his hazel eyes. 'I'm sorry if it hurts to
hear all this, but I have to tell you my side of the story.'

'Yes.' Roisin felt a flood of guilt wash over her. She realised there
was a grain of truth in what he said. More than a grain if she was
honest. She was bossy and wanted to make all the decisions and
she didn't allow arguments. She always saw the sensible solution in
everything and it had often saved them from disaster. She had just
marched ahead without even asking him for his opinion, as if he
didn't have one. That can't have been easy to live with. But it was
hard to swallow this lament of years of feeling second best. 'Why
didn't you say anything?' she asked. 'Why didn't you protest?'

He shrugged. 'Don't know. I was happy in a way not to have to
make any decisions or take responsibility. I loved looking after the
boys. With them, I was always number one. We worked so well as
a family, too. Didn't we?'

'Of course we did.'

'But *we* didn't work that well as a couple,' Cian continued. 'I
realised that when I had a chance to think about it all. I took the
easy option of leaving all the business decisions to you and just
agreed when we should have discussed it. I was too lazy to argue, I

suppose. Being away from you gave me a chance to see the whole picture, if you know what I mean. So…' He paused.

'So?' she urged.

'So I've decided that from now on, I'll be fully involved with any ventures in business or change of careers, even if that means we'll be arguing and maybe even shouting at each other. I'm not worried about conflicts, if that's what it takes. You okay with that?'

'Sounds good to me,' Roisin replied, slightly taken aback by the steely look in his eyes. She found she liked this new determination in him. But there was still one thing she needed to know. She took a deep breath. 'Okay, so tell me the rest. Greta, the German bombshell.'

Cian made a dismissive gesture. 'She isn't important. Yeah, she's pretty and young and cheerful. She came on to me big time. Her friend had a thing with Andrew and they spent a whole night in their campervan while Greta and I…'

Roisin stared at him. 'Yes?'

'We had to stay in my van. We just talked. Nothing happened. I told her I was happily married and she backed off and even apologised. Then we played Scrabble until two in the morning and then she slept on the bunk and I slept in the top bed. She snored, by the way. Nice girl, though. Very sporty.'

'I see.'

'You don't believe me?'

'Yes, I do,' she said without hesitation. Of course she did. Good, dependable Cian would never fool around with another woman, she was pretty sure of that. The look in his eyes told her she was right. 'I trust you.'

'Good. I'm sorry if that stupid photo Andrew posted upset you. I didn't even know he had done it until it was too late. So…' He paused, looking serious. 'Before you go on, I need to tell you that I didn't believe all that stuff about you in the papers. But it still rankled and made me wonder what was going on with you and the man you've had a crush on for years. He was your hero, remember? You were glued to all his stories and when he was on TV, you were enthralled. We used to joke and call him your boyfriend. And then you met him in real life and seem to have hit it off big time. Of course you would. You're one of a kind. Glamorous, pushy, intelligent, ruthless. How could he not fall for you? Or you for him at a vulnerable time when your marriage was in trouble.'

'Is it?' Roisin asked.

'You tell me.'

Roisin wrung her hands while she looked away, out the window at the willow tree, its branches swaying in the wind. Then she looked back at Cian. 'Yes. Maybe we're in a bit of trouble right now. We have both been stupid, me most of all. But we can fix it. If we want. I admit that meeting Declan here and getting to know him has been fun and exciting. And that I was a little starstruck for a while. And of course, flattered by his attention. But my night with him was, funnily enough, very similar to yours with Greta. I had too much to drink and he let me sleep it off in his room, on a bed that was bigger than a football field. Nothing happened, despite what those articles said. I was too out of it and in any case, I would never do that.'

'I know you wouldn't.'

Roisin sighed. 'Good. At least we still trust each other on that front. I can't deny that I'm attracted to Declan and he to me. But that's just chemistry and hormones, not real love. It's not important. What matters is how I feel about *you*.'

Cian looked at her without replying. 'And how do you feel?' he whispered. 'About me?'

Roisin got up and knelt in front of him, taking his hands, looking into his sad eyes. 'I love you, Cian. With all my heart. That's all.' She took a deep breath. 'I know I must have been hard to live with for a long time. Well, ever since we set up our company, I suppose. I was too controlling and wanted everything to work my way.'

'But your way was great,' he interrupted. 'Most of the time. Except maybe when you didn't ask me if I had other ideas. But it wouldn't all have worked if it hadn't been for you and your organising. But then, when the boys went away to school, I thought we'd want to be free and not have any projects for a while.'

Roisin sighed. 'I know. And you were right. Except the campervan was a little too much for me.' She paused. 'I think it was a good thing for us to be away from each other for a bit. I mean, apart from all this stuff that happened, which was a stupid accident, it was good for me to have a chance to think. During these weeks since I waved goodbye to you, my outlook on life has changed completely. Being here, in Sandy Cove and doing up Willow House has made me see that the little things in life can be just as important and beautiful as the big things. And it helped me understand what you wanted to do and why you took off like that. I mean…' She paused, trying to find the right words. 'Oh, I don't know how to tell you. You'll have to see for yourself. I just want us to be together and be in love again.'

His eyes softened as he pulled her up beside him and put his arms around her. 'Me too,' he whispered against her mouth, which made her start crying and then she couldn't stop.

'I'm sorry,' she sobbed. 'I never meant to hurt you. Well, maybe a little when I saw that photo of you and Greta. Then I wanted to clobber you. And her.'

He laughed. 'Yeah, I know how you must have felt. And when I saw those photos of you and O'Mahony in the papers, I wanted to… to…'

'Were you jealous?' she whispered into his chest.

'Yes,' he mumbled as he slid his hands under her shirt. 'Were you?'

'Of course I was.' She let out a sound between a laugh and a sob as his hands on her bare skin made her feel hot all over. 'You know what the best thing you ever said to me was?'

'No?' He undid the clasp of her bra. 'That Greta snores?'

'No, that she came on to you but you didn't respond. That you could have slept with her but you didn't because you only want me.' She started to cry again. 'You love me.'

'I do.'

She sniffed. 'Even when I'm such a mess?'

'Especially then.' He wiped her face with the sleeve of his shirt and kissed her. Then he put his hands back and they lay down on the couch and it was nearly like old times. Except his kiss was hotter, his touch more insistent and later, his lovemaking more sensual than ever before. She relaxed in his arms and gave herself up to his mouth and his soft touch, responding in kind. Oh, how good it was to be in his arms and feel so loved, to kiss him and touch him and know how right it was for them to be together. She gave herself up to their lovemaking, melting into his embrace and responding to his touch, feeling for the first time in months that this is where she wanted to be. Forever.

Afterwards, Roisin lay naked on the couch, touching Cian's face, thinking that their marriage hadn't been fixed quite yet, but it was a good start. 'I'm sorry about being so domineering,' she said. 'I'll try not to be so bossy in future. I liked what you said just now about us deciding everything together, even if it might mean a fight or two. Every decision won't be mine, or yours from now on, it'll be *ours*.'

'I'll hold you to that.'

She snuggled closer. 'Just hold me and never let go.'

He put his arms around her. 'You bet.' He kissed her nose. 'But sweetheart, you know what? I don't want you to try to be different. It's enough that we want to do the same things and enjoy being together and seeing the world the same way. I love you the way you are. We just have to try to be on the same page.'

'We will,' she promised, looking into his kind hazel eyes. 'From now on.'

He took her hand. 'Shh. No more talking. No discussions or recriminations. No promises we might not be able to keep. We'll carry on from here with a better understanding of each other. That's all, and that's enough.'

'You're right.' Roisin pulled away and disentangled herself from their discarded clothing. 'We have to go and get the boys.'

Cian got up and stretched. 'I'll go. You make the tea, woman.'

'Yes, sir.' Roisin laughed and picked up her underwear, feeling a surge of relief. Everything was going to be all right. Different but better, she felt.

*

That afternoon, Roisin dropped in on Maeve while Cian and the boys had their tea, Cian making pancakes as a treat after surfing. She decided it was a good idea to leave them on their own for a bit to catch up on some male bonding.

She found Maeve at the laptop, typing away. She looked up when Roisin came in. 'Hi. I was just going to call you.'

Roisin took off her jacket and put it on the back of the sofa. 'Oh? What's up?'

Maeve pointed at a newspaper on the small table by the window. 'That.'

Roisin gulped as she saw it was the *Evening Herald*. 'Not them again. What lies are they telling today?'

'Take a look. Page four.'

'Ugh, okay.' Roisin picked up the paper and turned to the page, where she discovered two photos side by side; one of Cian's campervan, the other a grainy photo of Declan. The headline read:

Love triangle takes a further twist.

'Oh, shit, they really are the pits. I don't think I want to read this.'
'I think you should,' Maeve remarked.
Roisin sighed and read the piece:

Declan O'Mahony's new girlfriend was shaken when her husband turned up unexpectedly at her holiday retreat last night, having driven all the way from Donegal in his

*campervan (which he called Rita after his first girlfriend)
in an attempt to save their marriage. This, however, seems
quite a hard task, as Declan and Roisin were spied in a
clinch at her house, she wearing only a flimsy dressing gown,
while her husband was busy minding the couple's three sons
on the main beach. What happened when he came back
home? one would wonder. We will keep you posted on all
developments.*

Roisin gasped and stared at Maeve. 'What? In a clinch? Wearing
a flimsy— that's a laugh. I was wearing Uncle Joe's moth-eaten wool
dressing gown.'

'But you were in a clinch? With Declan?' Maeve asked.

'No! I was not in any clinch with him at all. He came around to
tell me he… Oh, it doesn't matter. I got mad and threw him out,
that's what happened. And I came here to tell you that Cian and I
have sorted everything out. And then I read this. Those people are
truly despicable. But how… who?' A surge of rage rose in Roisin's
chest. 'I'll kill that bitch Olga.'

'Olga?' Maeve asked. 'What has she got to do with all of this?'

'She's the one who's been talking to the press all this time, telling
them stuff I told her in confidence. I thought she was nice. I thought
she was a friend who I could confide in. But then everything I've
told her gets into this rag the next day.'

'Are you sure it's her?'

'Who else could it be?'

Maeve shrugged. 'Could be anyone. You know how news spreads
in this place, especially this kind of news.'

'Yes, but there was stuff in those articles I had only told a few people, like you and Declan and Nuala – and Olga. She is the only possible source. Think about it, Maeve. She is Russian, and you know how they spy there.'

Maeve laughed. 'Don't be silly. That's such a stupid cliché.'

'Okay, maybe it is. But…'

'In any case, Olga isn't here. She went to Dublin on Monday to stay with a friend until next week. She couldn't possibly have known all that stuff.'

'Oh.' Roisin stared at Maeve while this sank in. It was true. If Olga had been in Dublin the past few days, she couldn't have known Cian was back or that he had driven from Donegal. There had to be some other explanation. She picked up the paper and read the piece again. One little detail she hadn't paid attention to before suddenly stood out as if written in bright red, and it all fell into place. Her face felt hot and her throat dry as she realised what had been going on, and who had been feeding the journalists all the information. She closed the newspaper and stuck it under her arm. 'I have to go. Back soon.' Roisin grabbed her jacket and ran out the door.

'What? Where are you going?' Maeve shouted after her.

'I'll tell you later,' Roisin shouted back and raced down the garden path, in through the back door to the kitchen where she picked up the key to her car. The boys and Cian were in the sitting room watching TV. 'Going out for a while. Back soon,' she panted, not waiting for a reply.

She got into her car and took off in a shower of gravel and raced down the lane and onto the main road, taking the bends like a rally driver. The house was on the coast road, on the top of a hill overlooking the sea. She had never been there as they had met in pubs and cafés or on the beach all through the past month. But now she could see that it was a charming one-storey house with a slate roof and large picture windows. The front garden had a well-tended lawn and a clump of camellia bushes in full bloom. She would normally have admired the house and its lovely setting, but she was here on a different mission. She parked the car at the front door, got out and leaned on the doorbell. The door flew open. They stared at each other for a loaded few seconds before Roisin let it rip.

'You piece of shit!' she yelled and threw the paper in his face. 'It was you all the time, wasn't it?'

'I don't know what you mean,' he said, looking at her coldly.

'Don't try to deny it. I know.'

'How?'

'Because of one little item in that report, that nobody knew except you.'

He leaned against the doorjamb. 'What item?'

'That Cian called his campervan Rita. I never told anyone except you, when I was drunk that night.'

'Oh. Oops. How stupid of me.'

'In a clinch wearing a flimsy dressing gown?' Roisin snarled. 'What a sleaze you are, Declan O'Mahony. First you spread all kinds of rubbish about me, hoping it will break up my marriage and then, when you couldn't have me, you dream up these lies.' She felt tears of rage and frustration well up in her eyes. 'And to think I admired you,' she sobbed. 'I thought you were a superhero who always knew right from wrong. The slayer of corruption and deceit, the whistleblower who revealed those who cheated. Well, you're just as bad as them yourself. It takes one to know one, doesn't it?'

'That's a little harsh, I have to say.'

'No, it isn't. It's the truth.' She backed away. 'I'm leaving now. Don't come near me or my family, or I will make life very difficult for you. And if you thought this latest piece would drive my husband away, I can tell you that we're back together and will never be apart again.'

Declan smiled stiffly. 'Congratulations. I could say I'm sorry and that I didn't mean to hurt you but you wouldn't believe that.'

'You bet.'

He sighed, looking suddenly sad. 'I admit it was a stupid, mean trick, though. I should have known better and maybe just have been happy to have you as a friend. I enjoyed all our chats and laughs.' He pushed his hand through his hair. 'It was more than that. It was the kind of friendship I've never had before. Something I should have left alone and appreciated. I really wanted it to continue.'

'So did I. It was really special because you're so different to Cian in many ways. I liked the way you didn't always agree with me and we could have arguments that neither of us could win but we kept at it just because it was fun to bounce the ball back and forth. It was like having a brother, I thought. It could have been so great. For a while, it felt like you were my best friend. Why did you go and ruin it?'

'I wanted more. I think I fell in love with you and I thought…' He shrugged and there was a sad tone to his voice. 'I was hoping you'd feel the same. I had the feeling you were as attracted to me as I was to you.'

'In some way I was, but only because…' Roisin stopped. 'Not the way you felt, anyway.'

'I misread the signals, I suppose. I thought you and your husband were in real trouble, but I was wrong. Obviously.'

'Yes, you were. Very wrong, thank goodness.' Roisin hesitated at the door of the car. 'I'm really sorry for you, Declan. You're just a sad, lonely man behind all your bravado. I won't tell anyone about what you did. It'll stay between you and me.'

'Can you forgive me?'

She looked at him without replying for a while. 'I was going to say when hell freezes over, but… Well… I think I'll forgive you even if it'll take a long time.'

His expression softened. 'That's very decent of you. And maybe one day, we might be – friends again?'

Roisin felt a surge of pity. 'Maybe. In about a hundred years. But there might be too much water under the bridge. Bye, Declan. Good luck with everything.'

'Thank you.'

Roisin drove away, watching Declan go back into the house in the rear-view mirror. She sighed deeply, relaxing her shoulders, turning her eyes to the road and the beautiful view. All the anger and frustration seemed to evaporate and disappear in the slipstream of the car as she drove back along the coast road, the sun warming her face, the thought of her husband and family waiting for her giving her a surge of pure joy. Peace at last – or at least everything all sorted out. She and Cian had come to a new understanding and would be closer than ever before. Nothing could break them apart now.

The future lay ahead, possibly full of potholes and pitfalls, but they would tackle them. Together.

Epilogue

The evening at Nuala's turned out to be a taco party in the kitchen, where the children did most of the cooking and eating, the adults most of the talking and drinking. It was lovely to have everyone around the big table, Roisin thought, even if she would have preferred a quiet evening at home, alone with Cian. They sat side by side, touching hands and legs under the table, smiling at each other now and then, longing to be alone.

Maeve, on Roisin's other side, looked at them with approval. 'Great to see you so happy,' she mumbled in Roisin's ear. 'You've been able to talk it through?'

'Oh, yes,' Roisin replied. 'More than that. We've turned over a new leaf. And in a way, it's all your doing.'

'Mine?' Maeve looked surprised. 'Why?'

'It's thanks to you I came back to Sandy Cove. And being here, being with you made me realise a few things. I saw the world differently after a while. Living in this village and seeing you and Paschal so happy and in tune showed me that all that chasing after projects was like running away from life. I was hooked on being stressed and having deadlines. It was like a drug. Then I went cold turkey and had serious withdrawal symptoms before I woke up and saw that the only project I should be concerned about was my marriage and my family. You were there for me when I needed to talk. And you always listened and pulled me back to earth.' Roisin kissed Maeve on the cheek. 'Thanks for all the tea and sympathy and for letting me moan. And the reality checks. You're the best.'

'Aww, shucks,' Maeve said and pushed at Roisin. 'It was nothing. I love having you here.'

Cian smiled at them. 'You might get sick of us.'

'Never,' Maeve protested.

Cian put his arm around Roisin and kissed her. 'I heard all of that,' he said in her ear. 'And it made me so happy.'

'Look at the lovebirds,' Nuala shouted from across the table. 'Flirting like teenagers.' She slipped a wedge of lime into her bottle of Mexican beer and held it up. 'I'd like to propose a toast to Cian and Roisin, who are together at last after all the hoopla in the press and on Instagram. What a rollercoaster ride, eh, lads?'

Cian laughed and clinked his bottle against Nuala's. 'Yeah, it sure was. But thanks to all our friends here and the kind people in the village, we've sorted it out and now we will carry on and run the guesthouse together, if Phil agrees.'

'What?' Roisin asked, staring at him. 'We haven't talked about this yet. Or said anything to Phil. We have to call her.'

'No need,' Cian replied. 'We'll iron out the details with her tomorrow during a Skype talk. I arranged it all with her while you were out. But I think she'll like it. And I will also…' He looked at Roisin. 'I have a business idea, but I haven't told Roisin about it yet. So maybe I'll wait till later.'

'Ah come on,' Paschal urged. 'Give us the idea. You can fight about it later.'

'Well…' Cian started. 'It's like this: my weeks spent living in a campervan taught me a thing or two on how things can be improved. I have already been in touch with a few campervan manufacturers in Germany and Italy and they liked my ideas. So… if it all works out, I will be importing vans and making them over to suit Irish conditions, and will be setting up a small garage here in the village. This is just a plan for the moment, but the bottom line is that we will be selling up in Dublin and moving down here permanently.'

'Oh.' Roisin blinked, trying to take it all in. There was a warmth in Cian's voice with a spark of love in his eyes as he glanced at her. She smiled back at him, feeling they shared a delicious secret and that they were more in tune than ever before. His announcement was a bit of a surprise, but she liked the idea. She sat back, feeling relaxed and happy. Cian had found a project he'd love that wouldn't be difficult to run. In any case, he wanted to move to Sandy Cove and run the guesthouse, which had been her own plan all along. The campervan business was a clever concept. It would give Cian what he needed: a business to run all on his own the way he wanted. This was a twist on the idea of having his own space and this way she would have hers, too. She raised her bottle of beer. 'Cheers to that, sweetheart.'

There was silence in the kitchen as they all stared at her, which made her laugh. 'Yes, you got it right. This is the new me. All sweet and submissive.'

'As long as it lasts,' Maeve muttered. 'But hey, why not? This will give us more time together, too.'

Roisin blew her sister a kiss. 'That's true. And we'll be neighbours for good. We're going to live in Sandy Cove permanently and run the new guesthouse. It'll be a bit of a squeeze when the boys are home for holidays, but I have had an idea. I was thinking of making the two maids' rooms in the attic into bedrooms for the lads when they're home. There's no heating up there, but we'll sort something out. This way we won't have to look for separate accommodation for us. What do you think, boys?'

Darragh looked up from his phone. 'Sounds good, Mum. And we can hang out with the guys here more often.'

'Yay,' Olwyn said. 'We'll turn you into Kerry lads in no time.'

Nuala laughed. 'That might be quite a challenge. But I'm glad the kids are such great friends already.'

'All fantastic news,' Sean Óg cut in. 'And now, as the kids have gobbled up anything edible, maybe the grown-ups could retire to the living room while you young things clean up.'

There was a communal groan from the teenagers, but Nuala and Roisin got them to get up and start clearing plates and glasses. 'I have coffee ready in a thermos in the living room,' Nuala announced. 'And there's a box of chocolates from that fancy shop in Cork.' She drew Roisin aside when nobody was watching. 'Have you said anything to Olga about – you know?'

Roisin shook her head. 'No. And I won't. I don't suspect her any more. I feel awful even having considered it.'

'Who was it then?' Nuala asked, looking mystified.

Roisin shrugged. 'No idea. But it doesn't matter now. It's all over, thank God.'

'Amen to that.' Nuala smiled. 'It was great fun tonight. But maybe I should have asked Declan if he'd like to join us? It must be a little lonely living on his own over there.'

'It wouldn't have been his thing at all, with all this family stuff,' Roisin declared.

Nuala nodded. 'Nah, probably not. And maybe he would have found it a little difficult to watch you and Cian snogging at the table.'

Roisin felt her face grow hot. 'I don't know what you mean. But let's not go there.'

'No,' Nuala agreed. 'Some things are better left alone, right?'

'Absolutely,' Roisin said with feeling.

The adults gathered in the living room, but Roisin pulled Cian into the hall. 'Hey,' she whispered in his ear, 'how about going for a spin to the beach to look at the moon?'

He grinned and nodded. 'Good idea. We'll just sneak off. We'll text the kids later.'

They carefully opened the door and went outside, closing the door softly behind them. The full moon cast a soft glow on the front garden and the campervan parked outside the gate. They got inside and Cian started the engine. Roisin settled into the passenger seat and they exchanged a conspiratorial smile as they drove off into the lovely spring-like evening, down the street and onto the main road to the public beach, where the moonlit ocean glimmered before them.

They sat there for a while, looking out at the dark water, the moon and the stars shimmering in the velvet sky. Roisin turned to Cian. 'I loved your ideas.'

He kissed her cheek. 'Good. I hope you didn't mind me talking about it before we had discussed it between us?'

'Not at all. It's a brilliant idea that works so well with what we want to do. It'll give us each our own thing – me with the guesthouse, you and your campervans. It's perfect.' She laughed softly, putting her head on his shoulder. 'You turned me on when you got all masterful and decisive.'

'That was my plan. We haven't really explored all the delights of this van,' he whispered against her cheek. 'And you know what? That half bottle of champagne is still in the fridge since that day in Wicklow. Let's open it and I'll show you a few things…'

'Brilliant idea.' Roisin followed Cian into the living room of the van and laughed as the champagne spilled all over her when he opened the bottle. They finished what was left and Cian quickly folded out the double bed and they drew the curtains. She stripped to her underwear while he undressed. 'You look lovely,' he said, kissing her shoulder. 'But I prefer you au naturel.'

'Okay,' she said and undid her bra. 'Au naturel it is, mon amour.'

'I love it when you speak French.'

'Moi aussi,' she murmured into his shoulder.

'I love you,' he declared as he looked at her naked body. 'You're beautiful and clever and wild and impossible.' He pulled her down onto the bed and did all the things he knew she loved. There was new feeling between them as they made love, nearly as if they had just met and were trying to get to know each other.

'How strange,' she panted afterwards, when they were lying in a heap, smiling into each other's eyes. 'We've always been good in bed, but this was…'

'As if we're different people?' he asked softly, running his hand over her hip. 'Yes. I feel that too. And…' he paused, 'it's beginning to sink in on me.'

'What?'

'That being apart for a while was just what we needed.'

'Except for all the misunderstandings. I don't want to do that again. Do you?' She felt tears stinging her eyes. 'I was so sad when I thought we'd split up. I don't think I've ever been so scared.'

'No need to be scared any more.' He stroked her hair and kissed her cheek. 'I'm here and I'll never leave you.'

She brushed away her tears, feeling she had never loved him more than at that moment. He had been willing to let her have her me-time, her space to think and plan. It had been a huge sacrifice for him but it had also been good for them. 'Willow House will be the best place for us to recover and find each other again. And running the guesthouse will be an amazing new experience.'

'My new business will be fun, too.'

'I can't wait for you to get started,' Roisin said, excitement bubbling inside her. 'It'll be good for you.'

'We'll be doing different things but still be together.'

She took his hand and kissed it. 'Yes. I hope this will work.'

'We'll be grand, sweetheart,' he assured her. 'After this we'll be stronger than ever. I just know it.'

'I hope you're right.' She snuggled into him under the duvet that smelled of the sea with an undertone of fried sausages. 'I'm getting to like this van. I feel like a gypsy sleeping with her lover in the wilderness. I can imagine what a buzz it gave you to take off into the wild like that.'

He wrapped his arms around her and kissed her nose. 'I'm getting more of a buzz lying here with you. But yes, it was amazing. Next time we'll go off somewhere together. In the summer. It would be too much of a challenge for you in the winter. It can be pretty rough when the wind is up and the rain is hitting us sideways.'

'Okay. In the summer.'

'Just for a bit of a break,' he said. 'Willow House will be our home from now on.'

'Until we change our minds again,' she said with a laugh. 'Let's not set anything in stone.'

They slowly drifted off to sleep to the sound of the waves, while the moon shone on them through the window of the campervan and the stars glinted in the dark sky. All was well in their world for now.

A Letter from Susanne

I want to say a big thank you for choosing to read *Sisters of Willow House*. I had huge fun returning to Sandy Cove and visiting all the wonderful places as I wrote the book. All the characters in the book are inspired by the people I meet in Kerry in real life. I feel so lucky to have the chance to go back there often. It is truly one of the most beautiful places in the world! In this book, I wanted to describe Kerry in the winter, with spectacular storms interspersed with lovely sunny days. It's that changeable weather that makes the wild beauty of Kerry so special. I hope to return to this part of the wild west of Ireland in further novels with even more loveable characters. If you want to keep up-to-date with all my latest releases, just sign up at the following link. Your email address will never be shared and you can unsubscribe at any time.

www.bookouture.com/susanne-oleary

I hope you loved *Sisters of Willow House* and if you did I would be very grateful if you could write a review. I'd love to hear what you think. Readers' feedback is hugely helpful and it makes such a difference helping new readers to discover one of my books for the first time.

I love hearing from my readers – you can get in touch on my Facebook page, through Twitter, Goodreads or my website.

Many thanks,
Susanne

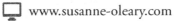 www.susanne-oleary.com

 authoroleary

@susl

Acknowledgements

Huge thanks to my editor, Jennifer Hunt, for her wonderful editorial work on this novel. And to Christina Demosthenous for her continued friendship and support. Thank you also, Kim Nash and Noelle Holten, for the amazing work with marketing and publicity. I would also like to thank Alex Crow for all the terrific graphic images and banners of my covers to use on social media, and all at Bookouture for being there at all times and making the hard work of writing a novel at break-neck speed a little easier. And thanks to the gang in 'the lounge' for the friendship, laughter and for being there when things get a little rough out there in author-land.

Many thanks also to my readers, many of whom help with caring and sharing of each book I produce, and for the kind messages and lovely reviews. I truly appreciate your enthusiasm and support!